PRAISE FOR *NEW YORK TIMES* AND *USA TODAY* BESTSELLING AUTHOR ANNE FRASIER

"Frasier has perfected the art of making a reader's skin crawl."

—*Publishers Weekly*

"A master."

—*Minneapolis Star Tribune*

"Anne Frasier delivers thoroughly engrossing, completely riveting suspense."

—Lisa Gardner

"Frasier's writing is fast and furious."

—Jayne Ann Krentz

PRAISE FOR *FIND ME*

An Amazon Charts #1 Bestseller
#26 Amazon Most Sold Fiction List of 2020

"[An] exquisitely crafted thriller . . . Frasier has outdone herself with this shocker."

—*Publishers Weekly* (starred review)

"For thriller fans who appreciate intricate and unconventional plots, with shocking twists."

—*Library Journal*

PRAISE FOR *THE BODY READER*

Winner of the International Thriller Writers 2017 Thriller Award for Best Paperback Original

"Absorbing."

—*Publishers Weekly*

"This is an electrifying murder mystery—one of the best of the year."

—Mysterious Reviews

"I see the name Anne Frasier on a book and I know I am in for a treat . . . I thought it was a very unique premise and coupled with the good characters, made for an almost non-stop read for me. I highly recommend this."

—Pure Textuality

"*The Body Reader* earned its five stars, a rarity for me, even for books I like. Kudos to Anne Frasier."

—The Wyrdd and the Bazaar

"A must read for mystery suspense fans."

—*Babbling About Books*

"I've long been a fan of Anne Frasier, but this book elevates her work to a whole new level, in my mind."

—Tale of a Shooting Star

PRAISE FOR *PLAY DEAD*

"This is a truly creepy and thrilling book. Frasier's skill at exposing the dark emotions and motivations of individuals gives it a gripping edge."
—RT Book Reviews

"*Play Dead* is a compelling and memorable police procedural, made even better by the way the characters interact with one another. Anne Frasier will be appreciated by fans who like Kay Hooper, Iris Johansen and Lisa Gardner."
—Blether: The Book Review Site

"A nicely constructed combination of mystery and thriller. Frasier is a talented writer whose forte is probing into the psyches of her characters, and she produces a fast-paced novel with a finale containing many surprises."
—I Love a Mystery

"Has all the essentials of an edge-of-your-seat story. There is suspense, believable characters, an interesting setting, and just the right amount of details to keep the reader's eyes always moving forward . . . I recommend *Play Dead* as a great addition to any mystery library."
—Roundtable Reviews

PRAISE FOR *PRETTY DEAD*

"Besides being beautifully written and tightly plotted, this book was that sort of great read you need on a regular basis to restore your faith in a genre."
—Lynn Viehl, *Paperback Writer* (Book of the Month)

"By far the best of the three books. I couldn't put my Kindle down till I'd read every last page."

—NetGalley

PRAISE FOR *HUSH*

"This is by far and away the best serial-killer story I've read in a long time . . . strong characters, with a truly twisted bad guy."

—Jayne Ann Krentz

"I couldn't put it down. Engrossing . . . scary . . . I loved it."

—Linda Howard

"A deeply engrossing read, *Hush* delivers a creepy villain, a chilling plot, and two remarkable investigators whose personal struggles are only equaled by their compelling need to stop a madman before he kills again. Warning: don't read this book if you are home alone."

—Lisa Gardner

"A wealth of procedural detail, a heart-thumping finale, and two scarred but indelible protagonists make this a first-rate read."

—*Publishers Weekly*

"Anne Frasier has crafted a taut and suspenseful thriller."

—Kay Hooper

"Well-realized characters and taut, suspenseful plotting."

—*Minneapolis Star Tribune*

PRAISE FOR *SLEEP TIGHT*

"Guaranteed to keep you awake at night."

—Lisa Jackson

"There'll be no sleeping after reading this one. Laced with forensic detail and psychological twists."

—Andrea Kane

"Gripping and intense . . . Along with a fine plot, Frasier delivers her characters as whole people, each trying to cope in the face of violence and jealousies."

—*Minneapolis Star Tribune*

"Enthralling. There's a lot more to this clever intrigue than graphic police procedures. Indeed, one of Frasier's many strengths is her ability to create characters and relationships that are as compelling as the mystery itself. Will linger with the reader after the killer is caught."

—*Publishers Weekly*

PRAISE FOR *THE ORCHARD*

"Eerie and atmospheric, this is an indie movie in print. You'll read and read to see where it is going, although it's clear early on that the future is not going to be kind to anyone involved. Weir's story is more proof that only love can break your heart."

—*Library Journal*

"A gripping account of divided loyalties, the real cost of farming and the shattered people on the front lines. Not since Jane Smiley's *A Thousand Acres* has there been so enrapturing a family drama percolating out from the back forty."

—*Maclean's*

"This poignant memoir of love, labor, and dangerous pesticides reveals the terrible true price."

—*Oprah Magazine* (Fall Book Pick)

"Equal parts moving love story and environmental warning."

—*Entertainment Weekly* (B+)

"While reading this extraordinarily moving memoir, I kept remembering the last two lines of Muriel Rukeyser's poem 'Käthe Kollwitz' ('What would happen if one woman told the truth about her life? / The world would split open'), for Weir proffers a worldview that is at once eloquent, sincere, and searing."

—*Library Journal* (Librarians' Best Books of 2011)

"[She] tells her story with grace, unflinching honesty and compassion all the while establishing a sense of place and time with a master storyteller's perspective so engaging you forget it is a memoir."

—Calvin Crosby, Books Inc. (Berkeley, CA)

"One of my favorite reads of 2011, *The Orchard* is easily mistakable as a novel for its engaging, page-turning flow and its seemingly imaginative plot."

—Susan McBeth, founder and owner of Adventures by the Book, San Diego, CA

"Moving and surprising."

—The Next Chapter (Fall 2011 Top 20 Best Books)

"Searing . . . the past is artfully juxtaposed with the present in this finely wrought work. Its haunting passages will linger long after the last page is turned."

—*Boston Globe* (Pick of the Week)

"If a writing instructor wanted an excellent example of voice in a piece of writing, this would be a five-star choice!"

—*San Diego Union-Tribune* (Recommended Read)

"This book produced a string of emotions that had my hand flying up to my mouth time and again, and not only made me realize, 'This woman can write!' but also made me appreciate the importance of this book, and how it reaches far beyond Weir's own story."

—Linda Grana, Diesel, a Bookstore

"*The Orchard* is a lovely book in all the ways that really matter, one of those rare and wonderful memoirs in which people you've never met become your friends."

—Nicholas Sparks

"A hypnotic tale of place, people, and of Midwestern family roots that run deep, stubbornly hidden, and equally menacing."

—Jamie Ford, *New York Times* bestselling author of *Hotel on the Corner of Bitter and Sweet*

TELL
ME

ALSO BY ANNE FRASIER

INLAND EMPIRE THRILLER

Find Me

DETECTIVE JUDE FONTAINE MYSTERIES

The Body Reader
The Body Counter
The Body Keeper

THE ELISE SANDBURG SERIES

Play Dead
Stay Dead
Pretty Dead
Truly Dead

OTHER NOVELS

Hush
Sleep Tight
Before I Wake
Pale Immortal
Garden of Darkness

NONFICTION (AS THERESA WEIR)

The Orchard: A Memoir
The Man Who Left

TELL ME

ANNE FRASIER

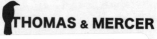
THOMAS & MERCER

Published by Thomas & Mercer, Seattle

www.apub.com

Amazon, the Amazon logo, and Thomas & Mercer are trademarks of Amazon.com, Inc., or its affiliates.

ISBN-13: 9781542025560
ISBN-10: 1542025567

Cover design by Damon Freeman

Printed in the United States of America

TELL
ME

CHAPTER 1

Four female hikers walked single file along the narrow, footworn Pacific Crest Trail in Southern California, with Emerson the last in line. The air was cold, but the sun was hot. From somewhere, an invisible bird called. The wind sounded hollow, with a repetitious pulse that increased, then fell away, increased, fell away. Emerson imagined a giant crater. In her mind, she pictured the pulse as a dark, swirling cloud inside the crater's vast space. At times, the sound of the wind was almost funny. Like a little kid under a sheet making ghost noises. *Ooh-ooh-ooh.* Her younger sister would do that very thing, trying to scare her. Emerson would pretend to be afraid and her sister would laugh.

Someone once told her sound could actually physically hurt a person. She wondered if it was true. It might be a lie. It was something called infrasound intrusion. But she was fifteen, not a kid anymore, definitely old enough to know adults couldn't always be trusted to tell the truth. Everybody lied, especially her mother.

Although she was an unwilling participant in the hike, Emerson couldn't ignore her emotional response to her surroundings. Several times already, at the vision of deep canyons and evergreen trees as tall as some of the buildings in downtown LA, she'd felt a blossoming in her chest at the wonder of it all. That blue, blue sky with no hint of clouds. The narrow trails and turns that brought her face-to-face with wind that tugged her long hair straight up, then slapped it back in her face. Steep and wild paths, clear streams, small animals scurrying away.

For the most part, the four of them walked in silence, occasionally passing through areas where fires had left charred tree trunks that still smelled like smoke even though the woman leading the hike told them the fire had been over a year ago. Among the acres of dead trees, blooming flowers of yellow and purple danced on delicate stems that somehow withstood the wind. But the beauty of the trail did nothing to change Emerson's resentment. So what if she was addicted to her phone? There were a lot worse things she could be addicted to. She'd never even tried anything like ecstasy or meth or LSD, when almost everybody her age had dabbled in at least one of them. Her parents should have been glad she was such a good kid.

"Think of it as a vacation," her mother had said.

As the glossy brochure stated, staying at Kaleidoscope *was* like an upscale vacation. She and the other guests had good food—*great* food, really, gourmet stuff cooked by some famous chef. There was a pool they could swim in, which was nice, and they could draw and read. But there were no televisions, and they weren't allowed to use any electronic devices. And they had group activities, which Emerson loathed with all the passion her body language could convey. And now, after being on site (locked up) for a week, they had to participate in a three-day hike—because the big thing at Kaleidoscope was nature. *Ta-da!* But the place was still a prison, and the hike still felt like discipline.

Despite her constant low-boil anger, her unease about the coming night, and her awe of the beauty around her, boredom still managed to creep in. Emerson caught herself mindlessly reaching for her phone. And even though she'd felt for it maybe twenty times since leaving the trailhead parking lot, where a dude from Kaleidoscope had dropped them off, panic still washed over her each time, before she remembered her mom had taken the device.

Yeah, she probably did have a problem. So what?

They could have just hidden her phone for a week. Or the whole family could have gone camping together and left their phones at home.

For free. She didn't need an intervention. She didn't have a crisis-level social media addiction.

Crisis-level. She rolled her eyes. The invisible bird continued to yell.

Was it the same bird? Or a new bird? Did birds follow people? It almost seemed like it was trying to communicate with them. She remembered learning about a bird in the Amazon jungle that lured lost people in the wrong direction. The people would follow and follow and just go deeper into the jungle, never to be seen or heard from again. Maybe this was a good bird, trying to warn her away from danger.

"What are you trying to tell me?" she shouted up at it.

The bird ignored her.

The others in the group turned and looked at her. She shrugged. They swiveled back around, hands gripping their pack straps, and continued on their mindless walk, three resentful girls, one person there because it was her job. That person was Janet Ravenscroft, employee of Kaleidoscope. She looked like a professional hiker with her brown braids, serious cap, dark sunglasses. She wore leather boots, thick socks, a wind jacket that snapped and popped like a flag with every strong gust. Earlier she'd told them she'd walked the whole Pacific Crest Trail. When no one reacted, she told them how long the trail was—2,650 miles, extending from Mexico to Canada.

Why? That was what Emerson had wondered but hadn't said. *Why* did you walk it?

And then Janet had proceeded to tell them she was a Triple Crown hiker. Again, all three of them blanked, and Janet had to shake her jacket sleeve to show them a thick silver bracelet on her wrist. The bracelet had a copper triangle on it.

"A Triple Crown hiker means you've hiked the three longest hiking trails in the US," she'd told them. "Pacific Crest Trail, Appalachian Trail, and the Continental Divide Trail. Altogether, they're nearly eight thousand miles."

They'd made sounds of appreciation, none interested but all trying to be polite. The lives of adults could be so boring and weird. The stuff they got excited about . . .

The two other girls were BFFs and went to a private high school in Palm Springs. They both had popular YouTube channels, but the blond, Portia Devine, had a lot more followers, maybe because her father was the famous actor Phillip Devine. Weird to think about that. Like, a guy Emerson had watched in a movie theater while eating popcorn actually having a kid and a real family, not a pretend family. Emerson wasn't into action movies, but she knew who he was, and she'd grown up seeing footage of him in dangerous situations. Fiction, of course. Hanging from cliffs, jumping out of helicopters, saving people from burning buildings. Stuff like that. Things she couldn't relate to but could imagine her father—her real father, not her stepdad—doing.

A blast of wind hit so hard it took her breath away, pulling her out of her daydream. The wind just snatched the inhalation from her mouth. Portia screamed as her teal bandanna blew off her head. All four of them watched it soar above the treetops, then vanish. They'd all gotten bandannas with their welcome backpacks. Kind of cute, with the retreat logo—round with evergreen trees. *Retreat. Resort.* These were words used at the addiction center. It hadn't taken Emerson long to understand they weren't supposed to call it what it was—an addiction center. It went against the whole vibe the place was trying to project.

As the elevation increased, the temperature continued to drop. At one point, they stopped to put on sweatshirts. These also matched and had the "resort" logo. They zipped them, pulled up hoods, got drinks and snacks. They shivered. They sniffled.

The cold air should have felt good after the heat of San Bernardino, but it just seemed like another insult and unfair punishment. Feeling awkward because of the sudden face-to-face, they all reached for phones that weren't there.

It surprised her that they didn't have the trail to themselves. She'd been expecting just them and nature. No. There were others, which made her nervous. She'd heard this was the slow time of year. Too hot for the whole trail. Most of the hikers they saw looked like they'd been walking forever, and a lot of them had started in Mexico. Their gear was worn, their eyes were glassy, their hiking shoes tattered, some with toes sticking out of holes. They moved like zombies, like maybe they'd forgotten why they'd even started in the first place. One guy they'd talked to said he was doing it to lose weight. Others, like Emerson and her group, were hiking to get away from the internet. Some were just plain doing it to get away from the world. And apparently hiking was also good for people who'd experienced trauma and loss. Emerson wondered if that was the real reason her parents were making her do it. Maybe it wasn't about the phone at all. Maybe they thought she needed more healing. But the school shooting had been years and years ago. She was fine.

They paused again, this time in a clearing. The dirt under their shoes was packed hard from the massive number of people who passed through in a week or a month or a year. The foursome briefly gathered around a wooden mileage sign that pointed in the direction of the next remarkable spot on the trail. It included their present elevation—eight thousand feet. Stapled to the wooden mile marker were faded photos of people who'd gone missing on the trail. The laminated sheets were yellowed and weathered. They seemed old. Were the hikers *still* missing? Or had they been found and nobody returned to remove the photos? Probably. Because why bother?

Without discussion—maybe all of them feeling a little fearful or a lot fearful—they turned their backs on the sad pictures. That's when Emerson noticed that Janet's head was down. She was looking at her phone.

Looking at her phone.
That's right, folks.

5

"You seem to have a problem yourself," Portia said.

Emerson let out a snort of surprise. She was still trying to figure out if she liked the girl, but Portia had guts. Emerson admired that.

Janet held a finger against the screen. "Okay, powered off." She tucked her phone away, seeming embarrassed, and everything about her response made her look guilty. "I was checking in," Janet said. "Updating Kaleidoscope on our location."

Ri-ight.

Janet sat down on a log and zeroed in on JoJo McGrath. JoJo seemed uneasy, looking around, watching over her shoulder like she was expecting someone to appear at any moment.

"Tell me how you feel, JoJo," Janet said.

Oh God. Emerson tried not to roll her eyes. Talk therapy. She was familiar with that too.

"I don't think I can do this," the girl said.

Her makeup was precise and professional, a work of art. It was hard to even guess what she might look like without it. Oddly enough, Emerson was hoping the hike might provide an answer to that question. Right now, JoJo's lids were painted with thick black eyeliner, her brows perfectly drawn, about twenty perfect freckles, along with sparkle on her cheeks. When you talked to her, it was hard to pull your eyes away or even concentrate on what she was saying because her face was such an intriguing mask. How did she even do that? Mad skills.

There were two kinds of traumatized people: those who embraced talk therapy, and those who just bullshitted their way through it. Emerson was a bullshitter and proud of it.

"I *can't* do this," JoJo said. Her eyes glistened. Careful of her liner and mascara, she wiped her tears with a long pink nail. "I do makeup tutorials," she said with a sob. "I have over a million followers. It's a *business*. It's not something frivolous I'm just doing for fun."

And yet the constant quest for content could wear a person out. Emerson was glad she didn't have millions of followers. But she got it.

Not about wearing makeup in the wilderness, but the loss of something that made a person feel important.

"I mean," JoJo said, "I feel like I don't exist right now. Like my identity has been taken from me. It's awful."

"That's understandable and expected," Janet said. "But we all have so many people inside us. This isn't about changing who you are or taking away from your life. It's about giving you an opportunity to consider something more." She rested her elbows on her knees, hands clasped.

So sincere.

"Some of the people who go through our program return to their old life without any adjustments," Janet continued. "Others take what they gain here and moderate their online lives. This is about adding, not taking away."

A scripted response. Emerson was familiar with those too. It was obviously something Janet had studied and memorized for moments like this. Emerson might have even read something similar in the Kaleidoscope brochure. Still, Janet's words held enough truth that even Emerson found them slightly comforting. She nodded in agreement.

Pep talk over, they gathered their things and continued the hike. They'd all done pretty well so far, but an hour later the complaining started. All three of them, Emerson included, reported headaches, sore legs, aching feet.

"This isn't as far as I'd hoped to go today," Janet said, "but we can stop for the night."

The girls glanced nervously at one another.

"Let's see if we can find a spot away from the trail," Janet added.

They cut into the woods to eventually come to a clearing. It was flat, bare ground, a firepit of rocks. Janet visually assessed the area, hands on hips. "This looks fine. Close to the trail, but not conspicuous."

"Do you think someone might try to hurt us?" Portia asked.

"I don't want to scare you, but there have been some instances of people being attacked on this trail. It's very rare, and the victims tend to be people who are hiking alone. So I wouldn't worry, but it's also good to be aware."

JoJo let out a low whimper, and Emerson fiddled with the ring she always wore.

While it was still light, they set up their tents, three in all, the two friends sharing one, Janet and Emerson each in their own. Once that chore was done, they cut open dehydrated-food packets and dumped them into four tins of water to heat over a tiny stove.

"I wish I could take an Instagram pic of our food," JoJo said with a forlorn voice.

They all agreed, even Janet.

It *was* curious how they felt the need to share what they were doing. Like sharing made them and the experience more real. How weird life must have been before the internet and cell phones. Emerson couldn't begin to imagine it. She knew people who'd lived both kinds of existences. Her mother, for one. It must have been awful.

Done eating, there was nothing else to do but sit around the fire. It was boring at first, but then Portia started talking about how she'd been in a bad car wreck when she was twelve.

"Like, a friend *died*," she said.

Emerson figured she'd regret it later, but the darkness and her exhaustion left her feeling reckless. Plus, these weren't her forever people. She wouldn't have to face them at school or in her real life once she returned to it, so she found herself sharing something she never shared. She told them how she'd survived a school shooting. Told them the name of the school and how old she'd been. "You probably heard about it on the news."

"Oh my God." Portia hugged herself. "I remember that. That must have been awful. I'm so sorry."

Before the shooting, school officials had told Emerson and her classmates that gunshots wouldn't sound the way they'd expect them to sound. Like they'd think they were something else, most likely firecrackers. So part of their shooter drills had involved listening to real gunshots recorded inside a school. Different kinds of guns. Like rifles and pistols, but mostly the nonstop rat-a-tat-tat of an AK-47.

She didn't know if listening to the gunshots had helped. None of it had seemed a real threat or like anything that would impact them. Those things happened in other places to other people. The day of the shooting, she'd gotten out of history class to use the restroom and was walking down the hall when she heard a popping sound and thought it might be people working on the building, using a nail gun or something.

Then she heard screams.

And more popping.

Doors burst open. Her history teacher, Mr. Bell, ran toward her, not speaking, waving his arms, blood coming from his mouth, staining his white shirt. Kids were behind him, scattering, screaming. Mr. Bell fell to the floor. Just dropped straight down and didn't move.

While Emerson was sharing her story with the girls, she also told them the name of her biological father and how he didn't have anything to do with her. Appropriate sounds of sympathy were made.

"You guys were right about the phone," Janet finally admitted. "Totally right. I was texting a friend. I was checking social media. I have a problem too."

Was this part of the whole thing? Emerson wondered. More scripted words, something to make them feel like they could open up and share? *Tell me.*

"What kind of ring is that?" Portia asked.

Emerson held out her hand so they could all see what Portia was talking about. "A self-defense ring. My stepdad gave it to me after the shooting. And he showed me how to jab it into someone's neck. And showed me where the jugular vein is." She dragged a finger down her own neck to demonstrate.

"Wow," JoJo said, freshly nervous.

Thirty minutes later, they were talked out. It was still early, much earlier than Emerson typically went to bed, but they crawled into their tents, Janet to probably sleep, Emerson and the girls to just get through the night.

Using the light of a tiny battery lantern, Emerson zipped the tent flap closed and blew air into a small inflatable pillow. She removed her boots, socks, and jeans and wriggled into her sleeping bag. In the darkness, she could hear Portia and JoJo talking and giggling, and almost wished she were in the tent with them.

Finally their conversation stopped.

Emerson tried to stay awake, straining to hear any sounds coming from outside the tent as she adjusted to the darkness, but the hours of hiking and the fresh air caught up with her. She fell asleep. Later, she awoke to a fresh visit from the howling wind, the seams of her tent whistling and loose fabric snapping. She felt a renewed surge of anger toward her mother and father for doing this to her. She was a good kid. This was punishment.

The wind changed until the sound felt more rhythmic, more like something vocal and hollow and scary. She held her breath and didn't move. Light pulsed across the outside of the tent. A moment later someone screamed.

CHAPTER 2

Three weeks into their hike on the Pacific Crest Trail, Jordan and his girlfriend, Deidra, had reached the point where they'd started to wonder what the hell they were doing. When putting one foot in front of the other in yet another day of stupefied hypnosis wasn't fun anymore. Hiking was supposed to be enjoyable, at least part of the time. A lot of the time, with some expected physical discomfort now and then. But whereas Jordan sometimes enjoyed the scenery, he often fixated on needing to step off-trail to go to the bathroom, or he worried about upcoming bad weather, or how good it was going to feel to stop, just stop, and eat shitty food cooked over a tiny stove.

Why? What was the objective? To say he'd done it? To find something that was lacking in his life? Maybe in retrospect he'd see the value in having done it, but right now he was too miserable to figure it out. Too busy living moment to moment, day to day.

At this particular moment they were looking forward to reaching the town of Big Bear Lake, California, before the post office closed. They were expecting packages. Stuff they'd ordered, like new shoes, because the tread was gone, and their toes were poking out. It was the miles, man. If you walked the whole trail you could expect to go through several pairs of hiking shoes. But Jordan was mostly looking forward to a birthday package from his mom. He was hoping for money and her soft oatmeal cookies.

Deidra had almost given up a few times already. The joke among hikers, and it was really no joke, was that the trail could solidify or break a relationship. Theirs had hit some rocky moments over the past weeks, usually brought on by miserable weather. But they were both learning to control their tantrums and suffer in silence, or together, rather than knock each other down. Still, last night had been rough. Rain, wet gear, and now walking with muddy and torn shoes. Neither of them speaking. No energy for conversation. Both of them fixated on getting to town, the post office, having a real shower in a motel, sleeping in a real bed. They just had to get through the day.

At one point they paused under the protection of some giant pine trees. They sloughed off packs and drank water they'd purified at the last water source. While Deidra rested in silence, Jordan took a trail that led to privacy. As he peed, he spotted a bit of orange in the distance. Maybe a tent.

If this had been his first week on the trail, he would have been excited to see signs of human life. And, being an extrovert, he would have walked up to the campsite and introduced himself. Today he was beyond caring.

Deidra showed up and they both silently eyed the patch of color, then each other. He read the exhaustion in her face and he felt bad for her. He felt bad for him. He had nothing to give, no words, no gestures. Without speaking, she reached for the zipper of her pants.

Before the hike, she would have died of embarrassment if he'd seen her pee. Now she didn't even think about waiting for him to leave. He left anyway. Someday when she looked back on this, she might care. Or not.

He pulled together some of his old self, tried to recall what it felt like to be social, and decided to check out the campers while giving Deidra the privacy she hadn't asked for. He walked down a narrow, beaten path, noting that the hikers had chosen a good spot. Not that visible from the trail, but close.

A clearing.

Three orange tents.

Most of the time, hikers got going shortly after dawn. But the sun had been up awhile now, and there was no sign of life in the camp. Maybe they were still sleeping. Maybe they'd decided to take a zero day. And yet he felt uneasy. Zero days were usually taken in town, where a person could shower and resupply.

His eyes were doing all the work as he tried to decide if he should call out, say hello, see if everything was okay. But then his ears kicked in and he heard buzzing.

Insects.

Flies?

In harmony with the buzzing was an odd and repetitious popping sound that seemed familiar even though he couldn't place it. He looked around, above his head, then at nearby flowers. A couple of bees hovered between blossoms. A gust of wind moved through the trees. Just a slight breeze, carrying with it a sweet and rotten smell.

Oof.

Something bad was going on.

His brain told him to leave, to get out of there. *Now. Fast. Do it.*

Instead of leaving, he moved closer. Close enough to see tiny black insect shadows inside the nearest tent.

Mystery solved.

The popping sound was coming from the flies throwing themselves against the taut fabric. How often had he experienced the same thing waking him in the morning? But it had been one or two flies, not hundreds. And without what seemed to be bees in the mix.

"Hello?" he ventured. His voice shook. "Anybody in there?"

The only answer was an increase in the movement and buzz of insects.

He spoke again, louder this time, his heart pounding. "Hello!"

He heard a sound, let out a gasp of alarm, turned. Relaxed. Just Deidra, walking toward him with a full stride as she adjusted her clothing, more intent on her misery than her surroundings.

"We need to get going," she said.

He put a finger to his lips.

Her eyes flared in anger at being shushed. That anger faded, and puzzlement washed over her face as her brain went through the same workings he'd gone through minutes earlier.

"Stay back," he warned her. "I'm gonna check the tent."

She swallowed and nodded, her eyes big, looking more alert than she'd looked in days.

Maybe this was a joke. Maybe someone had set this up and was filming them. Kind of a *Blair Witch* deal.

The tent flap was unzipped, which explained how the insects had gotten in. With a shaking hand, remaining as far back as he could while still able to grab the zipper, he pulled it the rest of the way down, the plastic teeth slowly separating until the flap fell open. Freed flies went airborne. A black cloud swarmed his face. He waved his arms, tripped, fell down, got back up. Didn't run away even though he wanted to. With a hand covering his mouth and nose, he forced himself to creep forward and look inside the tent.

He froze and remained frozen for what seemed like minutes but was probably seconds. Finally, he stumbled away and threw up. When he straightened, he saw Deidra walking past him, approaching the tent, phone in her hand, like she was making a video. *Was* this all something staged? His brain couldn't function. It didn't seem like something she'd be a part of.

"Don't go in there!" he half screamed, half sobbed, watching in horror as she pushed the tent flap aside.

She stood in the opening for a long time before turning to him. "We need to check the other tents." With amazing calm, she walked to the next one and looked inside. "Nobody here." Then the third. She straightened. "This one's empty too, but all their stuff is still inside. It's like they just vanished."

"That was a dead person, right?" he asked. "In the first tent?"

"Definitely."

"Have you ever seen a dead person before?"

"At a funeral."

He pulled out his phone. "No cell service." His brain was still trying to process the body in the tent. He almost needed to have another look. He replayed it in his head instead. A lot of blood, and a lot of flies. A phone next to the body. He should get it. The phone. See if he could figure out who the person was. No, what if this was a murder? You weren't supposed to touch a murder scene.

Not murder. That was ridiculous. Bear attack? And where were the others? The people from the other tents?

"We need to get somewhere else," he said. "Call 911."

Probably no hurry. That person wasn't going anywhere. But maybe he and Deidra needed to get away, far away, in case they were in danger.

Deidra returned to the tent, held up her phone, moved some distance away, then began poking at the screen.

"You aren't going to post that to social media, are you?" Jordan asked.

"Maybe. Once we have cell service."

"That's not cool, Deidra."

"Everybody does it."

"Not us. We don't do shit like that."

Who would have thought it would take a dead person to officially end their relationship? He would never have predicted that.

He heard rustling. Inhaling sharply, they both turned toward the woods. A mouse ran from under a bush, spotted them, squeaked, and ran back into the undergrowth. They let out their breath and laughed in relief.

Jordan began walking away from the campsite. "Let's get the hell out of here."

They hurried down the trail, back the way they'd come. An hour and several mountain miles later, Deidra was still periodically holding her phone high in the air trying to pick up a signal.

"Got it!" she finally shouted.

Jordan paused, checked his phone, saw he had two bars.

"I posted my video!" Deidra said defiantly.

Jordan ignored her. His finger was on the screen of his phone as he prepared to call 911. He was interrupted by another rustle similar to the sound they'd heard earlier. He turned, expecting to see another mouse. But no. It was a person. Two people, in fact.

"Hey, man," Jordan said. "Whatever you do, don't go that direction. We found a dead body." He pointed the way they'd come.

The guy smiled. "Thanks for the tip."

That's when the gun appeared and Jordan understood that this was the danger they'd been running from, but instead they'd run right to it.

Deidra was somewhere behind him. Before he could shout a warning, he heard a pop, felt a burn in his chest, and dropped to the ground.

CHAPTER 3

Piles of bright-orange carrots littered the highway, and traffic was backed up for miles as Detective Daniel Ellis headed for the San Bernardino County Sheriff's Department. High winds had blown a semitruck off the road, scattering the vegetables bound for a canning factory, closing both east and west lanes.

Carrots on a highway seemed more ludicrous than other things that could have spilled. Where did they come from? Where were they going? What story did they have to tell? Daniel wasn't sure why carrot trucks were often the victims of the high winds, but this was the third such accident he'd seen so far this year. Regardless of the how and why, it put him behind schedule, which meant he wasn't going to get to work as early as he liked.

In the sheriff's department parking lot, he was careful to face his SUV into the wind so the door wouldn't shear off when opened. He stepped out, his hair whipping about his head, his tie and suit snapping. He ducked, squinted, and headed for the two-story sprawling concrete building that also housed Homicide. Leaning into the wind, he kept a grip on the travel mug Bo had stuck in his hand as he'd left the house that morning. Bo, a retired detective and Daniel's adoptive father, considered himself in charge of Daniel's health and diet. And ever since Daniel had suffered a concussion, Bo's coffee had become part of his daily routine. The concoction was something Bo called "bulletproof" and was made with mysterious ingredients.

Daniel stepped inside, the double doors with tempered glass closing behind him, shutting out heat and noise. The immediate absence of wind was a relief, and the space suddenly felt hollow. Cool, canned air hit his face. After the roar of the wind, his ears rang. He attempted to tame his curly hair but didn't try very hard.

A nod and smile and hello to the regular at the front desk, Mabel Lennon, who was dressed in a neatly pressed beige shirt, gold badge on her pocket flap. She'd been with the department forty years, and he was going to miss her when she retired.

"Looks to be an interesting day," she said. "Santa Ana wind always brings the weirdness. I'm hearing there's been an alien abduction in the mountains."

He wasn't sure he wanted to know what she was talking about. Considered asking, figured he'd find out soon enough. Could be nothing. Night cops, like night nurses, were a superstitious bunch.

He passed through security and the metal detectors, gathering his belongings from a plastic container on the other end of the conveyor belt. As he did most mornings, he took the stairs. A quick jog up the cement-block fire entry to the second floor, his footsteps echoing, the heavy door slamming and latching solidly behind him. In the second-floor hallway, division commander Captain Edda Morris stopped him. From where they stood, he could see through the glass wall into Homicide. Everybody was in action, and it looked like a choreographed ballet. People passed by with coffee cups in hand, heading for workstations and monitors and ringing phones, ready to see what had transpired overnight and what they'd have to prioritize. He typically launched the day with a briefing and sharing of information. Today would be no different.

"Have you seen the crazy stuff floating around social media?" Edda asked.

Ah, what Mabel was talking about.

Edda had worked in Homicide thirty years, most of that time spent here in San Bernardino County. She knew her stuff, and Daniel had learned a lot in the three years he'd worked under her. She had feathered lines around her eyes, and her shoulder-length gray hair had been cut recently. She'd said she gave twelve inches to a charity that made wigs for chemo patients. He'd wondered if there was much demand for gray. Or did they dye it?

"A possible murder," she said. "But we don't have any details and don't even know if it's real. I even heard someone mention alien abduction. Hopefully a joke. People on social media are talking vampires, pointing out spots on the victim's neck." She rolled her eyes.

Daniel had an Instagram and a Twitter account, but he hadn't looked at either in several days. He'd been too busy dealing with the women who were coming forward claiming to be his mother, who'd vanished when he was a child. This sudden interest was the result of a recently aired true-crime show. One of their local medical examiners had been snagged for a series that featured a new story every week, and Daniel had agreed to be on an episode about the Inland Empire Killer. The show's focus was on his involvement in the case, with only peripheral attention to his missing mother, but it didn't matter—many people had followed up their viewing with a deep dive into his history and background. And what had seemed like a good idea at the time—allowing the posting of his contact info, asking for leads about the Inland Empire case and possible bodies they hadn't yet found—had ended up being a source of significant regret. His inbox was overflowing.

This wasn't uncommon in his field; people had a weird need to be a part of stories bigger than themselves. The police department tended to see similar bogus responses whenever they requested help from the public. Daniel called the responders "crisis parasites." They loved to latch on to whatever current drama was being fed to the public by the media. Some people thought they were helping; others just wanted to feel important. But he didn't get why so many were coming forward claiming to be his mother when a simple DNA test was all it took to rule them out.

So no. He hadn't had time to pay much attention to social media.

Edda produced her phone, poked at the screen, turned it around. He leaned close and saw an Instagram profile that belonged to someone named "Deidra Cat Lover." Her recently posted images were shadowy, but he could make out a body in a tent. Dead? No proof. Real? No proof.

There was also a video. It wasn't much better.

"The account owner is claiming to have come upon a campsite on the Pacific Crest Trail where she says she found a dead person," Edda said. "Two other tents at the site were empty, all the supplies left behind. The other hikers, if this is real, seem to have vanished into thin air. So far, we haven't been able to contact the poster for information, and we've had no reports of anyone missing. So the big question is—is this real?" She passed the phone to him.

Using his thumb and forefinger, Daniel enlarged one of the photos of the body. A woman. "Could be a gunshot wound to the chest. But it also has the feel of something staged."

"My thought too."

"The poor photo and video quality, the lack of any details or information about the possible victim. Add to that the massive number of likes and the way it's gone viral . . . It seems like something designed to get more followers." Even the tagged location was vague. Instead of exact coordinates, the poster seemed to have chosen a randomly generated Instagram tag, and everybody knew those weren't always accurate.

Pacific Crest Trail, Section C.

Daniel was more of an ocean person. Not much of a mountain or desert guy, although that was changing. He had no idea how much ground Section C covered. A lot, he'd guess. Which meant chasing this down would require time, and it might not lead anywhere. This thing had all the markings of the found-footage dramas that had gained and lost popularity over the years. Fiction disguised as something real. The poster had included a few hashtags: #PCT #PCThiker #hiker #thruhiker. And her post had thousands of comments.

He passed the phone back. "I'll try to track down the family of the girl who posted the images. If I don't get any satisfactory answers there, I'll have to dig deeper."

"If it comes down to that, I suggest you contact a local trail expert," Edda said. "And involve your intern. This seems like a good research project for him. He's already excited at the prospect of an alien abduction."

She was kidding, but he wasn't sure about the intern. Davenport seemed nice enough, but his eagerness could be exhausting. And yet Daniel had been like him once, and everybody deserved a break. He'd certainly been given one by his adoptive dad.

"I will," he said. "And I know somebody who should be familiar with that section of the Pacific Crest Trail." Someone who planned to hike the whole thing.

Reni Fisher.

He knew she was going through a rough patch right now. Understandably. She'd gone into hiding and wasn't answering his calls. Getting her involved in the case would mean he'd be working with a damn good detective, and also give him a chance to see how she was coping. Keep a closer eye on her. He was concerned.

He pulled out his phone and opened his contacts. Reni's face appeared in the profile circle. The photo had been taken shortly after they'd solved the Inland Empire case. She had the kind of direct, sober gaze that might compel a specific kind of annoying person to tell her she should smile more. Auburn shoulder-length hair and severe bangs, cut, as he understood it, in something called a pageboy. The hairstyle hadn't been her choice, but it looked good on her. He also understood her need to grow it out so it would stop reminding her of the mother who'd cut it. The mother who'd left Reni for dead in the middle of the desert. The mother he'd killed.

Reni was one of the strongest people he knew, but it was a lot for anybody, even someone of her strength, to process, bury, deal with. She tended to pour herself into her art, and over the past weeks of silence he'd imagined her furiously working at her potter's wheel. Throwing and shaping clay was said to be an excellent form of meditation; he'd recently discovered that books had been written on the subject. Maybe he'd try it himself.

He made the call.

She didn't answer.

He wouldn't give up.

CHAPTER 4

Reni Fisher and her dog, Edward, sat high on an elevated area overlooking the Mojave Desert. A 360-degree turn would reveal earth and sky in every direction. Not a house or road or vehicle in sight. They'd had a few heavy snows the past winter, and now, even in early June, flowers were still blooming. The unusual abundance was called a super bloom, and the mountainsides were lush with color, the most prominent shades being yellow and purple.

The desert was hard to describe to someone who'd never visited it. On the surface, in the heat of summer or during a dry year, it could seem like just sand and dirt and rocks. And it truly was raw and stark and vast, hot and cold and dry, with a wind that blew so hard it knocked a person down sometimes. And yet, when it finally stopped blowing and the hummingbirds and bees returned and a pack of coyotes crossed her path, Reni could easily forget about the wind that had sent her to her knees. Right when she thought she couldn't take it a moment longer, the gusts would go quiet and clouds would loom low and near, going from pastel to deep red. Then the moon would creep into the sky, bold, bigger than the mountains and towns, pouring down on the curved highways. At that point, if she was driving, she'd pull over to stare at the magnificence for that brief magical moment.

She and Edward were in a prime spot, high up, but not that far from home. She often hiked miles and sometimes days with no chance of communicating with the outside world. She liked that. A hermit by choice, she rarely got phone calls anyway. The one she used to wait for—that call from the prison letting her know that her father, the Inland Empire Killer, was dead—would not be coming. Or the calls she used to get from her mother, asking if she wanted to stop by for dinner. Neither of those things would be happening now.

Sitting cross-legged on the ground, watercolor pad on her lap, she dipped her soft brush into a can of water (she preferred using the old-school tin-can method because the sharp edge cleaned the brush so well), shook off the excess, and rolled the brush in the cerulean blue. The paper was still wet from the clear water wash she'd applied with a thicker brush moments earlier.

In the desert air, it was hard to maintain the proper dampness needed to create an adequate fade of watercolor sky. A person had to work fast. A challenge. The slight moisture allowed her to add a blush of color to the line of mountains, working it from intense navy to pale blue at the top of the paper. Satisfied with the result, she cleaned her brush with the hem of her shirt and moved to the brown and white in her palette, gently rolling the brush again, combining colors to create a creamy shade that would work perfectly for the giant bloom on the nearby human-looking Joshua tree that was reaching for the sky. She'd use the same shade for the boulder with the bird on it.

On a whim, she'd taken a couple of her watercolors to the craft fair where she sold her pottery. They were purchased before she'd even gotten her booth set up. She felt a nagging guilt for selling the art to strangers, not because she didn't want to let the pieces go, but because she hadn't told the buyers that the desert landscapes were depictions of the spots where her father had buried his victims. And now those paintings were hanging in someone's home for them to enjoy. Of course it made her uneasy.

Only two months had passed since her mother's betrayal and the revelation of the dark role she'd played in the killings that had defined Reni's childhood. Not that long in grief time, and Reni was still struggling, trying to come to terms with it all. And not doing that well. But she'd learned it was better to fixate on what had happened than to try to look away, even for a minute. Because it hurt too much to return unbidden to the memory and be taken unawares. It hurt too much to revisit it. It was better to stay, not leave at all. It was better to just hold the pain close, caress it, whisper to it, never let it go.

She was trying hard to heal, and painting helped. For a while. Maybe she saw her pieces as a duty. Or even a penance. Many of the victims would still be alive if not for her involvement. Yes, she'd been a kid, but even as a kid she'd known things weren't right.

All she knew was that once she was done with a painting, she felt an overwhelming sense of relief. But after a few days the itch would begin again, and she'd look at the map on the wall of her cabin and pick the next location, the whole process an eerie echo of what her father must have gone through when feeding his need to kill.

How long would it take? For her to memorialize them all? He'd killed so many that it might never end. And they just kept coming. The FBI was still looking for bodies, and last she'd heard the count was twenty-six. Twenty-six young women her father had killed and buried. With Reni's unwitting help. A lot of her help.

Some might wonder how she could even visit the desert, let alone live there, knowing what had transpired. But the desert was still a place her soul needed, a place that brought peace and comfort. Even with its whole truth. It was almost as if she had to defend the desert, document its beauty, honor it—rather than defile it in the way he had. But she knew that once she packed up her paints, once she'd hit the road to head home, the nagging anxiety would return. The replaying of things in her head. The telling and retelling herself she'd done all she could, the best she could. The questioning of whether that was really true. The knowing deep down that it wasn't. She wished she had someone to talk to about it.

Not someone. Her mother. There it was. She wished her mother were still alive. Even if Rosalind Fisher had gone to prison, Reni would have liked to know she was there, living, breathing. She would have visited her, talked to her, maybe even pretended for a short while that Rosalind was the mother Reni had been tricked into thinking she was, and not a cold-blooded killer. But there was no pretense now.

Her phone alerted her to a text. Checking the screen, she saw the message was from Detective Daniel Ellis.

The text brought Reni jolting back to reality and jerked her out of her elaborately constructed fantasy. She was not in the desert, but was instead sitting in a café in Joshua Tree, a stranger across the table from her as they waited for their food to arrive. She had a pen in her hand. On a napkin she'd created a black-ink version of the painting she'd been daydreaming about, the place where her father had buried a woman named Carmel Cortez. It was especially recognizable because of the large round boulder that loomed as big as a house. How much time had passed since she'd spoken to the man across from her? Maybe not that much, because his expression was one of polite patience and a little curiosity, tinged with an appreciation for her napkin art. She read Daniel's message.

I could use help on a case. You interested?

"I'm sorry." She lifted her phone. Her breakfast date had a nice calm vibe. "I'm going to have to reply to this."

"No problem." The man—his name was Greil, right?—reached across the table for the napkin, picked it up and turned it so he could get a better look, then nodded, giving her a quick smile before glancing back down.

Her therapist had suggested dating. This was her first test, and she could already see it was a fail. It was too soon, she was too messed up, too wounded. She couldn't even sit through a meal without frantically drawing death scenes and imagining herself elsewhere.

She tried to remember what had piqued her interest in Greil. He had a kind face. He was a widower. Young for that label, but they hadn't gotten to how his wife had died. Like Reni, he was wounded, not in the same way, but hurting. He had some old tattoos, and he was . . . a mechanic. Was that right? Specialized in motorcycles maybe? From the LA area, but had moved to the desert after his wife died. The desert healed.

She replied to Daniel's message.

Sorry, I can't.

He'd seen that response from her a lot lately, or no response at all, so much so that she was surprised he kept asking for her help. He was a good detective, and she doubted he really needed her. He was just trying to keep her active and involved. It was nice of him but getting a little repetitive. Until today, she'd been avoiding everyone but her dog. Had she told Greil about the dog? Did *he* have a dog?

She looked at his napkin, which was lying on the table, cushioning a fork that was waiting for his meal. She wanted to pull it out and draw on it too. A blank page. Blank pages were good. And what burial site this time? So many choices.

Her paintings were like her own personal tour. She was surprised someone hadn't done that. Made an app that took you from one Inland Empire Killer burial site to the next, while including background information on her father, the victims, and also anything interesting about the location. Her favorite death spot was Amboy Crater, an extinct cinder cone volcano about seventy-five miles outside Barstow. But there was also Giant Rock, a freestanding boulder and once-famous gathering point for UFO believers. So many great locations to choose from, she thought with dark humor.

She wanted to draw and paint both spots. Her fingers curled; her palms itched. Her mind was taking her away again, and she forced herself to pay attention to the room, the man, the phone in her hand.

Her therapist said drawing and painting were good for her. Nothing to be ashamed of. She called it an "excellent coping mechanism." But her therapist had no idea how bad it was. She had no idea how often

Reni employed it to calm herself, day and night. Her therapist definitely didn't know the paintings depicted burial sites.

It used to be that her pottery and the hypnotic spin of clay on the potter's wheel did it for her, took her away. But after her mother's death, the wheel was no longer enough, even as demand for her pottery had increased. So after her father's burial sites had been confirmed, she'd started going to them. First just going. Then taking photos. Then drawing every detail. And finally, buying a set of watercolors and paper. It wasn't until she'd placed the soft and pliant brush against the paper, wasn't until the wet paper caught the color and caused it to bloom and change as it took on a life of its own, that she'd felt a sense of calm come over her that she hadn't felt in years.

Daniel replied: *I'm not asking you to go to a party or something. I could use some help.*

Reni: *I can't.*

Daniel: *I get it.*

Reni: *No, you really don't.*

Daniel: *No, probably not.*

He was going through another kind of hell, something that had impacted him all of his adult life. When he was young, his mother had gone out one evening and had never returned. It was heartbreaking. Reni was doing all she could to find her, dead or alive. Her watercolors, taking care of Edward, and hoping to bring Daniel closure made up her life right now.

Daniel: *You're familiar with the Pacific Crest Trail near San Bernardino, right? Haven't you been hiking segments of it in preparation to hike the whole thing?*

She had.

Daniel: *We've got a possible homicide of a hiker. I'll wait for you, but I'd like to head out soon.*

Like she was coming.

Reni: *I'm on a date.*

Daniel: *Haha. Good one.*
Reni: *No, really.*
Daniel: *Weird. Maybe this will interest you. Alien abduction.*
Reni: *Har har.*
Her phone rang.

She looked at Greil, mouthed *Sorry*, got up, and moved toward the front door of the café. Outside she stepped into a sliver of shade next to the rough wood building that was supposed to look like an Old West saloon. She answered her phone, elbow resting on the arm crossed at her waist.

Daniel dove right into the conversation. "Conspiracy theorists are already latching on to this."

Sometimes she wished UFO sightings and alien abductions weren't such a big part of desert lore, but when you lived in a place with so much sky, people saw things they didn't understand. The last big observation, seen and reported by hundreds, had ended up being a Hollywood crew filming at night.

Daniel continued, "Even within the department I'm hearing comparisons to the Dyatlov Pass incident."

She was familiar with the incident, which had taken place in Russia in the fifties. Several hikers died under mysterious circumstances. Some conspiracy theorists liked to believe they'd been killed by aliens.

"That's gotta tempt you, right?"

"It's one of my favorite mysteries," she said reluctantly. She didn't want to care about anybody, not anymore, but she had to admit it was good to hear his voice. They'd been through a lot together. He worried about her. She knew that. She worried too, because she was having a hard time keeping it together. But her old and true joke was that she kept plugging along because of her pets—Sam, gone, and now Edward. She'd found Edward only recently, or rather he found her when she'd been left to die in the desert. Edward had been starving, his hair matted. She hadn't known it at the time, but his presence when she was dying

29

had given her strength and a desire to survive. In bad shape himself and probably almost just as near death, he'd almost seemed to cheer her along as she dragged her broken body across the desert. She and Edward were both desert rats.

Daniel must have guessed she was weakening. He brought her up to speed on the details of the case, then said, "I tracked down and contacted the Instagram poster's family through her account. Her mother said the daughter and her boyfriend began hiking the Pacific Crest Trail in Mexico about three weeks ago. She doesn't hear from her daily, but she dug a little deeper, contacting friends, and it doesn't sound like anybody's heard from her or her boyfriend since her post went live."

"A lot of places on the trail have no cell service. And if she doesn't have anything like a Garmin for emergencies, that's not unusual." Reni was often out of contact for days at a time. It was something Daniel nagged her about. "What are you feeling about the social media post?"

"It has elements of a hoax," he said. "The no contact could be part of it. I'm sending a chopper up to see if they can get a visual on anything, but I'd like to check out the mountain myself."

Her weak spots, if she had any, were kids and animals. And also ensuring Daniel didn't make any foolish decisions. It wouldn't be the first time he'd used his lack of wilderness skills to coax her into helping him.

CHAPTER 5

Back in the café, Reni sat down and told her date she had to leave. "It's business. I'm sorry."

"What about our food? At least stay and eat."

Reni shook her head.

Their server, a young girl with green hair and piercings, arrived with her arms loaded with plates that she placed on the table in front of them.

"I'm going to need a carryout container," Reni told her with apology. "I can't stay."

"No problem."

The server left, and returned in less than a minute. Reni put a twenty-dollar bill on the table and dumped the scrambled eggs, bacon, and toast into the container.

"I'm really sorry," she told Greil as she got to her feet.

"It's okay."

But she could see he thought she was making up the work to get out of the date. It was very possible he was a nice guy. Seemed like it. But he didn't know her history. Or even her full name. What had she been thinking when she agreed to this?

"I really *am* sorry," she said.

"No worries." He lifted her napkin. "Can I keep this?"

She almost recoiled, but caught herself. "Sure." What did it matter? He didn't know what it was. But as she tried to imagine the napkin's journey, it still bugged her. Would he save it for a while? Tuck it away? All of that seemed wrong. Throwing it away would be best.

"It was nice to meet you," he said. "I hope everything's okay, and that you'll be okay."

Aww. Damn. That was sweet of him. "Thank you."

She started to leave, paused, grabbed the napkin from his hand. "I think I want to keep this," she said. "As a reminder of our date." He smiled and looked even more confused. She didn't blame him. She tucked it into the back pocket of her jeans.

When she stepped outside, wind caught the café door, almost pulling it from her grip. She shoved it closed, then turned and spotted a homeless man who was often on this corner, always holding a cardboard sign. Not about his own plight, but rather the plight of the world. Most of the time she agreed with him. Today his big piece of cardboard was whipping around as he struggled to keep the wind from whisking it away. In a brief moment of calmer air, she was able to read what was written in Magic Marker.

SAVE THE JOSHUA TREES!

She wholeheartedly agreed. The trees were not only in danger due to a changing climate, they were also at great risk from human expansion. At the moment, there was a plea by the Center for Biological Diversity to list the western Joshua tree as a threatened species under the California Endangered Species Act, but there was strong opposition to it by land developers. The typical nature-versus-commerce struggle. Reni hoped the trees and nature won.

She found a cement area near the base of the restaurant sign that wasn't as windy. She put her food down in the protected spot, saying, "I brought you something."

The man smiled. "You're an angel."

"Not really, but I appreciate your confidence." She'd given him food before. Sometimes money.

A car honked. He turned and waved at a passing vehicle, someone who could be either friend or foe. It never seemed to matter to him. After the wave, he got a fresh grip on his sign. She told him goodbye and left.

In her truck, she turned the ignition key as texts from Daniel hit her phone. Before driving off, she checked the screen. A link to the Instagram feed he'd been talking about.

With two fingers, she enlarged the photos, one at a time, especially the images of the body. She noted lividity beneath the eyes and along the jawline. Some shine to the skin on an arm, suggesting early body bloat. The wall of the tent was covered in flies. Something staged most likely wouldn't include flies, but anything was possible. People had gotten good at making fakery look realistic.

The post had close to a million views and a couple hundred comments. She scrolled, looking for responses from Deidra, the account owner. She didn't see any. Exact coordinates weren't supplied, but rather a less exact location that anybody could change. It was an area of the Pacific Crest Trail that Reni had hiked several times: Section C.

As she pulled her truck out of the parking lot to head in the direction of home, she called Daniel. When he answered, she said, "That's a pretty tough hike."

"The location's going to be a challenge," he agreed. "It's one of the reasons I wanted you involved. You're involved, right?"

She laughed. "The good news is there are a lot of access points, some not well known. I think we can park relatively close."

"How close?"

"Something that might only require a couple of hours of hiking. I'm swinging by my cabin to grab supplies, then I'll drop Edward at the sitter and hit the road." She gave him her ETA.

"I'll be ready and waiting."

Her place was thirty minutes from the town of Joshua Tree and a couple hours east of Los Angeles, but much farther in the sense of geology, weather, traffic, and life in general. Going from city to desert dwelling was like taking a trip from the earth to the moon. The house wasn't easy to find. The dirt road was rutted and climbed steadily to an elevation that bothered some but not others. Her small cabin was situated on a steep rise that afforded a view of Goat Mountain in the distance and a flat basin below. On a clear day, Reni liked to think she could see all the way to Nevada. Maybe she could.

She didn't anticipate being gone overnight, but she never went into the wilderness without adequate survival supplies. She gathered her basics: water, energy food, sunscreen, small first aid kit, lighter, flashlight, compass. It didn't take long, because she always had a small pack ready to go at any given moment. Prepping to drop Edward at the sitter took a little more time. She hadn't had him long, and she rarely went anywhere without him, so she hadn't established a routine. But she'd used a local dog sitter named Joss a couple of times in the past. He was an artist who, like so many in the area, had fled LA. He lived in a shack he was making more livable as money allowed.

Fifteen minutes after leaving her cabin she pulled up to Joss's and cut the engine. Wind was making the wires of the chain-link fence vibrate at a frequency that sounded like music. Edward, recognizing the location, sat up straighter and stared out the window. He was such a good boy. He heeled well, didn't bark, was patient in any situation. But as soon as she opened the truck door, he bolted for the house and the happy pink door. Joss must have heard them pull up, because he was right there, barefoot, wearing beige shorts, a plaid cowboy shirt, sleeves removed, hair in a ponytail, full tattoos on both arms. Reni spotted the outline of a round tin through his shirt pocket. His edibles, which he pulled out at random times to offer anyone nearby.

He was a social butterfly, always sending texts, inviting her to local events. She never went, but that didn't discourage him. He continued to send invites. They'd met at a craft fair where they each had a booth. She'd been selling her bird-feather pottery, and he'd had a stand of metal sculptures, most cut into shapes that would appeal to tourists—cacti, coyotes, Joshua trees. Edward had been with her, and Joss had whipped out his pet-sitting business card. It had looked like he'd been carrying it around awhile. She'd told him she didn't need a sitter, that she never went anywhere, but after doing a quick background check on him, she found him to be clean, other than an arrest for marijuana before it had been legalized for recreational use.

"There's my boy!" Joss said.

Edward jumped into his arms, and Reni felt a little pang of jealousy. Edward was *her* boy. But it could be he'd never really be anybody's boy again. Some dogs were one-person dogs.

Holding Edward in his arms, Joss said, "You didn't come to my art opening at the gallery."

"Is that a surprise?"

"I thought maybe you would. I looked for you."

"I'm not really into socializing."

"That's not healthy."

"That's what Daniel says."

He put Edward down, looked taken aback. "Daniel?"

"Someone I work with sometimes."

His face brightened.

Was Joss interested in her? The thought hadn't even crossed her mind. She felt a million years old even though she hadn't yet hit forty. She and Joss were actually close to the same age, but he seemed younger. Like someone who hadn't experienced any serious tragedies, which was an unfair assumption. Some people pushed through better than others. Some people were good at covering up the pain. You could never tell what a person was dealing with.

Did he know about her? He had to. What had happened in her past and what had happened not that long ago—they were both still in the news. But wouldn't it be great if he didn't? It would be like shedding her skin, starting over. Maybe that's why she'd met up with Greil. What a freeing notion, to interact with someone who didn't know her past and would never know her past. There was a reason she kept to herself.

She might have been someone who liked to socialize if her life had unfolded in a different way. But everyone she now met had the potential to become an enemy, or be someone who, when they found out about her, would be sickened by her background and even her. Maybe that's why she was okay with Daniel even though she'd been avoiding him. He knew her story and didn't recoil from her.

"I'm going to San Bernardino," she said, "and I'm not sure when I'll be back. Could be tonight, but could be longer."

"No problem. I can keep him as long as you need," Joss said. "He and Petunia get along fine."

Petunia, his Siamese cat. Edward, being the gregarious oddball that he was, loved cats.

Back inside her truck, Reni checked her email in case Daniel had sent info on the case. Nothing from him, but she did have a message from Janine Masters, a woman she'd been trying hard to get ahold of. Janine was Daniel's childhood babysitter, the person who'd been watching him the night his mother vanished. It seemed that now, after weeks of Reni's relentless emails and voicemails, Janine was finally agreeing to meet.

Reni had interviewed several people who'd known Daniel's mother, but the key players—the babysitter, the babysitter's mother, and the only still-living cop who'd come to the house the next morning—had all been evasive, not returning voicemails or emails. This was the first response of any kind Reni had gotten from any of them. Janine lived in San Diego, less than three hours away. Not a bad drive.

The bad thing? Daniel had asked Reni to stop looking.

CHAPTER 6

After leaving Joss's, Reni headed down the steep Yucca grade toward San Bernardino and the sheriff's department, where Daniel was expecting her. It was an easy drive—low traffic, very few lights. There were actually two grades, Yucca and Morongo. Both provided a descent from the high desert to the low of Palm Springs and Coachella Valley, a drop of over two thousand feet in elevation, and, sometimes in summer, an increase of twenty degrees in temperature.

Reni was driving through what was known as Morongo Basin, an area of Southern California residing within the Inland Empire. The basin was east of Los Angeles and the coast, north of Coachella, south of Death Valley, and southwest of Las Vegas. The word *basin* itself was confusing to visitors and even locals, as it was situated in a part of the high desert that got very little rainfall. The term was purely topographical, not intended to indicate something that held water. There *were* oases in the area, but there were few bodies of standing water.

The borders of the Inland Empire weren't well defined. Some cities sat solidly within the region. Other claims were murkier, and depended on the source. But undisputed was that the Empire reached all the way to the Mojave Desert, was geographically situated northeast of Los Angeles, and encompassed several municipalities including San Bernardino, a city nestled not so romantically in the foothills of the San Bernardino Mountains. Not so romantically because San Bernardino could reach a heat index that often earned them a high-danger status in the middle of summer. And those infamous Santa Anas were more extreme in San Bernardino because of wind being funneled through Cajon Pass, where it burst upon the city at speeds of up to eighty miles per hour.

Right now, temps for early June weren't bad—unusually cool, actually—but the wind had been gusting for days, drying out air and eyeballs. It had been blowing for so long that the blue sky was hazy with dust probably carried all the way from the dry lakebeds of the Salton Sea. The tainted wind made for amazing sunsets but not for amazing breathing. Asthma in the Coachella Valley and beyond was on the rise. Along with some alarming health statistics was the fact that the county boasted the highest levels of ozone ever recorded in the United States. But earthquakes and fault lines and wildfires and toxic air—Reni took it all in stride, the way most people from California did.

After passing fields of giant white turbines to finally reach her exit in San Bernardino, she took Tippecanoe to Third Street and parked her truck in the guest lot of the sheriff's department, then sent Daniel a text to let him know she'd arrived. He must have been waiting, because the double glass doors of the police department opened and he appeared, moving toward the parking area, head down, looking at his phone and glancing in her direction. He was wearing jeans and leather boots. Sunglasses and a cap to shade him from the sun. In other words, prepared for a hike and the outdoors without her nagging. Not easy for a city dude.

She stepped from her truck and slung her pack over her shoulder. Their paths converged at his SUV, which was white like her truck. White was the color of choice in an area where the sun-scorched paint of a dark car could give a person a burn serious enough to earn them a trip to the ER.

He smiled and unlocked the doors.

If Reni were to paint Daniel, she'd bathe him in warm hues and give him a blue sky with no dark clouds. She'd give him sheltering trees and a bench to sit on. She'd give him his mother back, maybe standing far in the distance on a hill or looking out a window, raising a wistful hand in either farewell or hello. His eyes would be kind, and Reni would remove the pain from them.

Paintings weren't an entire life, but a captured moment. And paintings could wish for what a person didn't truly have. But she wouldn't ignore evidence of a hard life. She might even make it more pronounced. He'd be looking at a sunset or sunrise, the golden-hour light caressing cheekbones, his curly and shiny hair.

He put the vehicle in gear and they pulled from the parking lot. A few red lights and they were heading up the 215 toward Section C of the Pacific Crest Trail. As he drove, he filled her in on what he knew, and she gave him directions to the trailhead she thought might be the best to use. A secret spot.

He asked about her date.

"We'd just ordered our food when I got your text," she said. "And I was actually glad to get out of there."

"Bad match?" he asked.

"He had promise, but I'm just not ready for anything like that."

"That's a shame." He sounded oddly pleased.

They passed a bar that was famous for Willie Boy burgers, and Daniel shook his head. "Ah, Willie Boy. Haven't thought about him in a while. The Ruby Mountain incident happened almost in your backyard."

"It did. California has some very dark and shameful history." Like the Dyatlov Pass incident, Willie Boy was another of her favorite cases that had never actually been her case—because it happened in the early 1900s. "It's tough to find solid facts because there's so much misinformation to digest and discard," she added.

"I've always felt like the shooting of his girlfriend's father was self-defense and that Carlota wasn't kidnapped but went with Willie Boy willingly," Daniel said. "It felt like a plan. And he never shot anybody in the posse except by accident, when he hit a pair of hand-cuffs that caused a bullet to ricochet. He only shot the posse's horses."

"Which I absolutely hate, of course," Reni said. "But he could have shot the men and didn't, which leads me to believe he wasn't the psychotic killer some of the sensationalized news sources claimed."

"He was a guy in love who made some stupid mistakes," Daniel said. "And paid the price. When the woman he loved was accidentally killed by the posse, he was grief-stricken. And because of that grief, he might have been the dead man found on Ruby Mountain."

The body had been too bloated to ID. "I've always wanted to think he got away." Reni pointed to a dirt road.

Daniel slowed and turned. "So you like the romantic version. And now there are hamburgers named after Willie Boy. Bet he never saw that coming."

"Could be justifiably romantic. And yet we have a history of romanticizing outlaws here in the United States. People romanticized my father even though he killed so many innocent women. I hope to hell nobody ever names anything after him, but if they do, it might be pie. He loved peanut-butter pie." Thinking about Benjamin and his pie made her heart soften in the way thinking about his hummingbirds did. He'd carefully fed and cared for the tiny birds. And once when Reni was small, he had even cried when he found one dead.

"They're vicious little things," he'd explained through his tears. "They have plenty of food. They kill each other for no reason."

He really had known what he was talking about.

"The pie would be some deep normalization," Daniel said.

"No kidding." She pointed again, this time at a small dirt pull-off next to a trailhead. She was glad he couldn't see her face, because she suddenly felt close to tears herself. She hadn't heeded her own advice, which was to never look away, never let a memory catch her unawares.

The trailhead was mainly unused and definitely off-app, changed and redirected by fires, with a trail that wasn't well marked and could only be found on old maps or recommended by people who liked to reference the obscure. There were no other cars around, which was a relief. Despite the unpopular and relatively unknown entry point, Reni had worried about press. But the story wasn't really a story, not yet, and it might never be. Maybe this would end up being just a day in the mountains for both of them.

It was much cooler here than the desert. Beautiful and perfect. Blue sky, very little wind. Ideal. There was a reason people lived in California despite the threat of fires, earthquakes, and mudslides. It was hard to turn your back on days that were often perfect.

She was pleased to see Daniel with a pack. It was small, nothing like her overnight that contained close to everything they might possibly need, including her sketch pad and watercolor pencils, but it was a pack. With hopefully food and water.

Reni was more of a desert hiker, but after leaving her job with the FBI, she'd done quite a bit of mountain hiking, mainly one-to-three-day sections of the PCT, particularly where they now were, in the San Gorgonio Mountain region, and especially in the summer when it was too hot to hike in the Mojave and the temperatures of the mountains meant a person could be outside without fear of dying from the heat. She hoped to eventually hike the entire PCT from Mexico to Canada. She hadn't done it yet, because she was taking it in small steps, conditioning herself and Edward. Also, she wouldn't admit it aloud, but mountains, evergreen trees, made her uneasy and depressed her. The desert might have been the place her father had buried most of his victims, but the mountains had been the place he'd lured and trapped them. And the mountains had often been his killing field.

Standing at the trailhead as she and Daniel adjusted their packs, her mind returned to a time when her father had brought her to such places, and she'd helped him lure young women to their deaths. She wasn't supposed to have witnessed his atrocious acts. He'd tried to shield her from that. Make her see only little father-and-daughter outings. But a few times she broke the rules and left the car, where she'd been told to stay. She saw things no child should ever see. And now her mind tumbled back there . . .

She hears a scream and other weird noises. Does her daddy need help?

Scared, but concerned for her father, she tiptoes down the trail and into the woods, stopping to listen. More than once she thinks about turning around and running back to the car. But her daddy might need her.

And then she sees them, her father on top of the girl with long braids. And it looks like he is slamming her head with a rock. That was the weird sound she'd heard.

Words that don't belong to the game come out of her mouth before she can stop them. "You're hurting her!"

Her father looks up, his face shadowed and ugly, like the mean wolf in a book. "Go to the car!"

She doesn't move. Can't move. But she can still talk. "Don't hurt her! Stop hurting her!"

"It's the game!" the wolf snarls.

The girl on the ground is quiet now, and something dark is crawling out from under her head. That's good. She isn't screaming. She isn't in pain. Just the game.

"Go back to the car!" Her father's voice is high, like a lady's.

She turns and runs, trying not to think about anything but his weird voice. She climbs into the back seat and covers her ears. Her heart is beating as fast as hummingbird wings.

Everything's going to be all right. Just close your eyes and take a little nap.

She feels a bounce and hears the trunk slam shut. Keeping her head down and her eyes closed, she hears her father slide behind the steering wheel, breathing hard like a dragon. Without a word, he drives away fast, tires squealing. Later, as the car takes them home, he reminds her, "Just a game."

As an adult, she feared she'd always associate the scent of evergreens with her father. So deep in Ponderosa pine and western juniper wasn't a place she wanted to be. But, as she did with most things in her life, she dove in and accepted the pain like a penance. Her form of cutting. And the scent was everywhere in the world right now anyway. It wasn't only used in candles, it was used in deodorant and soap. And those damn air fresheners people hung from car mirrors. Even aftershave. She sometimes thought she caught a whiff coming from Daniel, and she wondered if he'd ever noticed her slight recoil. Her own mother used to spray it around the house. Reni wondered if Rosalind had known and had specifically chosen that scent for Reni's visits. But that seemed a little too aware for Rosalind. No, Ben Fisher was the one who'd actually twisted his ability to feel what others felt into a tool for his crimes. A killer with the ability to empathize was the most dangerous killer of all.

As she and Daniel took off up the trail, Reni in the lead, her heart pounded, but not from exertion. She knew how to pace herself. She didn't give in to the temptation of going fast when the path was easy, and she took the steep areas slowly. As she moved up and forward, her mind struggled with three things: the beauty of the day, the memories of her father, and the mystery of what had brought them here. She didn't know if she was heading into a crime scene or a hoax. Or if they'd find the spot at all.

The Santa Ana winds were typically most active October through March, but weather had gotten more volatile in recent years, and the winds that people liked to personify and blame for everything from a stubbed toe to disease and death had become even more unpredictable. As they walked and the elevation increased, the wind went from a slight breeze to a steady thirty miles per hour, with gusts close to fifty, the movement through the swaying branches producing a strange low howl. The temperatures fluctuated as well; they marched through patches of cold and patches of warm air. A switchback curved sharply, a sheer drop to certain death below, and as Reni rounded the point, a gust almost knocked her off her feet. She flattened herself against a rock and finished the turn, Daniel close behind. Then they dipped into a stand of dense trees, the roar in her ears going hollow. After making it through that excitement, they took a water and food break in a shaded area.

Reni was sweating from the exertion, but the air moving across her bare arms was cool. She'd brought a dry shirt, but right now the damp felt good. They were in a nice spot, one just begging for a nature photograph with the deep ravine on one side, layers of mountains in the distance, the tallest peak still covered in snow. It had been a good idea to prepare for both cool and hot temps.

Daniel offered her some of a mandarin orange he'd pulled from his bag. "Shall we bet? Hoax or real? Are you leaning toward anything?"

She peeled off a couple of slices, took a bite, gave his question some thought. "The flies. I keep coming back to the flies."

"Twenty bucks it's a hoax," Daniel said.

The Instagram girl *had* gone hiking, according to her mother. "I'm on the fence, but I'll go with no hoax," Reni said. "Twenty bucks."

"Deal."

They put water bottles away and slung their packs over their shoulders.

"It's pretty out here, right?" Daniel asked.

"It really is."

"But I'll bet it's not an easy place for you to be."

She looked at him for a few beats.

His sunglasses were perched on top of his cap. He had dark eyes and dark lashes. A scar on his brow she'd noticed the first time they'd met. Maybe from an old piercing. She was grateful for him and his sensitive astuteness. But that sensitivity was also the reason he hadn't been able to let his mother's death go for so long. Was he really ready to give up the search?

"It's not easy being here," she admitted. She was getting cold now but didn't want to swap her shirt yet. Needed to save it for later, when the temps dropped even more. "Thanks for realizing that."

They resumed their walk, the trail her focus. The wind continued to increase. The movement through the swaying branches included a new and different kind of howl as she leaned into her steps and the repetitious movement of just putting one foot in front of the other. As often happened when hiking, she zoned out and almost missed something important. This time it was a bit of orange fabric off the trail, through the trees and brush. A perfect place for someone to camp.

She stopped, and Daniel caught up. She pointed to the unnatural color between the trees. He adjusted his sunglasses, then nodded. They both slipped off their packs.

He motioned for her to circle to his right. He went left. As silently as two people could creep through low brush, they moved toward the target, knees bent, heads down. Like riding a bike. After years of FBI training and fieldwork, Reni Fisher knew how to do this. It came naturally.

CHAPTER 7

Reni approached the campsite, keeping an eye on the ground for signs of recent passage or any evidence that should be left undisturbed if the area turned out to actually be a crime scene. Keeping track of each other, she and Daniel moved forward. There were three tents, all a pretty shade of orange. She stepped into the clearing, crouched, and dipped her fingers in the ashes of the firepit. Cold. She looked up at Daniel and shook her head.

Nobody and nothing in the clearing. The secluded spot was located in a pocket of trees. She couldn't feel the wind anymore, but she could hear it. She could also hear insects. Popping against the side of one of the tents. She knew that sound, and she'd already noted the cause. Flies. She straightened. Back-to-back, she and Daniel slowly turned, doing a visual sweep of the area. Clear. Without speaking, he motioned toward the tents.

They were identical. Small, for one or two people. All appeared brand-new, all with flaps unzipped and hanging open. She was pretty sure Daniel was going to owe her twenty bucks. She no longer trusted herself with a gun, but right now she wished she still carried.

As if reading her mind about the need for a weapon, Daniel lifted his sweatshirt to reveal a holster at his waist. And a Glock 43. Small and lightweight, with a shorter muzzle than the 48. Dependable. It used to be her weapon of choice.

There'd been an incident when she worked for the FBI. Some might call it a breakdown. She wasn't sure. But one evening when she was closing in on a perp, her partner's face seemed to change and turn into the face of her father.

She drew on him. She almost pulled the trigger.

That night she went home and decided she needed help. She turned in her gun, took a mental-health leave that became permanent, and hadn't touched a gun since. She'd been all the more freaked out because of her personal legacy of death, courtesy of Benjamin Fisher. In her work for the FBI, she'd never expected to actually shoot a living thing. The weapon, at least for her, had been a deterrent, a prop.

She and Daniel stood very still, glancing at each other, turning their heads, looking, watching, listening. He finally moved forward and lifted the flap of the nearest tent. After a moment, he motioned for her to join him at the opening.

The body inside belonged to a woman with braided hair. Very obviously dead, and currently with cadaveric rigidity, which typically started a couple of hours after death. A body tended to hit full rigor around the twelve-hour mark and would remain that way for another twelve before slowly reversing. The rigor of this body put the killing at fewer than twenty-four hours ago.

Reni spotted two matching dark wounds on the neck. They could have been caused by a camping fork or even a Taser. Nothing that spoke to her of vampires or the aliens social media was talking about. The victim was probably around thirty, dressed in a teal T-shirt and gray shorts. The T-shirt had a logo across the front. *Kaleidoscope.* What was Kaleidoscope?

"Gunshot wound to the chest," Daniel noted.

No obvious weapon inside the tent that Reni could see. "Not a suicide."

"Nope."

I especially like the girls with long braids, her father had told her years ago.

The braids . . . she couldn't stop staring at the braids. That visual was mixed with the dead body and the scent of blood, the T-shirt logo with triangular evergreen trees. The combination worked against her and turned her legs to lead. Flies and bees were making so much noise it seemed like they were inside Reni's head. Maybe they were.

She finally managed to move her feet and stagger back, almost tripping. She caught herself, tried to keep her reactions to a minimum even though she was screaming inside. She needed to run, needed to grab pencil and paper and draw, draw, draw like a madwoman.

"Check the other tents," Daniel said in a low voice, not taking his eyes from the body. He hadn't seen her reaction.

Moving robotically, she stepped away, braced herself at the next tent, lifted a flap, and looked inside. Clothing, and backpacks with the same logo as the T-shirt. No body. She let out a tight breath and moved to the third one. Same. No human. She let the flap drop closed. And realized she was shaking. Not a little. This was the kind of shaking she'd seen in friends or relatives of murder victims. The kind of thing a person might call overacting if they saw it in a movie.

Only one thing to do.

She moved with long, deliberate strides, the world out of focus except a pinpoint that revealed her waiting backpack and her art supplies. As she moved, everything to her left and right was a blur. She was like a horse with blinders put in place to keep it from panicking.

Just look straight ahead. Look at the goal, the thing that will make this okay.

When she reached the pack, she dropped to her knees, unzipped the large compartment, and pulled out her sketch pad, followed by her little container of paint pencils she preferred for fieldwork. She frantically riffled through pages of her notebook, past sketch after sketch of burial and death sites, until she reached a blank page.

Had someone called her name? Her father, maybe? Chastising her for not staying in the car? No. That was over. That happened years ago.

This was new. This was happening now. A killer in the woods. A killer killing a female with long braids. The scent of evergreens.

She sat and crossed her legs, propped the tablet against her knee, chose a color. Orange. She would start with the tent and finish with the body. Or should she start with the body?

People die every day, little bird. It's not a big deal.

She drew the tent. All sharp angles and violent gestures, flaps open. Next came what was inside the tent. She chose Light Apricot for the swollen arms and legs. Burnt Umber for the hair. Bordeaux Red for the dried blood. The woman had been wearing a teal T-shirt with a white logo. *Kaleidoscope.* A circle with evergreen trees and a stream. Peaceful.

They're only pretending, little bird.

Normally she would have lightly sketched the scene in first, but she felt compelled to get it down as quickly as possible before it flew from her head. Working backward, she picked up another colored paint pencil and began to shade the hair and the face, the clothing and arms and legs.

Years ago, she'd drawn for her father. He'd criticized her work due to its lack of realism, so she'd learned to suppress the desire to go for the abstract or anything inaccurate. He taught her to be exact. And so she learned to note every fine detail, things most people wouldn't even notice. Things you might not even see in a photo. Like the lip balm on the ground with a logo that said *Made in the Mojave* and included a silhouette of a Joshua tree. The way the dead woman's tongue had already turned black, the tongue itself swollen, half outside the mouth so it looked almost like a growth on her face.

Reni worked quickly, shading in the correct colors for the clothing, even paying close attention to the accuracy of the sunlight that tried to penetrate the thin cloth of the shelter. This would give them another time-of-day reference.

Some deaths were beautiful, but most weren't. She hadn't learned that from her father. Just a fact. A peaceful death was what everyone wished for, but very few received. Nobody wanted to know that, though, and she'd been known to lie a few times when talking to a family member who asked that tough question: *Did she suffer?*

After her father's arrest, she hadn't seen him again until recently, but she'd read something he'd said in the transcript of an early interview.

I gave them a good death.

So much delusion. Had he believed that nonsense? Probably not. Had his victims suffered? Most likely.

He was calling her name again.

She ignored him.

Time passed. Maybe a few minutes. Maybe seconds. Then a shadow fell across her paper. She didn't lift her eyes. Instead she pressed her pencil so hard against the tablet that the point snapped. Finally she forced herself to look up, expecting to see Ben Fisher standing over her.

"You okay?" the shadow asked.

Daniel.

She looked back down. A moment later, she brushed the broken pieces of colored wax away with her hand. The drawing was done. She pulled in a deep breath. Let it out. This was what it took. Drawing removed the pain from her heart and put it outside her body, on paper.

She recalled a short story, maybe something written by Edgar Allan Poe, about how the subject slowly died as she was painted, as if the paint sucked the life from her. This was the opposite of that. The sound of the pencil on the paper, the re-creation of the scene, the colors, the act of reproducing it, all worked together to ease the ache and panic deep in her stomach.

She managed a smile. Probably not a very good one, but maybe convincing enough even for someone as perceptive as Daniel. "I'm fine."

CHAPTER 8

He didn't fall for it. Reni could tell.

"You don't look fine." Daniel dropped to the ground beside her, grabbed his pack, and dug out two bottles of water. He handed one to Reni, along with a ridiculously big cookie. Chocolate chip.

She drank some of the water and took a mindless bite of cookie just because it was in her hand. Her eyes widened at the soft texture and burst of rich flavor.

"Good, right?" Daniel took a bite of his, chewed, swallowed. "I keep telling Bo he needs to start selling these things. Open up a cookie shop."

Reni wasn't much into food, period, but the cookie was good enough to distract her from her present state of mind. "Definitely better than his pizza." And knowing Bo had made the cookie added another layer of comfort to it. Also endearing that he'd sent cookies with Daniel. She imagined Bo standing at the kitchen door, handing Daniel his lunch as he left. Their entire relationship was charming. A gruff single detective adopting a precocious motherless child.

"I found a billfold and ID with the dead woman," Daniel told her. "California license. She was from San Bernardino. Janet Ravenscroft."

"Her T-shirt had a logo. Kaleidoscope. I don't know if that means anything. Have you heard of it?"

"It's a fairly new business," Daniel said. "A place where teenagers go to break their social media and smartphone addictions. Started about a year ago, marketed toward the upscale crowd. I first noticed the expensive ads that ran after the local news feeds in the evening. Then I began seeing brochures in cafés. Don't know for sure, but judging from the money they're pouring into advertising, I got the idea it's very expensive and prestigious. They tout high-end lodging, a gourmet chef, yoga classes, hiking. Clientele tends to be kids of famous people. A lot of actors. Politicians. One of the focuses is on health, but I believe the biggest is on nature. Getting the kids out in nature. Without any electronics."

"The nature emphasis makes sense," Reni said. "It's always good to replace the hole left by whatever addiction you're removing." She finished her cookie, then drank more of the water. Felt better. It reminded her of the old trick used to get a toddler to stop crying. Give them a drink. Give them a treat. She tucked her sketch pad away.

He got to his feet, extended a hand, pulled her up. "If you don't want to go back to the crime scene, I can meet you at the trailhead. You can wait for me there."

"I really am fine. The cookie helped. Maybe I needed some sugar."

At his expression of doubt and curiosity, she shrugged and added, "Drawing is something I do now. When I'm stressed. It makes me feel better."

"Like pottery?"

"Yeah."

"I still haven't tried that."

"I could teach you to paint if you ever feel the need for some art therapy. It can be very effective." She'd offered to let him use her wheel, but watercolor might be more his thing. And yet art as therapy didn't work for everybody. Sometimes it just made a person frustrated, especially if they weren't interested in art in the first place.

"I might take you up on that." He moved away to stand on an overlook. Remaining in the open area, he wandered around, holding his phone high, finally climbing to a higher elevation on a rocky perch.

Cell service could be spotty in the mountains. Nothing in one location, and a good signal in another. It took patience to find the magical spot.

"Two bars," he announced with satisfaction. "I need to contact the department."

He made the call and requested a crew to process the scene, along with a search team to comb the area. The helicopter already in the air was given their location and the location of the trailhead. Then he made another call, asked someone on the other end to get more info on Kaleidoscope, specifically the owner's name and number.

After disconnecting, he said, "San Bernardino Search and Rescue dogs are occupied with two other searches, so I don't know if or when they can offer assistance."

"I know somebody." A woman who'd helped Reni on a few missing persons cases. "I'll reach out to her."

While they waited for a processing crew to arrive, they returned to the crime scene and continued with a cursory investigation, this time focusing on the tents with no bodies, Reni deliberately avoiding the shelter with the dead woman. She'd seen a lot of death in her life, but this trigger had hit hard.

They hadn't come with crime-scene gear, so they had to be careful about disturbing evidence, but they also needed basic information. The second tent had two sleeping bags and two open backpacks, both with the Kaleidoscope logo, some of the contents spread out on the floor. Most of it was makeup. A lot of makeup, including very non-camping items like false eyelashes and bottles of nail polish in colors like orange and teal. The items didn't look ransacked. They carefully examined the bags, but couldn't find any IDs or phones.

"No sign of a struggle here." Reni found that as odd and interesting as everything else. Had they been taken by surprise? Had they known the perpetrator? Had they run, leaving everything behind while the victim was being murdered in the nearby tent?

They moved to the third tent. One sleeping bag. Again, no ID. No phone. They carefully stepped away.

"Just gone," Daniel said.

"Are we looking at a stranger abduction?" Reni asked. "Something random?" Wouldn't have been the first time someone was attacked and killed on the PCT by a person they didn't know.

"Or was the perp someone in the group?"

"It might not be a kidnapping," she said. "The occupants might have gotten away." A kidnapping would be time sensitive. It used to be that anyone not found after the first seventy-two hours was most likely dead. And while they'd seen a shift in that trend over the past several years, such that many victims were staying alive much longer—today there was more hope for survival even weeks out—those early hours were still crucial. Especially when you considered that the victims would suffer until they were found. And after.

Daniel received a text message and read it. Tucking his phone in his pocket, he said, "Here's what the intern found out: Janet Ravenscroft worked for Kaleidoscope and apparently took some girls hiking yesterday. They were to be gone three days, and right now nobody has been reported missing. Four people altogether."

"And let's not forget about Deidra Cat Lover and her boyfriend."

"Right. Jordan Rice. I left a voicemail with his parents and will try to reach them again later."

Two hours after they found the body, a crime-scene crew arrived and a perimeter was established. Wilderness areas were always a challenge to contain, and it was easy to overlook evidence. People moved with care, and everyone wore paper slippers over their shoes.

Having done everything they could do on site, Reni and Daniel left the scene and walked back down the trail, moving much faster this time because of the descent, quickly reaching the base station that was already set up near the trailhead, officers monitoring who came and went. Family, friends, and news crews, once they began to arrive, would have to remain at the trailhead staging area.

Reni and Daniel tossed their packs into the SUV and headed down the mountain. They needed to focus on the next phase of the investigation before the press picked it up. First on their list was a talk with the owner of Kaleidoscope. Before reaching San Bernardino, Daniel got another message from his intern. He passed the phone to Reni. "Read that, will you?"

The sender profile photo was a smiling young man in stylish green glasses. Lucas Davenport. She read the text aloud. "'The story has leaked. One of the missing kids is Portia Devine, actor Phillip Devine's daughter. And he's taken the matter into his own hands.'"

Never good when parents took over the investigation.

The message was followed by the names of the other two clients who'd been on the hike. Reni read those too. "'JoJo McGrath and Emerson Rose.'"

Daniel let out a sound of surprise.

"Someone you know?" she asked. Obviously it was. From his reaction, it might have been someone he knew well.

"Emerson Rose's mother is an old friend from college."

"I'm sorry." College was a long time ago, though, too long to merit such a strong response. The mother must have been more than just a friend.

"It's fine," he said. "Just caught me off guard, that's all."

Reni got the feeling there was more to the story, but she wasn't the type of person to pry. He'd tell her if and when he wanted to.

CHAPTER 9

Actor Phillip Devine and his wife, Gwendolyn, ducked and ran for their private helicopter. Two hours earlier Phillip had gotten calls from both his agent and publicist about a disturbing social media post that had gone viral. Phillip had contacted someone he knew in the San Bernardino County Sheriff's office and the story was confirmed. The contact also supplied him with information that hadn't yet been released to the press. The woman leading his daughter's camping trip had been found dead, the other two tents empty. His daughter, Portia, was missing.

Harnesses latched, Gwen sobbing beside him, Phillip gave a nod to the pilot and the craft lifted from the helipad, hovered, then shot away in the direction of San Bernardino and Kaleidoscope.

Phillip had spent the past two hours reaching out to everybody he knew, pulling strings. He'd even made a call to the governor of California to get all the assistance he could possibly get. Amber Alerts were only used when there was a known vehicle, which they didn't have. But in a short amount of time, his daughter's face and a contact phone number were everywhere, splashed across social media, and his team and personal assistant were already fielding calls. He was used to getting whatever he wanted, and he refused to believe that anything bad had happened to his daughter. He'd find her.

Rumors were swirling about the event being a hoax, something perpetrated by the girls in order to get more social media attention. Maybe. He hoped to hell it was true and she was safe somewhere. That was exactly like something Portia's friend JoJo would do. But if the rumors *weren't* true, it meant someone was really dead. It meant his daughter was really missing.

In the city of San Bernardino, deep in a gated community, dressed in a business skirt and jacket and carrying a briefcase, Ava Brown, owner of Kaleidoscope, ran for her car, ducked into the passenger seat, and pulled the belt across her chest. Her driver drove to the front gate, which opened, then closed after them. Twenty minutes later, they were pulling up to the retreat.

Ava slipped on her glasses and raised a hand to shield her face from a small cluster of reporters already gathered outside the perimeter of the exclusive establishment she'd worked so hard to build. It hadn't been open long, and they'd already done a lot of good. But this, *this*. How would they ever recover from this? And how had it happened? Was it her fault? No, couldn't be. The world had just gotten out of control. Bad people were everywhere.

She blamed it on social media. Clients weren't supposed to do it, but some of the guests sent out media blasts before entering the program. People knew where they were going. Those goodbye posts were often promises to return as soon as the two weeks were over. The good news was some were cured and didn't go back online. The bad news was she couldn't save them all. Because that's how she thought of it. Saving.

This news was far worse. The awful video of Janet Ravenscroft was nothing Ava could have possibly dreamed of or prepared for. None of it was her fault, but she'd be crucified by the press. She also didn't like hearing that Reni Fisher was part of the investigation. Hopefully Reni wouldn't recognize her. If she did, things were going to be awkward.

CHAPTER 10

Kaleidoscope looked more like a college campus than a recovery center. In fact, according to the online information Reni found, it had been a college campus at one time, before it was bought and converted to house people addicted to their devices. Everything was beautifully landscaped, with clusters of duplicate plants ranging from barrel cacti, some in bloom, to tall cardon grande, a cactus that could rapidly reach twenty-five feet. Rows of palm trees lined walkways and the parking area. Everything looked new, and the place screamed money.

The investigation was still in the early controlled-chaos stage of initial outreach. Reni and Daniel now knew some of the possible players, but nothing concrete other than a visual confirmation of the dead woman in the tent. Not enough. Certainly nothing to release to the press. They were still awaiting the formality of a confirmed ID of Janet Ravenscroft from a close relative or the owner of Kaleidoscope. But the name and face of one of the girls was already being blasted across social media, with a tip-line number scrolling across the bottom of the screen. Not their doing, and Reni could only assume Phillip Devine was behind it.

After checking in at Kaleidoscope's main desk, where they were required to have IDs scanned and sign a confidentiality agreement, they were led down a pristine and soothing hall to an office, their guide giving them a serene smile and soft wave of her hand as she motioned for them to step inside.

A small blond woman with the straightest hair Reni had ever seen got up from her desk to greet them both with a confident handshake. Even the part in her hair was precise, right down the middle, no bangs. She had the kind of skin that took time and work: glowing, unblemished, very pale for California. Behind her was a wall of windows overlooking a courtyard, where groundskeepers worked near a utility cart. The woman's name was Ava Brown.

They sat down and Ava gave them a brief history of the business, an overview, including how she'd gotten a grant to partially fund what she kept calling a *retreat*. "I wanted to create a place where people could take care of their bodies and minds," she said. "I've been in recovery for ten years. I recognize addiction when I see it, and I wanted to help."

Reni wasn't sure about that. Help, or make money? The center wasn't something low-income households could afford. This was for the wealthy. And as Ava talked, Reni kept getting the sense she knew her. She must have reacted in some way, because Daniel shot her a questioning glance. And then it hit her. Reni *did* know her. Not a recent acquaintance, but old. She'd known her as a child. Ava had lived on the same block in Palm Springs, and she and Reni had been friends at one time. She didn't look anything like the child Reni remembered, but some mannerisms were still there. The way she blinked, and the way she smiled.

"You're Ava Boyce," Reni said.

"You two know each other?" Daniel asked with a curious expression.

"We lived on the same block when we were kids," Reni said. She didn't mention that they'd been best friends. Ava had to have known who Reni was from the beginning, maybe even before they'd arrived— so why hadn't she mentioned it right away? But things hadn't ended well between them. Ava's mother had put together a petition to have Reni removed from grade school, citing her as a distraction and possible danger. At that time, and even today, some people believed Reni had been behind her father's murders. That he'd killed people because she'd begged him to.

"Brown is my married name," Ava said. "I'm divorced now." She glanced at Daniel. "I just kept it."

She seemed a little uncomfortable now. Not really much to say about the old life in the old neighborhood. *Hey, remember that time your dad was arrested because he was a serial killer?* Reni didn't blame Ava's parents for being afraid, and she tried to tell herself she didn't blame Ava for what had transpired years ago. They'd been kids. But what had transpired recently—Ava's failure to report a possible problem—was suspect, and that was what Daniel immediately dove into.

"Why didn't you call the police about the missing girls?" he asked.

"As far as I knew, they *weren't* missing. Missing would be if they didn't return."

"But surely you kept in touch with the employee leading the group," Reni said. "These were young adults. I would think Janet Ravenscroft would have reported in at the very least once a day."

"You were up there. You know it's not easy to get cell service in that area. It was not unusual not to hear from her."

Daniel gave her one of his pained looks. Sometimes silence worked better than words.

"Okay, I did think it was odd," Ava admitted in a way that felt reluctant. "But the girls don't have cell phones. That's our whole strategy for recovery. They're completely unplugged. Janet, the team captain, was the only person with a communication device. I did try to contact her. It went straight to voicemail. I thought she was out of tower range or maybe something had happened to her phone. Maybe she forgot her charger. Maybe she lost it. It could have been any number of things, and I saw no reason to panic."

"And you don't have any protocol established for such a break in communication?" Reni asked.

"We're still learning. The overnights were an expansion of our day-hike packages. This was only the third group to go."

"A more expensive outing, as I understand it." Reni recalled the price list she'd viewed online as she and Daniel had headed back to San Bernardino.

"So?" Ava asked. "What does the price of the packages have to do with anything?"

"I think you might be more worried about the reputation of your new business than you are the girls," Reni said.

"That's ridiculous. This is exactly what I was afraid of. You're just using what happened to us as kids to attack me."

Not true, but Reni picked up on some old guilt from Ava. If the roles had been reversed, Reni wouldn't have ghosted a friend, even as a kid. So Ava's past character traits could suggest she was now watching out for herself instead of the girls. People could force themselves to change, basically stuffing a square peg into a round hole, but the core person usually remained the same.

Daniel redirected the conversation, and Reni settled deeper into her chair. Let him take over. Maybe she *was* harboring some resentment.

"We're going to need all the information you have on your team leader," he said. "And everything you have on the girls."

"All info on the girls is confidential." Still pushing back.

"Three people are missing," Reni pointed out, her silence not lasting even fifteen seconds. "I suspect the parents would want us to do everything in our power to get them home."

"We'll also need a list of all employees and anyone who had contact with the girls after their arrival," Daniel said. He went on to ask if she'd noticed anything odd. "Did Janet have any enemies? Fight with anybody? Anything going on in her personal life?"

"I can't confirm any of those things," Ava said, still coming across as defensive. Her demeanor changed when she seemed to consider a way out for herself and Kaleidoscope. "Do you think she was the target?" A perpetrator after Janet and not the girls.

"We don't know. We have to start somewhere, and since she's the only confirmed death we have from the group . . ."

"We're also going to need numbers for all those employees," Reni said. "Officers from the police department will be taking their formal statements."

"You're right," Ava said, seeming to ride a fresh wave of hope. "I should have called the police. I know that now. But I honestly thought it was just a communication issue. And yes, I'm worried about the reputation of this place. Everybody is going to pull their kids out of the program and demand their money back. It's . . ." She took in a shaky, calming breath. "It's already over for me. I'll help you in any way I can."

Reni's attitude toward Ava softened.

"We'd like to see their rooms," Daniel said.

"The parents . . . They'll be here soon . . ."

"We have to move quickly," Reni said, more kindly now, "and we've already lost valuable time."

"Of course, of course." Ava rose. "Follow me."

They left her office, her shoes loud against the tile, the sound oddly abrasive in a place that was supposed to convey peace. Daniel's and Reni's quieter steps left behind dusty footprints from the mountain trails. As they walked, Ava pointed out the dining hall and kitchen, a cozy library with comfortable-looking chairs and a fireplace, currently not in use, plus a game room with pool tables.

"We also have a tennis court and saltwater pool," she said.

Another few turns landed them in a wing that looked like a hotel with rows of doors. She went from one private space to the next, waving a code card in front of the handles, the sensors responding one after the other as she opened doors to reveal suites.

All the beds had been made in the same way, everything tidy.

Ava got a text. She checked her phone, tucked it away, explained. "That was a message from my assistant. We've been able to reach all of the parents, and some of them are on their way here."

"Some?" Daniel asked.

"Rachel and Stanley Rose are requesting you meet at their home," she told Daniel. "I can give you their phone number."

"I have it," Daniel said.

Interesting, Reni thought. To make that demand of a detective was unusual, but the mother and father might have been too hysterical to drive, or they might have needed the comfort of their home space while dealing with such a horrible event.

"We'd like to talk with the parents in a private area," Daniel said.

"I assumed as much." Ava appeared completely resigned now. "I'll have a private room set up, and someone will let you know when they arrive." She left them alone in the hallway with the unlocked doors.

The first room was like a high-end hotel with a comfortable-looking bed and a bathroom with a fancy shower and gold fixtures. A balcony overlooked a nearby preserve. Such excess. This wasn't the real world, Reni thought as they began their search.

Girl stuff. Makeup. Clothing that was probably expensive. They didn't find diaries or hard copy of any kind. "It's interesting how teens don't write anything down anymore," Reni said. Normally in this situation, personal devices would be logged as evidence. The girls had come without them. The rooms, even with the clothing and makeup, felt devoid of personality. Maybe that was the idea. A monastic stay. The surroundings, although plush, were still stripped down to necessities. Nothing more. A reset. She understood such things.

"It *is* strange," Daniel said. "And it makes it especially tough for us."

Phones and cell tower pings could be an excellent tool for tracking the missing.

They were about finished with the rooms when they got a text informing them that Portia Devine's parents had arrived, and they could meet them in the atrium.

"I don't feel we got any information here," Daniel said.

"Although the absence is something."

"What's the deal with Ava Brown?" he asked.

"Not really anything. We were best friends until my father was arrested. And we never spoke again after that."

"What were you? Eight? That's old enough to understand loyalty. She turned away when you needed a friend the most."

"I never blamed her, but of course it hurt at the time."

"Maybe I'm being a little reactive since it's you. Just don't like the idea of someone hurting you, even if you were kids."

She looked him in the eye. "You might be too soft-hearted for this business."

He smiled. "That's something we can agree on."

They left to meet up with the parents.

Portia's father, Phillip Devine, had one of those names that was a brand, the first and last name rarely hanging out alone. He was dressed in black jeans and a crisp white shirt, too many buttons unbuttoned, his hair looking as if it had been styled that morning, but maybe it just did that naturally. Reni was surprised to see how short he was in person. She had a good six inches on him. She recalled reading something about how he had to stand on a box sometimes, especially when working with a tall costar.

In true blockbuster fashion, the couple had arrived in a helicopter. Through a narrow set of windows, Reni saw the aircraft's blades still turning slowly before coming to a full, droopy stop.

Reni didn't watch many movies, but it was impossible to be unaware of the actor's existence. His face was everywhere, even on buses and buildings, whenever he had a new movie release. She'd seen him interviewed a time or two. His wife, Gwendolyn Darby Devine, was also an actor, not as well known. She'd stepped away from the business to manage a line of organic skin care products. She was almost too beautiful in person. Daniel looked a little entranced, like he was watching a sunset. Reni caught his eye. With one finger, she pushed her chin up to close her mouth. He recovered before anybody else noticed.

Reni asked about their daughter. What she was like.

"She has a YouTube channel and a lot of followers," Phillip explained, his focus immediately landing on the guilt he was feeling for sending his daughter here. A typical response. Trying to make sense of how they got to this point. The path they'd taken, which they might now question. "She doesn't need the money," he added. "We were just trying to be responsible parents."

"I blame Kaleidoscope," Gwen said. Her brows didn't move even though she was obviously distressed. "They should have had better security. I can't believe they took those girls out there without some kind of plan." Her eyes were red-rimmed. So were his.

Reni had to agree, but that didn't stop her from getting right to the point. "Some people are saying it was a stunt gone wrong. Do either of you have any reason to think that might be true?"

Everyone, including Daniel, looked surprised at the direct question, but Reni hoped to catch them off guard.

"No," Phillip Devine said. He seemed to grow distracted and annoyed. "She'd never be part of something like that."

"She bragged on a live feed about how she promised to be back soon, and here she is in the news," Reni pointed out.

"That's something we need to think about," Gwen admitted softly. It was obvious she thought it could be true.

Phillip shot his wife a stern look. "Our daughter is not a murderer."

"I don't think that's what anybody is suggesting," Daniel said. "Sometimes teenagers get caught up with unscrupulous people, and situations can escalate. We have to remain open to all possibilities."

There was a commotion at the door. Crying. Some shushing. Another couple had arrived—the parents of JoJo McGrath. The father wore a shirt with snap pockets and snaps on the sleeves, something vintage that had been updated with teal and orange embroidery on the collar. His wife, Belinda, wore the sort of flowing cotton dress that could be found in a lot of the little desert boutiques. Both of them were tan and healthy-looking, the quintessential middle-class California couple.

Jim McGrath told them he owned a sewing machine repair company. "I have five employees. We basically make and repair the machines."

Seemed an odd thing to share without being questioned about it.

"My mother was a seamstress," Daniel said, "so I have an affinity for sewing machines. I even have a few old Singers in my garage."

The things you could learn about a person during a subtle investigation, Reni thought. Sharing his own personal story was a good technique to help alleviate some tension in order to get to the real questions, and the father seemed to welcome the mundane diversion.

Jim McGrath lifted the flap on his shirt pocket and pulled out business cards, handing one to Daniel. "If you have a machine in need of repair, let me know and I'll work you in." He gave a card to Reni. "You too."

"I don't sew, but thanks." However, once this settled down, she planned to contact him and see if he had ever repaired a machine owned by a woman who might be Daniel's mother.

Ava returned to show them to a private meeting room. She didn't stick around. The way she kept vanishing and reappearing had Reni imagining her running back to her office to have short meltdowns before materializing again.

A pitcher of water with sliced cucumbers had been left in the middle of a long table. It seemed oddly inappropriate—spa-like and frivolous—under the circumstances. There was nothing else to drink, so Reni filled enough glasses for them all. They sat down at the conference table, a wall of windows on one side, tranquil nature prints and possibly original art on the other. All very tasteful but sterile.

The group meeting revealed more about the girls; fears and worries were shared among the parents. How they felt to blame, how the children hadn't wanted to go. Responses that were common, and no matter how many times they were told it wasn't their fault, nothing would remove the sense of guilt.

"We're going to need their computers and phones," Daniel said. "Passwords if you have them. We have an excellent digital forensics team that might be able to determine if there is any connection between any of the people involved," he added. Daniel also gave them an assignment. "Contact friends, family, neighbors. See if there's a way we can connect Jordan Rice and Deidra Lundy to the girls. In cases like these, we look for commonalities that might lead us to a reason, which could in turn lead us to the missing girls. I'd like to especially know if any of them knew the girl who posted the Instagram video."

Throughout the meeting, Phillip Devine kept answering his phone, sometimes stepping off to one side, sometimes remaining at the table. From his side of the phone conversations, the only side Reni could hear, it appeared he was continuing to guide his own investigation through the use of media and contacts. At one point, he got up and left the room altogether. Reni shot Daniel a look before following Devine, closing the door behind her.

She entered the hall in time to hear the movie star ending the conversation and saying something about getting his daughter's face on the side of city buses. Once his phone was in his pocket, he looked at Reni as he patted his shirt pocket. "I don't have a pen on me."

"What?" *A pen?* "Oh, no. I'm not here for an autograph." It was a sad commentary on celebrity culture and how people in the spotlight could rarely have real interactions with people. Even now, when his daughter was missing, he was expecting new people within his orbit to seek something from him.

"I wanted to remind you that we're the ones in charge," Reni said. Back in the meeting room she'd gotten the idea she and Daniel were just an annoyance to him, and now she was sure of it. But this was not one of Devine's movies. He couldn't dangle from a helicopter and pluck Portia from a mountaintop even if that's what he wanted to do. This was real life. "We're the detectives. If you're thinking of taking any action like putting your daughter's face on the side of buses, you need to run that past us. Let us do our job."

He looked at her, *really* looked at her, for the first time. He probably spent a lot of time avoiding eye contact with strangers. "Will you do it?" he asked. "Your job? I'm not feeling confident about that."

She wasn't feeling confident either. Missing people often turned up dead, but his disrupting the investigation was dangerous and risky. "Detective Ellis might seem laid-back, and he is, but his cool head actually works to his benefit," she told him. "He's good, one of the best. And I'm not too shabby either." As she spoke those words, she realized she was committing to this, to finding the missing girls. Of course she wanted to help, to bring them home, but she wasn't going to fool herself. The search, especially when it involved young women, was another form of atonement.

"The important thing is to keep us in the loop, don't get in Detective Ellis's way, and don't undermine the investigation," she said. "That's all we ask."

"How do you honestly investigate something you think is fake? That's what I want to know. You said as much earlier."

"I was just checking all the boxes. That's all. We want your help. We need your help, but sometimes helping means restraint. And sometimes it doesn't take the form of having to be the hero."

He stared at her for several beats, then pulled in a deep breath and said, "Thank you." He rubbed his face, swiped a knuckle under his eyes. His hand was shaking, and her heart softened again. His voice, when he spoke again, was shaking too. "That makes me feel better."

She nodded. "Good."

While they'd been in the hall, the meeting inside the room had broken up. The three parents and Daniel filed out. As Daniel and Reni walked away, the parents huddled and comforted one another. It was good for them to have some private bonding time without the intrusion of detectives.

Outside, Daniel checked his phone. "Text from Evangeline," he said. "The body of Janet Ravenscroft has been officially identified by a relative, and Evangeline has adjusted her schedule to accommodate us. She'll begin the autopsy in three hours."

Reni thought about the conversation she'd just had with Phillip Devine. Had it been too positive? Made Daniel seem invincible? She'd never tell a parent that everything would be okay. She, more than anyone, knew that was something a detective should never do. Not in this world. Maybe she should have offered more of a warning so he'd be prepared for the worst thing that might ever happen in his life. She sincerely hoped Phillip and Gwen Devine wouldn't end up having to ID their daughter at the county morgue.

Daniel looked at his phone. "I got several texts from Emerson Rose's mother while we were inside. She wants to meet at her home in Redlands."

"When?" Reni asked.

"Now."

Things were moving quickly. That was good.

CHAPTER 11

One week earlier

He noticed her right away. She was shorter than him, which was good because he didn't like tall girls. She had perfect skin, not dark and not light. He hated girls with really white skin because you could see their veins. He didn't like to think about what was under there, didn't like the reminder of how a person's heart pumped blood through their body all the way to their capillaries. He could hardly look at his mother anymore because of her transparent skin, but the girl in the dining room was almost perfect.

When he walked past her table, she glanced up from her baked squash, looked right at him, and smiled. That direct gaze opened the door and told him so many things. She liked him. She was interested in him. She would like to get to know him. She would like to live with him and maybe even eventually have sex with him if and when he was ready.

How could they make it happen? That was the silent question she asked with her smile and her eyes. He moved closer so he could hear her voice again, and maybe learn something about her. She was talking to some other girls, these with skin that was too white, the kind of white that made him shudder. They were complaining about how their parents had made them come here. Eating some fancy meal he couldn't even pronounce, and they were complaining. But he found out her name. Emerson. He wasn't sure how he felt about that. Might need to be changed. Seemed a little too different to him.

As he hovered near her table, he heard her talking about her stepdad and how he'd betrayed her by sending her there, how she would never feel the same about him now. He nodded to himself. Oh, she needed to be rescued. That was for sure. He could do it too. He had guns and he had a car. He had a good place to hide that not many people even knew about. He swallowed and asked if she wanted more water.

She said, "Yes."

That *yes* was a cry for help. *Get me out of here, take me away with you.*

"I will," he said.

She blinked and looked as if she hadn't heard him right.

He didn't like when girls gave him that face. It meant the relationship was already falling apart. He ducked and grabbed her glass. "I'll get you more water." He hurried to the kitchen, filled the glass from the sink faucet.

"What the hell are you doing?" the chef asked.

He didn't answer as he ran back to the dining room. Gave her the glass.

She smiled and thanked him.

Yeah, she likes me. A lot.

He could fix everything for her. He could fix everything for him. *She* could fix everything for him and make his life right. He'd never had a girlfriend, and now here was someone who wanted that, and more.

She'd never have to see her stepfather again. Never have to go to school again. Never have to do anything she didn't want to do. Never have to eat raw fish he couldn't pronounce.

As the hours passed, he asked questions of other people working at the resort. He learned about the girls' hiking trip, saw the map and the places they were likely to stop for the night. He didn't like the outdoors, hated camping, but he would tolerate it for Emerson. That's what love was about. Sacrifice. Going that extra mile, both mentally and literally.

At home, he made his plans, collected gear, packed his car. He had a lot of guns, but he bought more ammunition. At work, he continued to watch for her in the dining room. He wanted to tell her his plans, see her face light up. But he also wanted to surprise her.

CHAPTER 12

"You okay?" Reni asked him.

Daniel glanced away from the road to see her looking at her phone while tugging at a strand of hair as if subconsciously willing it to grow back. It was a habit she'd recently acquired that could only be tied to the haircut Rosalind Fisher had given her shortly before leaving her to die.

"I'm fine, thanks."

They were in his SUV heading toward the Rose house in Redlands, which was twenty minutes from San Bernardino depending on lights and traffic. He wasn't sure how he felt about Reni coming along. *Uncomfortable* was the word that came to mind, but then the idea of seeing his old girlfriend under these circumstances—period—made him uneasy. He was also thinking maybe Reni should have gone to the Rose house by herself. It was never good to work a case involving family or friends. Or old girlfriends. But they were almost there, and it would be foolish to turn around. Time was precious.

After hitting the city, it took an additional twenty minutes to get through town and arrive at a house in upscale Wimbleton Heights. Wimbleton was an older neighborhood, with Victorians mixed with modern ranch-style homes, mature shade trees that spoke of time and history, the Rose house nestled on a hillside that provided views of near and far mountains.

Shaking off his apprehension, noting the glances Reni kept shooting him, Daniel parked in the driveway and they got out and approached the house. The front door opened before he knocked. Rachel Rose,

Emerson's mother, stood there. This was his first face-to-face since college. She must have been doing all the right things, like exercising and eating healthy. Her skin was still smooth and clear, her hair still dark and shiny.

For a moment, he wondered if she recognized him. It had been a while. Maybe she'd figured more prominently in his past than he'd figured in hers. But then she spoke his name. The snag in her voice, the terror on her face, had him shedding all pretense of formality. This was an old friend in pain.

"I thought you'd come by yourself," she said.

Something he'd *really* wanted to avoid.

Reni gestured toward the driveway. "I can wait in the car."

In near panic at the idea of being alone with Rachel, he said, "Stay."

"I need to make some calls. I'll wait in the car."

He gave up and tossed her his keys. "Turn on the AC."

She strode away, and he and Rachel with the shiny dark hair were left facing each other in what felt like an isolated bubble.

Time was such a curious thing. They'd dated for less than a year. He'd been fixated on finding his mother, and Rachel had been more into the relationship than he was. Things had moved too quickly. One day she'd asked if he'd ever consider getting married and having kids. That had thrown him.

But she'd been his first real . . . love. Yeah, maybe *love* was right. And when you're hardly more than a kid—they'd both been maybe twenty—you don't realize this might really be the one. You don't realize that the relationship is special. You kinda think they might all be like this to some extent. And that there were more near-perfect women out there. But for him, she truly was the one who got away. He'd told her he wasn't ready, told her he didn't know if he'd ever want kids. She'd wanted a commitment, even if it was just verbal.

At the time, he'd thought he was close to finding his mother. Now he couldn't even recall the details of that particular thread. He also hadn't known it would be just one of the many times he'd feel close to finding her. And one of the many times his girlfriend—and later the one woman, now his ex, who'd foolishly married him—would beg him to let it go. Those pleas had frustrated and annoyed him. His quest for his mother had been a part of his life, and they should have known better than to ask him to quit looking. And so the relationship had ended. Much too abruptly. Not one of those slow things that gradually led to his moving out. This was overnight and she was gone. Leaving behind a kind of bittersweet regret that was mingling with another dead end in his search for his mother. It had been a dark time in his life.

"I'm sorry, Rachel."

He stepped inside.

She closed the door.

Her husband stood in the center of a living room that made Daniel painfully aware of the inferiority of his own meager home, even though having an expensive place wasn't and had never been on his radar. It seemed her leaving him had been a damn good move.

What he knew about them: Rachel was a successful CEO of an organic food company. She was involved in philanthropy. Her husband, Stanley, was a stay-at-home dad who was also involved in the food company.

The entry and living room were minimalistic. The kind of minimalism that didn't come cheaply. It spoke of a successful life. Tile floors and white walls and art had probably been chosen and hung by a designer. It looked ready to put on the market—that's how perfect it was—but Daniel knew they'd lived in the same house for ten years. He'd looked it up long ago. They'd lived there back when she called him for help in saving her daughter during the school shooting. During and after that event, he'd never seen Rachel in person, only talked to her on the phone. He would have preferred a phone conversation again today. If he remembered correctly, he'd gotten a lead on his missing mother during the school rescue operation. Immediately afterward he caught a flight to Florida. He might have preferred to avoid Rachel even if there had been no quick trip to Florida.

It had been another dead end.

Right now the husband looked lost, helpless. He seemed in shock. Anything less would have been suspicious. It was Daniel's job to find their child, but he also wanted to leave them with something else today. Hope.

He understood how it felt to have someone disappear, and it was strange that the very thing he and Rachel had fought over was the reason he was here now, in her living room, as he prepared to tell her everything was being done that could be done. He also couldn't avoid wondering if she was thinking about the day she'd begged him to quit searching. To stop. To get on with his life. He could feel the memory of that day in the room.

The three of them stood there, her husband with possibly no knowledge of their past relationship, and probably no knowledge of a day that suddenly seemed so real and close, all the way to Daniel's memory of the yellow curtains that had fluttered in the kitchen window as she cried and he didn't. But this wasn't about the past or that old relationship. It was about a missing girl. It was about finding her before she was killed, if she hadn't been killed already. It was about finding her before horrible things happened to her. That was unlikely, but not impossible.

The house was made up of odd angles. One of those California homes from the sixties that was reminiscent of a hotel in the way everything faced the pool. Low white ceiling that reflected light. Walls of windows. Hazy and layered mountains way off in the distance, beyond the palm trees. Quintessential California, with a touch of Frank Sinatra. He almost expected someone to appear and ask if he'd like a cocktail.

He followed the couple down a long hallway, where Rachel opened a bedroom door and stood back, arms crossed. She didn't want to go inside. Most parents reacted that way. He'd had a case once where the mother didn't seem upset by the room. She ended up being the child's killer.

"I can't go in there," the husband said. He looked ready to cry, and Daniel suspected he needed to be alone. Over the years, he'd come to understand it was the fathers who had the hardest time dealing with harsh news about their little girls. The man left and Rachel pulled in a bracing breath before walking into the bedroom like she was walking through a force field. Daniel followed.

"Stanley feels a little inadequate in your presence," Rachel said.

Daniel's face must have mirrored his bafflement. From Daniel's perspective and in a different scenario, Rachel's husband had everything a father could possibly want if his daughter hadn't been missing.

"You rescue people," she explained.

"I'm just a guy doing my oftentimes boring job." He moved across the room, drawn to a framed yellowed newspaper clipping on the wall. He expected to see an announcement of an award, or any number of things kids liked to hang up. When he was close enough, he realized what it really was. And flinched. A five-by-seven media photo of him running from the school, a girl in his arms. The girl was Emerson.

Back then, when Rachel had reached out to him, he hadn't been able to understand why she was calling. That was in part because she was crying on the phone, hysterical, and he was unable to make out anything. It had taken him a few breaths to realize she was talking about the school currently on lockdown. He was aware of it, but school shootings weren't his field. He dealt with murders.

Several squads from his building were either there or on their way. Like others in the department, he'd been at his desk watching live footage of the unfolding event. Several children had been reported dead, many more injured. One shooter had died from a self-inflicted gunshot. At the time, they hadn't known if there were any more shooters at large. As she sobbed into his ear, he finally put it together that Rachel's daughter *was in the school.*

He'd worked some SWAT and hostage negotiations in his career, but he wasn't connected to either of those units at the time of the shooting, even though departments overlapped.

"She's inside," Rachel said.

"She might not be," Daniel told her. The situation was controlled chaos. All available officers had been tapped. "I'll see what I can do." In another life, the child might have been his.

He grabbed his jacket and walked briskly out of Homicide. Almost flew down the fire stairs to join a multitude of police and squad cars racing to the scene. On the way, he spotted helicopters overhead, moving in the same direction. The computer in his unmarked car kept him updated with visuals while the crawler at the bottom of the screen reported everything in an emotionally absent way, using a font that could convey bad or good news.

Two security guards dead, along with the first two officers who arrived on the scene.

New reports of shots fired. At least one shooter still suspected to be in the building.

Sadly, it was a familiar occurrence, played out too many times in schools across America. Lines of children running toward buses. Zoom lenses catching frozen and silent images of terrified faces. The difference in this shooting was the age of the kids. These were younger than most, but the trend toward shooters in middle schools and even grade schools was increasing. Children should not have to experience a war like this.

It took a half hour for Daniel to reach the location. He parked in a grassy field filled with cars—some ambulances, some media, many belonging to parents. Rachel was probably somewhere on the grounds, but he wouldn't waste time trying to find her. Instead he sent her a text, letting her know he was there. It took him another fifteen minutes to locate the main staging area, where officers and techs were in the process of setting up. Inside a large tent, the current concentration was on trying to grab feeds from cameras mounted in the building.

"I'm in," a woman shouted. She had a laptop balanced in one hand and was working the keyboard with the other. Behind her, two people were setting up a long table and running cables for power. Others were unpacking equipment. Someone plugged in a large monitor. Another person spread out a physical floor plan of the school. The woman with the laptop clicked keys, and the monitor filled with a checkerboard of security-camera footage from various areas of the building. Some screens were eerily empty. Others revealed the chaos inside. Bodies on the floor. Definitely more dead than the earliest reports. They needed to move fast.

Daniel's phone vibrated. He checked the screen, saw a text from Rachel.

She's in the library restroom. I got a message from her. I responded but haven't gotten a reply. She's twelve.

She sent a photo. A pretty young girl with black hair and golden skin. A bold and direct gaze.

He silenced his phone.

A plan was formulated.

Daniel was part of it, but not in charge. He and three other officers put on bulletproof vests. Nobody questioned his involvement. The SWAT team, carrying heavy shields and wearing armor, led the way, Daniel and the two other cops behind them.

Unexpected gunfire erupted from an area that had been determined by cameras to be clear. That was followed by explosions that blew out more windows. The SWAT team pivoted and cut down a hall. Daniel dove the opposite direction. He didn't know why. Instinct, maybe.

The sprinkler system malfunctioned. Water rained down. In a distant area, a semiautomatic was blasting away and the SWAT team was returning fire. Daniel went momentarily deaf from the noise and was forced to rely on his vision. And what he saw through the rain were two people running straight for him. One was a guy waving a revolver. He had an AK-47 slung over one shoulder, the weapon possibly empty with no time to reload. His other hand gripped a girl's arm.

Emerson Rose.

The shooter fit a familiar profile with very little divergence. White. Hair dyed black. Hand and neck tattoos. Facial hair and pimples. Military clothing. Long black coat for hiding weapons. Laced military boots and tucked black pants.

The kid pressed the end of the barrel against the girl's temple.

He'd already killed without mercy. If he got out of the building with the girl, he'd kill her. Daniel had no doubt about that.

Water continued to pour from the ceiling, dousing them. Daniel didn't allow the water to distract him. He didn't say *Drop the gun* or *Let the girl go*. Instead, he said something anybody and everybody would want to hear no matter the situation. Because everybody was in pain. Even killers.

"Everything is going to be okay."

That took the kid by surprise.

He was so young. Younger than Daniel had originally thought. Probably not old enough to drive. Hardly old enough to date.

The girl did something unexpected, and yet he'd seen the promise of such a reaction in the photo Rachel had sent. She broke away and ran. Straight for Daniel, her movements awkward as she sloshed through the rising water.

The guy with the handgun shot.

The girl let out a shout of surprise and fell.

Daniel had no choice or even time to think. Training kicked in. He pulled his weapon and fired. The shooter dropped like a stone. Daniel's heart dropped too. Now he could add child-killer to his résumé, but he'd been left no choice. Behind him, down another hall, shots were still being fired. Rapid. He caught a whiff of mace. The girl was bleeding, but alive.

He picked her up and began moving in the direction she and the guy had come from, away from the noise and the smoke, wading through the water. The wet ceiling began to collapse. He ran. Pushed through the door into the light and fresh air, running with the girl in his arms, Rachel's daughter.

CHAPTER 13

Sitting in Daniel's SUV, Reni took the opportunity to reply to the text she'd gotten on the way to Redlands. It was another message from Daniel's old babysitter, and she was suddenly open to talking today. Sometimes, once the decision was made, contacts wanted it over with as quickly as possible. And sometimes they changed their minds and refused the interview. Reni couldn't let the opportunity slip away, so she suggested communicating through FaceTime immediately. It wasn't ideal, but video interviews were becoming more common and it was better than losing her completely.

Janine agreed, and Reni made the call.

Social media made things easy today too. By going through Janine Masters's Instagram feed, Reni had learned a lot about her. The person who'd been taking care of Daniel the night his mother vanished was in her late forties, single, never married, a house musician and violin player who toured with bands. She was one of those people whose face hadn't changed a lot over the years. You could look at a case-file photo and easily match it with the current person. Straight auburn hair parted in the center and falling to her shoulders.

"I ignored your emails at first." Janine was sitting in a bright living room, framed art and photos on a nearby wall, a shelf of books arranged by color behind her. "My mother and I had both made the decision to never talk about it again because it took over our lives for so long. But, as you might already know, ten years ago she and I both agreed to talk to Daniel. Just for our own closure and so he'd quit bugging us. I basically agreed to this call for the same reason—so you'd stop trying to contact me. I can't help you, and talking about it only drags me back to a horrible, horrible time."

"I'm sorry," Reni said. She really was, and what Janine said was true. There was a good chance she'd have nothing to add to the story, and Reni would end the call with an even vaguer narrative than the one that currently existed in the files. But a conversation could also reveal something new.

In hopes of making the woman feel more at ease, Reni went into a little of her own background. Not her being the daughter of a serial killer—Janine most likely knew about that, because who in California didn't—but her skill as a profiler. "After I left the FBI, I had requests to work on missing persons cases. I didn't want to do it. I was over anything even related to police work and crime. I wanted to get away from it. But what I'm getting at is that I *did* take the cases," she said. "They were tough, unsolved. And I found the people. All of them."

"That's good."

"Unfortunately, in all three cases, the missing were dead. But it did provide closure. And that's what I'd like to provide for Daniel. And I'm sure you would too. Not trying to guilt you into this, but I'm a pragmatic person. Even though I'd like to put this kind of work aside because it can do a number on me, I also have to realize that while I might not be the best in the country for the job, I'm *one* of the best." It was true. She was surprised she could admit that. "But if at any point you want it to stop, we can stop."

Janine's eyes watered and she blinked several times, pressed her lips together, and nodded. "I'll do it for Daniel. It's already in my head, and the upcoming days have already been set in motion. I won't be able to sleep tonight or tomorrow or maybe even next week regardless of whether we stop now or continue. I will warn you that every single piece of that night has been gone over again and again and again. And I *do not* want you to contact my mother."

Janine's mother was in a nursing home and Reni was unaware of the health details, but she'd try to honor the request. She made a point of not making the kind of deal Janine wanted, because a person never knew where a lead might take them, but she made a mental note to avoid it if at all possible, and certainly not without contacting Janine first.

Daniel could be returning soon, so Reni dove right in, opening her notebook to her list of possible questions about Daniel's mother, and went straight to the ones marked *urgent*.

"What kind of person was Alice Vargas?"

Janine repeated descriptions from the police interviews with friends and neighbors, using words like *friendly* and *sweet*. "A good mother. Quiet. Soft-spoken."

"Was she happy?"

"I don't know." Janine shrugged. "I was a kid. She seemed happy, but we both know that means nothing."

"Did she like being a mother?"

"Again, it seemed like it. But I was a kid."

"Was she struggling? Emotionally? Financially?" Reni knew the answer to both was *yes*.

"I don't know."

"Did she ever not pay you?"

Silence, thought. A nod followed by a reluctant admission. "A couple of times, yeah. But she always eventually paid. My mom said I should start asking for the money up front, but I didn't have the nerve. And I didn't really care about money that much. I liked babysitting. It made me feel like a responsible adult."

"What about boyfriends? Did you ever meet any of them?"

"Yeah. The last one. He lived with them sometimes, but he moved out, and I think the night she vanished was the first date she'd had since he left. All stuff I told the cops."

"They interviewed him, and he was never a suspect."

Janine looked up and away, then back. "I'm going to have to go soon," she warned.

Feeling fresh urgency, Reni scanned her list, targeting the most important items. "Can you tell me about that night? I know you've shared this many times, but let's go over it again. I'll make it easier. You came over to babysit. Alice was wearing a new dress. Daniel ate fish sticks and french fries. You made popcorn and watched a Disney movie. Does all of that sound right?"

"Yes."

"Before Alice left, how did she seem? Nervous? Upset? Scared?"

Janine gave that some thought, her brow furrowing. "I'd say distracted."

Reni pulled out a copy of a photo from between the pages of her notebook and held it up. The photo was of Daniel and Alice, taken inside their home, both of them standing in front of the door, Alice with her hands on Daniel's shoulders. "This was taken that night," Reni said, keeping the photo high so Janine would have time to get a good look at it. "The original has a date in the margin, the date it was developed, which was about a week later." She lowered the image. "Who took it?"

"I did."

"There was no one else there?"

"Nope. I took it with Daniel's little Instamatic camera."

"Then what?"

"I gave the camera back to Daniel. Oh, and I said something about it being the last picture on the roll."

Reni nodded. Nothing new here. "Then what? Did Alice say anything before she left?"

Janine thought again. Nodded again. "She said something about getting the film developed. Oh, wait." A revelation of an old memory. "She said to ask my mom to get the film developed."

This was new information. "Daniel claims she said she'd have to get it developed."

"No. I'm pretty sure she said my mother. I remember because it didn't make sense to me. Like, why would my mom get it developed? I thought maybe it was something they did. Like maybe my mom did that for her."

"I agree it was an odd thing for her to say."

Janine frowned again, puzzled. "Yeah."

Reni could see Janine was done. Better to stop now on a good note. "I think that's enough." She gave her the spiel about calling if the conversation had triggered anything new. They said their goodbyes and Reni ended the call, her mind racing.

From what Janine had said, it seemed there was a chance Alice had known she was leaving and not coming back. The question: Why? And where did she go? And why didn't she take Daniel with her?

Reni thought back to her own mother, who couldn't tolerate motherhood. It sounded like Daniel's mother was sweet and that she loved him. But she was single, no money in the bank, trying to make a living as a seamstress. Kids cost money. All along, Reni had been against the pervasive theory that Daniel's mother had just walked away. It had always felt like an excuse for lazy police work. Blaming the mother, making assumptions, ignoring and not following up on clues. But this new information moved the runaway mom theory to the top of her list.

She glanced at the house. It was still quiet, so she called an artist friend who specialized in age progression. "I'm looking for someone to progress an adult thirty years," Reni said. She'd seen some drawings of Daniel's mother, but nothing that had been done recently or even in the last decade. And it was never a bad idea to involve a few different artists.

"No problem." He sounded as if he was munching chips. "Send me an image."

She scrolled through her photos and sent him a JPEG. At the same time, she heard and saw a side gate to the Rose house open and close. A man with dark hair stepped out. Not Daniel. The person was about the same age, slight frame, dressed in shorts and sandals and a gray T-shirt. He looked confused and lost.

"Gotta go," she said into her phone. "Thank you." She ended the call and held perfectly still, watching the man who'd come through the gate. The person who'd killed Janet Ravenscroft could very well be staking out the Rose house.

The man dropped to the ground and hid behind a shrub.

Reni pulled the car door lever and pushed with her shoulder, wincing at the squeak. She slipped out, ran softly to the front of the house, then crept along the wall to peer around the side of the building. She could see the man's knees and feet. And she could hear him sobbing.

Her heart contracted. This was the father, Stanley Rose. She didn't want to intrude on such a private and vulnerable moment, but she also felt compelled, for both compassionate and investigative reasons, to at least attempt to engage him in conversation. She straightened and walked down the sidewalk, stopping a few yards away. Most people might ask if he was okay, but of course he wasn't.

"I'm sorry," she said softly.

He glanced up and wiped at his face as he attempted to pull himself together. She was excruciatingly aware of Daniel and Rachel not all that far away, inside the house. Stanley must have been hiding from them.

She settled herself nearby, close enough for them to talk privately but not so close to make him more uncomfortable. Sitting cross-legged, arms resting on her knees, she introduced herself.

"I had to get out of the house," he admitted with a head-to-shoulder bob that was both sheepish and honest. "This whole thing is so awful, and I can't deal with that guy."

"Detective Ellis?"

"Yeah. He's been a figure in our lives for so long, and I could never live up to the narrative Emerson designed for him. I call him the what-could-have-been guy. It's hard to compete with someone who doesn't even exist. Well, he exists, but not her larger-than-life version." He let out a sigh. "I guess the truth is, he might be everything she seems to think he is. He might be the hero."

He told Reni other things too, things she'd already known about Daniel, and things she hadn't. It seemed Stanley had been feeling like a stranger in his own home for quite some time, and the fact that he was hiding outside backed up that theory.

"So I've been living with two women who are obsessed with him," he said.

"And now one of them is gone," Reni said softly. How many times in the past few years had a father been behind a child's disappearance? Far too many. She'd never not suspect the parents. She wasn't a gut feeling kind of investigator, because gut feelings could be wrong. She was a facts person. And yet she got the impression she was dealing with a soft-hearted, sincere, and wounded man. But what about the mother? Maybe Reni shouldn't have been so eager to stay outside and use the time to speak to Janine. It had left her with no take on Rachel Rose.

Stanley looked up at her with red-rimmed eyes. "This doesn't look very good, does it? I want you to know I adore her. I love her like she's my own kid. And if he can find her, I don't care if that makes her even more obsessed. Hell, I'll hang his photo on the wall and light a candle under it every day." He started crying again. "Just find my girl."

Rachel wasn't the only mystery here. Stanley's revelations, combined with Daniel's reaction when he'd heard the names of the missing girls, left her with one big question that felt like it had been lifted right out of a soap opera plot: Could Daniel be Emerson's biological father?

CHAPTER 14

"After the shooting, Emerson became obsessed with you," Rachel told Daniel. They were still standing in the missing child's bedroom. "And you became a superhero to her." She moved around the room, fell silent at times, often avoiding eye contact. "And I know this seems really weird, but she decided you were her father."

She wasn't the only person to wonder such a thing. Daniel had thought about it himself, but once he'd checked her birth date, he knew it wasn't possible.

Rachel read his reaction, saw he'd done the math. "I know. After you and I broke up, I jumped into another relationship that didn't last."

As one did.

"I got pregnant. I didn't marry the guy. After the shooting, Emerson found an old photo of you and me together. And you know how girls can get. She and her stepfather used to be so close. I know this hurts him deeply, but she started talking about how he wasn't her real dad, and she started obsessing about you."

No wonder the guy had acted so uneasy.

"And to make it even worse, she's had a hard time dealing with reality since the shooting," Rachel said.

"I'm sorry."

He really was. He wished he could take away her pain. He wanted to find her daughter alive and at least fairly well. One hundred percent well was not possible.

"At about that same time," Rachel said, "she started spending way too many hours a day online. And it's been that way ever since. That was the reason we sent her to Kaleidoscope. Nothing else worked. We saw something on television about the center and decided no matter the cost, we'd do it. Cold turkey. Get her away from everything, because it had gotten to the point where we couldn't even talk to her. Her face was in her phone or staring at her laptop. We thought we were doing the right thing. We felt like we were saving her. That was the pitch, but now here we are." Her voice cracked on the last words.

Daniel tried to reassure her. Nothing good could come from self-blame right now. "It was an excellent idea. I might have done the same." He didn't mention Ava Brown's questionable behavior. There would undoubtedly be lawsuits.

"I'm going to need her electronic devices," he said. "Phone, tablets, laptops. I'll have our digital forensics team go over everything, see if we can connect her to someone you didn't know about. Or someone you did know about. Abductions are often perpetrated by an acquaintance, and many don't happen randomly. Although that's not to say they can't. We do see it, but not much. It takes planning today. Unlike the crimes of years ago, before cell phones."

He went on to explain other possibilities. "At the same time, the abduction might have nothing to do with Emerson. Three girls went missing. Two other hikers are missing. Emerson might have just been in the wrong place with the wrong people."

"People are saying this was faked by the YouTube girl, Portia Devine. Not the murder, but possibly something else, something that got out of hand."

"We're considering it. It could even have something to do with Phillip Devine. Someone trying to get his attention. An obsessed fan, or someone after ransom money." He hoped that wasn't it, because it meant Emerson had little value in such an equation. But they'd been talking too long—he had to search the room.

Beyond another wall of glass, he could see the pool. The bedroom was big for a kid. But the décor was still that of a younger person—something he found of note. Pink walls, turquoise trim. A bed with a fuzzy spread. A dresser with a funky lamp, a jewelry box, a mirror full of stickers and small photos of what looked like classmates. As though her life had stopped after the shooting. Sad to think about. Tragedies had a way of locking people into the age they were when the disaster hit.

His mind jumped away again, to the past and those yellow curtains billowing in the breeze. The scent of dish soap. That shared existence had felt close to real life and he hadn't even realized it.

"I found this earlier." Rachel handed him a journal. "I don't think she's used it in a long time." The cover was also pink and turquoise.

As he opened the book to the last entries, years old, something fluttered to the floor. He picked it up. It was an old photo, one he remembered now that he was looking at it. Of him and Rachel, taken back when they'd lived together. God, they were so young. Those were such sweet days. College. First real girlfriend. But decidedly odd for Rachel's daughter to have it in her private journal. And not only that, it meant Rachel had saved it to begin with. He'd gotten rid of everything that had reminded him of her.

He put it back, flipped more pages, came upon something else tucked into the gutter of the book. A newspaper clipping that wasn't faded the way clippings tended to get, like the framed one on the wall. He put the book down on the little ornate desk and unfolded the clipping. It was an article about him and his involvement in the Inland Empire Killer case. He looked up at Rachel.

"I had no idea she'd cut that from the paper," she said. "But I'm not surprised. And the photo is the one she came across a few years ago." She started crying. Walked away quickly, picked up a stuffed animal, a rabbit, hugged it, put it on the bed so it was sitting up surveying the room.

He took a breath, dove into a topic no parents responded well to. "Did Emerson ever do anything dangerous? Anything that worried you?"

"Like what?"

"Sometimes people who survive things like shootings or a near-death experience feel invincible. Though I know it can be a little hard to separate that from normal teen behavior, where they think nothing will ever harm them. The response can also go the other way, where they fear everything. I know of someone who won't ride in a car and is fearful to leave the house."

"I'd give that a no."

"What about hurting herself?"

"Another no."

"Hurting someone else?"

"No. She was—*is* a sweetheart." She looked annoyed now. "I don't even understand why you'd talk about such a thing. Emerson is a gentle soul. Easily hurt. Easily bullied."

People who were bullied sometimes snapped.

"She hurt me."

Daniel swiveled toward the open door.

A girl stood there, hands and face resting on the doorframe. Daniel had forgotten that Emerson had a younger sister. Unfortunately it was easy to forget about the siblings of traumatized children.

"She was mean," the girl stated with no emotion.

Rachel strode quickly across the room. "Come on. You know better than that." To Daniel, she explained, "They fought. Sibling stuff. It was something we were aware of and were working on."

Daniel grabbed a chair from the desk, carried it across the room, and sat down near the girl, but not so near as to be intimidating. She was about ten, a few years older than Daniel had been when his mother vanished. She was also what some psychologists called a collateral victim. She hadn't been at the shooting, but had suffered in her own way due to the spotlight rarely shining on her anymore.

"I get it," Daniel told her. "And I'd like to know a little more about what Emerson did."

"This is a waste of time."

Daniel glanced up. Rachel's jaw was tight, her arms locked across her chest.

"Just give me a couple of minutes," Daniel said. He felt bad about putting her through this, but it was important.

Back to the girl and her dark eyes. "Did she ever physically hurt you?"

"Sometimes."

Rachel gasped. "That's not true."

This could simply be a bid for attention, a child who wanted the spotlight for a change. Or it could be legitimate. Or just typical sibling rivalry. He didn't have any brothers or sisters, but he knew siblings could be vicious to each other while being good kids otherwise. Without taking his eyes from the girl, he asked, "Like what?"

"She tried to drown me once."

"Arial!"

"Anything else? Did she ever hit you? With her hands or anything else?"

"You're feeding her ideas," Rachel said. "You have to go. Leave. Now."

"She tried to stab me once."

"That's a lie!" Rachel said to Daniel. To Arial, she pointed and said, "Go to your room! Now!"

The girl stomped off.

Rachel turned her anger on Daniel. He understood some of that anger was misdirected fear. "That's a lie, and now you're going to be blaming this on Emerson instead of looking for her," she said.

"I'm going to look for her just as hard as I was minutes ago. That doesn't change. But we have to consider everything, and it's important to have an accurate and complete picture for our personality profile. Not just the glowing one parents tend to paint." Everybody was a saint once they went missing.

"Arial's profile is incorrect. So you want an incorrect profile?" She paced, then turned, her face red with anger. "No wonder I dumped you."

He chose to ignore that comment. "It's standard procedure. And think about it, Rachel," he said calmly. "The truth leads to clues, and clues lead to answers and rescues. This is what I do. I'm good at it, but I need the truth. Was she ever violent?"

His reassurance about his skill seemed to calm her. She was under enormous stress. He was fine with her lashing out at him, although he'd bank her comment about dumping him to replay in his head later, at a more appropriate time.

She pulled herself together. Took a deep, stabilizing breath. Looked a little embarrassed. "Yes."

He tried not to act surprised. Tried not to act anything. "Did she try to stab her sister?"

"I'm not sure about that. I would hate to think she'd ever do anything so horrible."

"But?"

"Maybe." She was uneasy, which meant he'd hit a nerve.

"Did she ever try to hurt you?"

"She's not a violent person."

He hoped not, but the truth would eventually come out. "Parents aren't always the best judge of their own child's character."

"You'll just have to trust me on this." She opened a drawer, pulled out a laptop case and phone, tucked the phone in the side pocket, handed the case to him. "You're going down the wrong path."

"There are no wrong paths in detective work."

He checked his phone, was relieved to see it was time to leave and that he and Reni had an hour to get to the medical examiner's office. He had a text message from Davenport letting him know the McGrath and Devine devices had been picked up and logged as evidence. He told Rachel he'd be in touch and left.

CHAPTER 15

Reni was sitting in Daniel's SUV trying to process everything that had occurred in the past thirty minutes, from her conversation with Janine to the face-to-face with Stanley, when the front door of the house opened and Daniel stepped out. He was carrying a pink laptop case.

He got in the vehicle and put the case between the seats. "Emerson's laptop and phone," he said. "After we finish with the autopsy, I want to give them an examination of my own before handing them off to our specialists." As he drove, he made a hands-free call, telling the person at the other end to get Digital Forensics on the devices belonging to the other girls ASAP, and to flag the job as high priority, extremely urgent. "And I'll be turning in another cell and laptop soon."

"On it," the person replied.

"I just had an interesting conversation," Reni told Daniel after he ended the call. "And I have one big question: Is Emerson Rose your biological daughter?"

He made a choking sound but quickly recovered. "I had the same thought several years ago, but the math doesn't work. It's not possible. Although I have to admit I still feel a little too close to this case."

News traveled fast in a small town. And also a midsize town. By the time they arrived at the medical examiner's office, TV crews were set up along the circle drive's entrance to the main campus, which was composed of a cluster of professional buildings located within walking distance of the San Bernardino County Sheriff's Department. Some people were in lawn chairs, most under umbrellas. Feet were propped on equipment. From somewhere, music was playing on a tinny speaker. "Bad to the Bone."

B-b-b-bad.

Upon spotting Reni, reporters jumped to their feet and shouted her name. Cameras silently clicked.

She'd never gotten over the unsettling ugliness of being stalked by the press. Even now, even as a grown woman and someone who knew and appreciated them when working a tough case. Reporters were invaluable, especially in today's fast-moving world of information. But after her father's arrest, news crews began parking outside the home where she'd lived with her mother. She and her mother became prisoners, her mother unable to even go to the grocery store and Reni unable to return to grade school. At some point in that string of endless days, their neighbor Maurice hatched a plan to sneak them to the nearby mountains, where he had a luxury cabin. Under cover of darkness, they crept from their house to his, and as the sun rose the next morning, Reni and her mother, hiding under blankets on the back-seat floor of his Cadillac, rode to freedom.

That memory took on a whole new meaning today. At that time, Reni had thought of her mother as innocent—even though she'd never understood how Rosalind could have been so blissfully unaware, missing the signs that she was living with the Inland Empire Killer, the signs that her own daughter was being used as bait to lure young women to their deaths. It turned out there was an easy reason. Her mother had missed nothing. She'd always known. She might even have been the mastermind.

There was no escaping the press during their stay in the mountains. Eventually someone recognized them, and reporters descended again, this time on the little mountain town where they'd been hiding. So they adopted a new strategy of no eye contact, no matter how insulting the questions hurled at them.

She employed that same strategy today, still keeping her head down, still refusing to make eye contact unless confronted in a way she couldn't ignore, or if her job demanded interaction. Her childhood experience had left her traumatized in many ways, and the press was mixed up in that trauma.

Daniel paused long enough to let reporters know they had no information to share yet, but that they would soon. Questions were shot at them. He held up a hand and ducked into the building. They checked in at the front desk, and together they entered the prep room of the autopsy suites, where Medical Examiner Evangeline Fry waited. She was already gowned, with a bright cap on her head and blue face mask below her chin. She had straight mahogany hair pulled back in a ponytail, and a dark complexion that didn't look like it had ever seen a blemish. Her eyes, behind stylish frames, were green.

If Reni were to sketch her, she'd take particular note of the glow of her dark skin, the shape and arch of her brows, along with a small mole. Today Reni noted the exhaustion in Evangeline's young face. The workload of two jobs was stretching her thin. As they chatted and caught up with small talk, Reni and Daniel slipped into paper gowns. Blue ones today.

"I heard my producer tried to talk you into being on another episode," Evangeline said.

They'd been guests on her reality show—unfortunately titled *The Corpse Whisperer*—Reni more reluctant than Daniel. The episode had managed to generate "great numbers" that the streaming platform had been thrilled with. So much so, they'd tried to convince Reni and Daniel to become regulars. Evangeline had liked the idea. Reni, not so much.

"I think once was enough," Reni said as she tied her mask behind her head.

Daniel seemed over it too. It had generated too much unwanted attention for both of them, especially for him.

They followed Evangeline into an autopsy suite, the three of them rustling as they walked. As always, Evangeline's casual demeanor changed as soon as they gathered around the sheet-covered body on the stainless-steel autopsy table. The thing about Evangeline was that she didn't become a medical examiner until she stepped into the autopsy suite. Reni liked that about her. She seemed able to turn it off and on, which was a healthy way to live. Reni wasn't there yet.

"Cause of death appears to be gunshot wounds to head and chest," Evangeline said. She pulled down the sheet and uncovered the body of Janet Ravenscroft. Here, in a removed medical setting, Reni felt none of the panic she'd experienced out on the mountain. Now she could give her full attention to the victim.

Even dead, Janet gave off the impression of being athletic. "She was a hiker, as we know," Reni said. "She was awarded the Triple Crown, meaning she hiked all three major United States trails. The Pacific Crest Trail, the Appalachian Trail, and the Continental Divide Trail."

"She should have known her stuff," Daniel said.

Reni agreed. "I wouldn't have been concerned about having my children go hiking with her. And I'm not sure how much a person can prepare for something like this."

Autopsies adhered to a specific methodology. Evangeline began by dictating details into a mic hanging from the ceiling and attached to a digital recorder she operated with her foot. The time and date, victim name, age, weight, and height, notes that would all be transferred to the case file.

She then moved on to the Y incision. Once made, she weighed the organs and documented everything. There was never any telling when something from the autopsy would end up being crucial during a trial. Along with the weighing of organs, she extracted bullets from the skull and chest, dropping them with a ping into a stainless-steel kidney-shaped tray.

"Looks like it could be .22 TCM round," Daniel noted.

Everything at this point was open to speculation. So far, they didn't know what kind of gun had been used, and no expelled cartridges had been found at the crime scene.

"Bottleneck cartridges aren't that popular," Reni said. "Those are proprietary, and you don't tend to see civilians with them that much."

"So you're speculating our perp is military?" Daniel asked.

"Just brainstorming," Reni said. "Twenty-two TCMs *are* popular with preppers, though. The weapon could have been a Rock Island Armory 1911."

Daniel leaned in for a closer look. "Could be a .357 SIG round. Those are a little more common."

"You guys," Evangeline said with enthusiasm and a lilt of humor in her voice. "This is why you'd be perfect as regulars on my show! That stuff is so sexy."

Reni and Daniel both laughed.

"Geeky, I know," Reni said.

"Regardless, we'll get this to our firearms expert and get an answer," Daniel said.

Moving on, Reni said, "I really want to figure out the cause of the puncture wounds." The "vampire bites," as a few people on social media were calling them.

Daniel agreed.

Evangeline took photos. She measured the width and depth of the wounds. "They're identical." She adjusted a light with a magnifying glass on a hinged arm. "If you look closely enough, the wounds aren't round. Like a tooth or fang would be."

"Sharp angles," Daniel said.

"I think I know what could have made the wounds." Reni pulled out her phone and searched Google, enlarging images, then turning her phone around so they could see the screen. "Self-defense jewelry. They come as necklaces and bracelets, even rings. This might have been a ring." The metal bits protruding from the ring looked almost like cat ears. In fact, the rings were called cat rings.

Evangeline looked closely. "I'd say that's probably the weapon we're looking at."

"It's typically not used to kill, only deter," Reni said. "So maybe just incidental." She tucked her phone away. "But a clue."

As the fans in the room continued to hum, Evangeline covered the body, snapped off her gloves, and said, "Vampires are so ten years ago." That kind of comment was why Evangeline's show was so popular.

Reni's phone vibrated, and she checked the screen. It was a text from the woman with the search and rescue dog, letting her know she was available to help with the missing girls first thing in the morning. Reni hated that they had to wait, but there was no way the search could be continued at night on a dangerous mountain, and darkness had fallen hard by the time they stepped out of the medical examiner's office.

After a quick stop at a drive-thru for food, they settled into a private room on the second floor of the San Bernardino Sheriff's Department. White walls, bright lights. Daniel pulled out Emerson's laptop and cell phone. He took the cell, Reni took the laptop. With a list of possible passwords supplied by Emerson's mom, they were able to log in.

It was a balancing act. While remaining aware of the urgency of the situation, they still had to be thorough. As they searched the devices, Daniel told Reni what he'd learned at Emerson's house, and of his recent history with the family. Reni hadn't known about his involvement at the school shooting. That wasn't that unusual, especially since it sounded as if he wasn't a formal part of the rescue effort. But it was odd that he was now connected to the Roses a second time.

Luckily the laptop automatically logged in to sites, and Reni was able to access Emerson's profile and activity on social media. "I'm looking at a Reddit group called Victims of School Shootings," she said. "Emerson seemed to be pretty active on it."

Daniel pulled his chair closer so they could view the screen together. "That's not a surprise. People look for support in all sorts of places."

"Right, but she might have connected with people she shouldn't have. I want to go through the threads, look at some of the people she's interacted with."

"I agree."

"Do you think the mother could have anything to do with it?" she asked.

He looked up sharply. "Rachel?" He seemed surprised and defensive. "No."

He obviously still had feelings for her. That could cloud a person's judgment. "You don't think it's odd that you're now involved in a second traumatic event in their life?" Reni asked.

"It's definitely odd. An odd coincidence. But because of your past, you're projecting. Not all mothers are evil."

Yeah, but some of them were.

CHAPTER 16

Nineteen hours after finding the body, Reni and Daniel were back at the campsite on the mountain. San Bernardino Search and Rescue had been working the area since yesterday, only breaking when it got too dark. So far, the helicopter in the air and volunteers on the ground had found no sign of the missing girls.

The wind that had been blowing for days had finally brought a biting rain. Most people in California knew better than to gripe about precipitation after so many years of droughts and wildfires, but in the back of everyone's mind was concern about too much too fast, which could cause flash floods and mudslides. Reni had once seen a million-dollar home slide right down the side of a hill. But their immediate concern was the washing away of evidence.

Due to the involvement of a canine in this round of searching, the number of people on site was being kept to a minimum to avoid distraction and misdirection. Yellow tape was still strung around the perimeter. The temperature was on the rise and now about sixty, steam floating in from a distant valley, everyone in rain gear, droplets pattering against the hood of Reni's poncho.

Upon their arrival, Betty, the rescue dog, an Australian shepherd, ran to Reni, who crouched to greet her. Betty and Nadine had helped in a few of Reni's missing persons cases. Those hadn't ended well, but Betty had found the bodies. Reni was afraid of a replay this time.

Nadine looked like someone who'd rather be sitting at home in front of the TV, sipping wine, watching a British baking show, and crocheting. Gray hair, a little plump, a big laugh. The kind of person who brought a sense of calm to any scene. She had a friendly confidence and zero attitude—which some people in the business could learn from. Plus, she was a civilian. That alone gave her leeway to act a little more casual. Like Reni, she could walk away at any time if she wanted.

Betty had been air-scent trained, meaning she wasn't a dog that sniffed a garment before tracking a person. Air-scent training was something Reni preferred because you didn't need to worry about lost trails—especially important right now due to the rain. Air-scent dogs were simply trained to find people, dead or alive.

Nadine secured Betty's GPS collar. Once she was certain it was sending a signal to her handheld device, they were ready. With Reni acting as Nadine's assistant, keeping track of location and terrain, Betty cruised a large area, moving in and out of brush, up and down hills. Betty kept going away and coming back.

After several hours, they returned to the campsite disappointed, needing to refuel and regroup. In the supply tent, out of the rain, they drank coffee, ate some warm soup with sourdough bread, and stood around a loud generator attached to a heater. Reni took note of the change in weather. The rain had stopped. She looked down at Betty the dog, who didn't appear tired or cold. "What about giving it another shot?"

Nadine was game.

Leaving Daniel to discuss strategies with the team, Reni and Nadine headed in a direction they hadn't yet explored. The tree trunks were dark, and leaves glistened in the sun. The air was so clean it didn't even seem like real air, but something filtered. Twenty minutes into the walk, Nadine gave Betty the command. "Find."

The dog took off.

Betty's behavior seemed different this time. She moved without hesitation, zigzagging, with only an occasional stop to sniff before moving forward fast, with purpose and intent. Reni's heart quickened as she zeroed in on the behavior of the dog. At one point, she lost sight of Betty, but spotted rustling brush as the dog continued to move forward. Then they heard a bark, the first sound she'd made that day.

"An alert," Nadine said.

They tracked the dog by GPS until they found her standing near a sheer cliff face, looking over the edge at something below, tail wagging. She barked again and ran back and forth, as if searching for a way down. Nadine called her from the edge, grabbed her collar, and snapped on the leash. It wasn't until the dog was safe from possible harm that both women moved forward to look over the razor-sharp drop.

They were on a dizzying precipice. Beneath them, evergreen tops swayed. Between moving branches, Reni spotted a patch of bright, unnatural color. Possibly clothing, and what might have been a person lying on the ground.

Nadine hugged and praised the dog as Reni pulled out a pair of binoculars. She brought them into focus and scanned the area, stopping on the patch of pink brightness. Yes, it was fabric. Yes, it was a person. She spotted blond hair. "It could be Portia Devine," she said. Portia was the only girl on the hiking trip with blond hair.

She felt a burst of hope as she passed the binoculars to Nadine. While Nadine held them to her face, Reni radioed Daniel, giving him coordinates and terrain details. "We need a helicopter immediately. And rescue personnel on standby."

"Is the person alive?" Daniel asked.

To Nadine, Reni asked, "Any movement?"

"No."

"Don't know," Reni said. "Wait on my follow-up." She disconnected so he could deal with his end of the rescue. Beside her, Betty was whining and struggling to remain in a "sit" position.

"I'm going down," Reni said.

Nadine looked skeptical. "That's steep."

"I'll be careful." Reni knew the last thing they needed was for her to require rescue too.

She eyeballed the topography, searching for a place with footholds, and spotted a few areas to her right, away from the overhang, that looked like possible animal trails. Nadine remained in position while Reni moved from the precipice and quickly backtracked to the trail they'd been following.

Now she spotted a worn path she'd missed before, a section that split off, dropped, and turned, to finally converge with the narrow path she'd seen from above. If the girl was still alive, it meant she'd been out in the elements for at least thirty-six hours. Reni had to rein in her desire to move too quickly. She took the path.

It wasn't straight down, but loose rocks made it hard for the soles of her boots to find anything to grab. The surface was also slick from the rain, adding another layer of danger. Rocks shifted under her heels and she ended up crab-crawling and sliding as she made her way down. Once it seemed she'd dropped enough, she changed direction and began to move horizontally. Nadine, who had a clearer view of the location of Reni in relationship to the body, shouted directions from above until Reni was at the girl's side.

Initial observations.

The girl was barefoot, wearing pink pajama shorts and a matching pink T-shirt with purple llamas on it. Her legs and arms were covered in scratches. Blue lips, her face scratched and bruised and swollen. But Reni could tell it was Portia Devine.

She dropped to her knees beside her, noting the lack of bloat and lack of fetid smell. Reni's heart was already slamming from the descent, but it quickened even more. She lifted the girl's ice-cold, blue wrist. She shifted her fingers, finally feeling a faint pulse. Paused, made sure she wasn't detecting her own blood pounding through her fingertips.

In her head, Reni played a possible scenario that had led to this. She imagined Portia hearing a commotion and coming awake in her tent.

Maybe seeing something else, the killer. In a panic, she ran blindly into the dark, eventually plunging over the precipice. And what about the other girls? Were they also nearby?

She shouted to Nadine. "Alive!"

Then, turning her full attention back to the girl, she gently touched her face, stroked her cheek with her knuckles, softly spoke her name, trying to rouse her.

No response.

Reni stripped off her poncho and sweatshirt and covered the girl as best she could, then she pulled out her two-way and contacted Daniel again, giving him the news. The radio cut in and out, but she could hear the relief in his voice. They tended to brace for the worst. It was easier that way.

"Do you have an ETA on the chopper?" she asked.

"Twenty minutes." His voice sounded uneven, and his next words explained his breathlessness. "I'm heading your direction on foot. Be there soon." The communication ended.

Reni rubbed Portia's cold hand and spoke her name again. She watched the girl's face, looking for the slightest muscle or eyelid flicker. Instead she felt Portia squeeze her hand. Reni let out a small sob of joy, leaned closer, spoke the girl's name again.

Another squeeze.

"Good girl! You're going to be fine. You're going to be fine." The words were like a chant, a vow to both of them. She thought about Portia's father, about how she hadn't been able to promise him anything yesterday. Now she could.

She heard skittering rocks.

It was Daniel, heading toward her.

His descent was awkward, rocks bouncing down the hillside and flying through the air, but he finally arrived. Once on level ground, he began talking to the helicopter pilot on his radio. He said something about wind and wind direction. Then he disconnected and joined Reni near the victim. "The gusts will make this tough. Some are clocking at forty miles per hour."

"You need to contact the parents."

"Already did. They're heading to the hospital where she'll be taken."

Considering the remoteness of their location, it didn't take long to hear the whip of chopper blades. A black-and-white helicopter appeared and hovered above them, the draft flattening shrubs before dying down as the blades created a center with very little air flow. A yellow rescue cage was lowered, along with two crew members.

Reni was concerned about the wind too, but she told herself the rescuers were experts, and given the shape Portia was in, speed was on all their minds right now. Carrying her down the mountain would add hours to the rescue and delay urgent care.

The injured girl was eased into a neck brace and swaddled in a silver hypothermia blanket that was then plugged into a small portable generator. A switch was flipped and the cells inflated with warm air. At one point, the girl mumbled something without opening her eyes.

Reni leaned closer.

"I'm scared," Portia whispered. Then, louder, "Come with me. Please."

The female in the rescue team said, "We can take you both."

Not what Reni had expected to do today, but if her presence brought the girl some measure of comfort, she'd do it.

"Absolutely not."

She looked up to see Daniel standing nearby.

"It's too dangerous in this wind," he said.

That was pretty much all it took for Reni to come to a decision. "I'm going."

"Reni—"

"I'm going."

"It's not your job. These people are professionals."

"I'm going."

He gave up. Not the time or place to argue.

Reni and one of the rescuers were attached to harnesses. After making sure everything was secure, both of them, along with Portia, were lifted off the ground. Above the trees, the basket began to sway and spin in the wind. Reni wasn't afraid, not for herself anyway. The spin slowed and finally stabilized.

The journey from the pickup point to the trailhead, where an ambulance was waiting, was long, not in miles but time. Upon arrival, Portia was loaded quickly into the ambulance, and Reni, unstrapped, climbed in after. Doors slammed. The siren was engaged. The ambulance took off. One of the techs braced himself, finally managing to find a vein in Portia's arm. The other tech applied a pulse oximeter to her finger, checked the readout. "Decent pulse, all things considered."

Portia began to cry and shiver. Her heart rate jumped. "I want my mom."

"Your parents are meeting us at the hospital," Reni said.

"Where's JoJo?" Portia asked weakly. "Is she okay?"

"We're still looking for her," Reni told her. She noted that Portia didn't ask about Emerson.

Thirty minutes later they pulled up to the emergency entrance at the San Bernardino Medical Center. A waiting team ran for the vehicle. Vitals were given as the girl was wheeled inside. Elevator, then a series of hallways until they reached the ER.

Portia's parents were already there. Teary and wide-eyed. They and a group of doctors and nurses converged on the moving gurney, leaning over the girl, Phillip and Gwen talking to their daughter, holding her hand.

It was more than the usual response to an emergency. Phillip Devine had obviously called some people.

Swinging double doors opened, then closed behind them, leaving Reni standing in the hallway. She felt relieved to no longer be responsible for Portia, but also emotionally and physically drained. She managed to turn and leave, walking through a maze of doors and a set of stairs until she reached an exit. Outside, she dropped down onto a bench in the shade. At this lower elevation, it was hot. No sign of rain, and the sun was shining. In the bright light, Reni realized her clothes were caked in dry mud. She checked the time. Late afternoon.

She called Daniel to update him. He didn't mention her stubbornness on the mountain. She filled him in on Portia, then asked, "Any sign of the other girls?"

"Nothing. Nadine plans to come back again tomorrow."

Reni was disappointed to hear they were leaving before dark, but she understood. Both Nadine and Betty needed to recharge.

"I know a dangerous helicopter ride wasn't in your plans," Daniel said. "Or mine. I'm glad you made it safely."

"Thanks. I'll catch a cab to the police department, get my truck, and be back up." Finding Portia was wonderful, but it also instilled fresh urgency and fear. She didn't want to think of the remaining girls being there another night.

"We're going to have to call off the search in a couple of hours. I hate it, but we can't have people on the mountain in the dark. Go home. Get some rest. I plan to put the word out for civilian volunteers to help with a grid search."

What he said made sense. "Good call about the volunteers." She would have done the same. Some people might have waited and let Nadine and Betty have another shot without volunteers around to confuse the dog, but she and Daniel had seen the shape Portia was in.

"You and I will be of better use speaking to Portia as soon as she's able, hopefully first thing in the morning," Daniel added.

"I'd rather be on the mountain."

"I know you would, but we have a good team up here. I trust them to do everything that can be done. And Nadine will be back. Plus Portia Devine obviously likes you, so I need you there for the interview.

Getting an accurate report from her as quickly as possible is the best thing we can do to help find the missing girls."

Portia might not have lasted another twenty-four hours. If the remaining girls were still alive, they might not have much time left.

After taking a cab to the sheriff's office, Reni got in her truck and checked the gas gauge. She had a half tank and all the supplies she'd need if she headed to the mountain right now.

Her phone rang. It was Daniel. She answered, hoping for more good news.

"You're thinking about coming back up here right now, aren't you?"

"It's not a bad idea."

"It is a bad idea. You don't have a gun, and the killer could still be up here. And we both need a good night's sleep so we can function adequately."

She really doubted he planned to do much sleeping. "I can take care of myself."

"Oh, I know that. But we don't know what we're dealing with. Think about Edward."

"My dog?"

"He'd be lost if anything happened to you." His next words were harder for her to catch. "So would I."

CHAPTER 17

After spending the night at home in her own bed, Edward beside her, Reni dropped him off again at Joss's early the next morning and headed down the grade to San Bernardino. She was still feeling optimistic after the success of yesterday. She wasn't used to finding people alive, and it was a nice reminder that outcomes weren't always the worst-case scenario. There were still people missing, but finding Portia Devine had given everyone hope. Which left Reni feeling torn—wishing she could return to the mountain and help search for the others, while also knowing she needed to speak with the injured girl.

She was equally distracted by what Daniel had said last night, about being lost without her. She tried to tell herself that was just Daniel. He was a warm and sensitive person, and he might just as readily say the same thing to someone else. She also recognized her reaction as the kind of denial she'd engaged in with her parents. Not healthy. But it wasn't the time to dwell on it. She'd pack it up and save it to contemplate or forget later, once the case was done.

Portia's hospital was in an upscale area of San Bernardino. The streets were lined with palm trees and real grass, not rocks or sand or the fake stuff some people used for their dogs to pee on. The parking lot was laid out in Zen-like pockets with curves and angles, surrounding an ultra-modern structure, mounds of soil covered in blooming flowers that made a person feel relaxed just being there, no matter how dire the situation. Directly in front of the entry was a fountain with fish that added to the serenity of the space. Unlike the desert, where things tended to be old and weathered, everything here seemed new.

She caught up with Daniel in the third-floor waiting area. As she'd suspected, it didn't look like he'd slept much. He hadn't shaved, and his hair was in even more disarray than usual, dark jacket open over a white shirt. In contrast, Reni was casually dressed in jeans and a black T-shirt.

Daniel looked up from his phone. "The tip line just got an anonymous call that claims not all the workers at Kaleidoscope go through background checks," he said. "This person says none of the last-minute help is reviewed."

"You mean if someone calls in sick."

"Yep. I also talked to Deidra Lundy's and Jordan Rice's families again. They haven't heard from either of them."

It was sounding more and more like the two hikers might have stumbled upon a crime scene and ended up victims themselves.

"There you are." Phillip Devine was striding toward them, arms out. Before Reni could discern his plan, he wrapped his arms around her and gave her a hug. He smelled like coffee and mints. Thankfully, the hug didn't last long.

"Sorry I didn't get a chance to talk to you yesterday," he said. "Portia told me you were the one who found her. Thank you. Thank you so much." He looked near tears, his eyes red-rimmed, and he wasn't nearly as put together as yesterday. He'd probably been at the hospital all night. But like so many beautiful people from Hollywood, his good looks couldn't be dampened by a few sleepless nights. Cut his light in half, and it was still like staring into the sun.

"It wasn't me," Reni said. "It was Betty, the search and rescue dog. And her owner."

"I plan to thank Betty with a lifetime supply of dog treats and a donation to the San Bernardino Search and Rescue."

"I'm sure that would be greatly appreciated," Reni said. "Their work is invaluable."

"We hoped to talk to Portia if she's up to it," Daniel said.

"She's already posting to social media," Phillip told them. At their dual look of surprise, he went on to say he and Gwen had given up. "We should never have sent her to Kaleidoscope. She's a good kid, with an amazing following. We need to support her for her entrepreneurship, not punish her."

They moved down the hall to his daughter's room. Outside the door stood an armed officer, a stern expression on her face. They weren't taking any chances since news of the girl's rescue was being blasted to the public. Sixteen-year-old Portia had somehow survived in the wilderness with no shelter, low temps of forty-five degrees, and rain, wearing only pajama shorts and a T-shirt. The media was loving the story. But that meant anyone and everyone knew she was alive, knew where she was. And if somebody was taking out witnesses—if Lundy and Rice had been killed—Portia could still be in danger. Anybody who encountered the killer could be in danger.

In Portia's room, both mother and daughter had an aura of calm after a storm, Gwen looking almost as radiant as she had days ago. The room smelled like sterile cotton sheets dried at a high temperature, and expensive perfume, the kind that stung your nose but didn't give you a migraine.

Reni and Daniel were after information that might help locate the other girls, but they had to be careful. People who'd experienced trauma could sometimes be pushed too hard, causing them to shut down and share nothing. They started by talking a little about the day prior to the incident. Unthreatening details. The Kaleidoscope driver dropping them off, the hike, setting up camp. Only then did Reni softly ask about the night of.

"I remember hearing screams. I remember running," Portia said. "That's about it. I was so scared. Just running through the dark." Her voice was quiet, barely a whisper, and both Reni and Daniel had to lean in to catch her words.

"Do you have any idea what happened to JoJo and Emerson?" Reni asked.

"It looks as if you were sharing a tent with JoJo," Daniel added. "Did she run too?"

"We both ran. At one point, we were holding hands. But we kept tripping and finally lost each other. I think we both kept running." She spoke numbly, with no real emotion. Sometimes better than tears, but not always.

"Do you remember seeing anything?" Reni asked.

"No."

"Or anybody?" Daniel asked.

"I just remember hearing the screams, and a popping sound I thought was fireworks. At first. Now I know it was gunshots."

Daniel glanced at Reni, then back at the girl. "What about Emerson? Do you have any memory of her that night?"

Portia frowned, trying to remember. "I don't. I don't think she was with us." She glanced up sharply. "Is she dead?"

Reni took over. "We hope not. Right now we have as much reason to believe she's alive. We found you, after all. What about Jordan Rice and Deidra Lundy?" Reni asked. "Do those names sound familiar?"

The girl shook her head.

Daniel pulled out his phone and showed her photos of the couple. "Did you happen to see these people on the trail?"

Portia shook her head again. "Dad gave me my phone back, though, and I know that's the girl who posted the video." She became more alert and animated. "She has like a million followers now even though the video was taken down and she hasn't even interacted. I'd be interacting."

Reni didn't point out that Deidra might be injured or lost or dead.

The girl's short burst of energy quickly faded. Her shoulders sagged and she began to cry. Daniel shot Reni a concerned look. *Enough.* That feeling was echoed by Portia's parents.

"She's tired," Gwen said.

"We know." Reni spoke gently. "But there are two girls still out there, and two other people possibly missing. Moving quickly is crucial."

"We understand. We do," Phillip told them. "We'll keep trying to get information, and if we learn anything, we'll call you immediately. And if there's anything I can do, let me know."

Reni and Daniel were moving toward the door when Portia stopped them.

"I just remembered something." She sat up straighter in bed, her mother hovering over her with water and a bent straw. "Before the screams. JoJo and I were in our tent, whispering and laughing. And we thought we heard talking from Emerson's tent. But she was by herself. We just looked at each other and laughed because, well"—she glanced at her parents, then back at Reni and Daniel—"she's a little weird. But now I wonder if she was really talking to somebody."

Since Portia seemed to have recovered from her tears, Reni took the opportunity to ask more questions. "Did you see anyone on the hiking trail that gave you any kind of a feeling? A bad vibe?"

"That could be a lot of people. But nobody I can really think of."

"Did you ever see Emerson talking to any hikers you passed or met on the trail?" Daniel asked.

"We all talked to the other hikers. Some more than others, but no. Nothing that seemed strange."

"What about at the resort? Anybody there who stood out?" Reni asked. "Other guests? People who worked there?"

Portia thought about that for a long while and finally shook her head. "No." She leaned her head against her pillow and closed her eyes. Phillip and Gwen gave Reni and Daniel a look. The message was clear. All of the Devines wanted them to leave. With no more questions to ask right now, Reni and Daniel did just that.

"I think we got kicked out without really being kicked out," Daniel said as they walked down the hall to the elevators.

"We'd reached the limit of what they would or could share," Reni said. "And it's always better not to piss people off."

Outside the building, Daniel received a call. He answered, putting it on speakerphone. It was from his intern.

"I got a list of all the people who work at the center, even the cooks," Davenport said. "I was able to get businesses, electricians, anybody who's been there over the past few weeks. I uploaded the list to the private database for you to access. All personnel are required to go through a background check. Also a drug check."

Daniel thanked him and disconnected, saying, "And yet a tip-line caller said last-minute help can get in the building without a background check."

"Not what Ava told us," Reni said.

"Nope. Guess we need to make another visit to Kaleidoscope."

CHAPTER 18

"We've heard you might have had some workers in the complex that weren't on the list of names you gave us," Reni said. She and Daniel had just arrived in Ava Brown's office, and Reni wasn't wasting time getting to the point.

"I don't think that's correct," Ava said. Her part was not straight. Her eyes were bloodshot. On her desk was a bottle of pain medication.

"Are you sure about that?" With hands in his pockets, Daniel turned away from one of the big windows that overlooked the grounds. "What about temps who fill in when someone's sick?"

Looking faint, Ava dropped hard into her chair, opened the pills, shook out three, then looked around, realizing she didn't have any water. She tossed them down anyway and immediately began choking.

Reni pulled an almost empty bottle of water from her bag. Two years ago, she wouldn't have thought much about offering an unfinished bottle to someone. Today, since the recent pandemic, it was a whole different story. She unscrewed the cap and handed the bottle to Ava.

Eyes watering, Ava took several swallows, the coughing subsiding but still there.

"I'll get more," Reni announced as she stepped out into the hallway. Her plan was to investigate at the same time. She passed the conference space where they'd met the two sets of parents—no cucumber water this time—and headed in the direction of the dining room. Chairs were turned upside down on round tables. Hit the kitchen, grabbed a glass from a stainless-steel tray, where it rested rim down on a rubber mat along with rows of other clean glasses.

It was always a little unsettling to see the similarity between kitchens and morgues. White walls and stainless steel everywhere, stainless steel being one of the easiest surfaces to sterilize. She filled the glass from the sink.

From behind her a deep voice said, "That's not drinking water. I don't know why you temp workers always want to give guests nasty city water straight from the tap."

Temp. To be fair, Reni supposed her black attire could be mistaken for waitstaff.

She turned to see a man dressed in a chef's jacket and cap stepping from a walk-in freezer. As the door clicked shut behind him, even the sound of it was reminiscent of a morgue. With the air of someone confident about his skill and weary of those who weren't or didn't care, he crossed to a prep counter and set down a giant metal tray loaded with some kind of pastry dessert. Then he opened an upright fridge, pulled out a green bottle of sparkling water, took the glass from Reni, dumped the contents in the sink, and refilled the glass with water from the bottle.

He passed the glass back. "I don't know who wants this," he said. "Going to guess it's Ava since nobody else is here right now. She would not be happy to get a glass of water from the tap."

"Temp?" Reni asked.

"After delivering that"—he nodded to the water—"you need to get back here to help prep for tonight's banquet. We're having twenty people for a six-course meal, and so far you're the only kitchen help to show up."

"Do you have a lot of banquets here?" she asked.

"It's a way to bring in more money, I guess."

That's what she'd figured. "I'm actually not here to help with the banquet." She introduced herself.

The chef asked to see ID. She wasn't a detective anymore, not one with a badge, so she handed him a business card. It must have done the trick, because he asked what she needed. She repeated her question about temp workers.

He perched a hip on a stool. He wasn't young, probably close to sixty, and standing all day meant any break was a good time to rest.

"This place is like a revolving door," he told her.

Busted.

"Nobody stays long. I've never had any problem, but then, I'm the chef." He told her his name, didn't ring a bell, he didn't care. "I'm sought after, and Ava's not going to risk losing me. But I've heard some people have had a hard time getting paid. And if a guy is living from paycheck to paycheck, nobody wants to deal with tracking down what's owed him every month."

Either the place wasn't doing well, or Ava didn't like to part with her money. Or both.

"You don't happen to have an ice pack, do you?" Reni asked.

He did.

She thanked him and returned to Ava's office with her haul.

Ava took a long drink of the sparkling water, then held the ice pack against the back of her neck. While Reni was away, Daniel had settled into a chair across from Ava's desk. Reni sat down beside him.

"I was talking to the chef," Reni said, "and he mentioned that you have a lot of temporary help. We're going to need all of those names."

As if it was too heavy to hold up any longer, Ava lowered the ice pack and rested her arm on the desk. "Oh, that's right. I honestly forgot."

Reni glanced at Daniel. Though his face might seem unreadable, she could see her disbelief reflected there. Neither of them were fools. They knew that when a person's livelihood was at stake, many of those people lied. That was one of the toughest things about this business. Sorting the lies from the truth.

Reni watched with interest as Ava tried to keep her expression under control. It was hard not to remember her as a child, and Reni recalled seeing that same face when Ava had been caught doing something she shouldn't have. Interesting how some things didn't change. They might try for a while, but most of the time people defaulted back to the person they were comfortable with, the one who took the least amount of effort. Being a better person was work.

With her back against the wall, Ava had no choice but to admit the truth. She was quiet, then looked up with an air of defeat and confessed, "I don't know who the temps are."

"We signed nondisclosures both times we came here," Daniel pointed out. "If you could find the paperwork for the temps, it should be easy to determine who isn't permanent help."

Daniel had a good approach in these situations. He remained relaxed and nonthreatening. Even when he knew they were dealing with bullshit, he didn't let on. He went with it so the subject wouldn't freak out and caution would remain low. But Ava seemed to suspect he was on to her. She didn't answer.

Reni's approach was much more straightforward. Ava would get no softness or faux sympathy and understanding from her. Maybe that made her and Daniel a good team. "You didn't get NDAs from them," Reni said.

Ava rushed to defend herself. "You have to understand that the kitchen is a separate entity. People come in the back service door. We can't possibly monitor that level of activity. It would be impossible. Not all the deliveries to both the kitchen *and* the supply area."

Poor Ava had begun with a dream, but she hadn't thought everything through. Reni didn't know if she was deserving of sympathy in the face of such incompetent yet arrogant actions. Signing NDAs at the front desk had been just for looks, to give people the sense of privacy and security that it seemed didn't really exist.

The lie exposed, Daniel had no problem unleashing now. "You had a responsibility to those girls. Their safety should have been your main priority."

"I know."

"We need to look at your security footage," he said.

"I've already had my building engineer gather all of it. There's a lot."

"Any undocumented help probably worked in the kitchen or housekeeping," Reni said.

Daniel piggybacked on her reply. "Let's start with dining room footage on the days the girls were here. That shouldn't take too long."

Reni wasn't so sure about that.

Ava led them to a dark, windowless room, where a man sat at a three-section desk in front of a row of monitors. He seemed not to have noticed them come in. Odd, because the opening and closing of the outer door would have clued him in even though he was wearing headphones. Then Reni realized he was asleep. Further evidence of lax security.

Ava touched his shoulder and he jumped, pulled his headphones down around his neck, trying to act alert and awake.

The room was small and claustrophobic, the screens bright and disorienting in the darkness. The desktop was strewn with personal items, like a small stuffed elephant and a framed photo of a girl standing in front of the entrance to Disneyland. Snacks to alleviate boredom. A can of cranberry soda that fizzed and popped every now and then. A bag of tortilla chips.

Ava explained why they were there. As Reni, Daniel, and Ava hovered behind him, the guy clicked his keyboard and brought up the timeline screen. Ava gave him a date to check. He opened the file. The dining room. Groups of people seated at tables.

"Keep an eye on the servers and look for anybody you don't recognize," Daniel said.

Reni noticed a person who seemed a little out of place. He was oddly disheveled for such an upscale joint. She pointed. They were viewing a feed from a camera mounted high in a hallway that led from the kitchen to the dining room. The man in question appeared several times, sometimes pushing a cart, returning to the kitchen, moving back and forth. It looked like he was busing dirty plates and refilling water glasses.

"There's Emerson," Reni said. "And JoJo and Portia." They were all at the same table. The guy put a glass down in front of Emerson. She glanced up at him. Smiled. "Who is that?"

Ava leaned closer to the screen, squinting. "I don't know."

Reni and Daniel glanced at each other, then back at the screen. The man was looking down, his features unclear.

"Can you zoom in on his face?" Daniel asked.

The tech clicked some keys. The close-up was no help. Once it was enlarged, the image became too pixelated to make out the features. Ava had apparently scrimped when it came to her security cameras.

"We need to find out who this person is," Daniel said.

They continued looking and found two other people who didn't match any faces of the workers on file. The sheriff's department already had phone numbers and email addresses, and most employees had been interviewed by officers.

"It might not have anything to do with anybody here," Ava said.

She still seemed to be trying to convince them nothing serious had happened, even though one of her employees was dead. "You're exactly right," Reni said. "We're just following up on every lead we have." She didn't add that this was one of the only leads they had so far.

"A lot of people think this was a prank," Ava said. "I think so too."

"Pranks don't usually kill people," Reni said.

"I'm not saying any of the girls were behind the murder, if it was a murder. It could have been suicide."

Another untrue theory already being tossed around on social media.

"They could have gotten mixed up with someone they shouldn't have," Ava continued. "It happens, especially when these girls are online all the time. They meet people. It's one of the things we try to teach them. They can't trust everybody they meet through the internet."

The tech looked at the clock on the wall and stretched elaborately. "Time for me to go."

"I'll bet you could stay a little longer," Reni said. "We'd like to see more footage." They didn't have time for the tech to go home and start the search again in the morning.

He shot her an irritated look before returning his hands to the keyboard. Thirty more minutes, with Daniel and Reni giving directions so they didn't miss anything, and they stumbled upon something else of interest.

A girl by herself in a hallway.

"This is the dorm-wing camera," the tech said.

The angle didn't reveal her face. A barefoot girl, wearing pajamas, pink hoodie over her head, covering her hair. She vanished through a door at the end of the hall.

"Can you follow her with another camera?" Reni asked.

He pulled up footage of another angle. It was in a stairwell. Still no face.

"Are there any other cameras in this hall or stairwell?" Daniel asked.

"No."

The girl stopped by a fire door that appeared to lead outside. She looked around, but not at the camera.

"I always laugh when people do that," the tech said. "You'd think by now people would realize they need to look up, and that they're on camera practically anywhere and everywhere."

"We have no camera in the girls' rooms or in any restrooms," Ava said, always on the defensive.

"Not talking about here," the tech said. "You know. People do things. Gotta be careful of that stuff." He tapped the photo on his desk. "That's what I tell my girlfriend."

As they watched, the girl opened the fire door several inches.

"Why didn't that set off an alarm?" Ava asked. Then to Daniel and Reni, "That should have set off the alarm."

"It either wasn't set for the night yet or someone turned it off," the tech said with a shrug. More damning evidence of less-than-stellar security.

The girl leaned out the door and was talking to someone, but the person on the other side of the glass was just a dark blur. A hand reached through the opening. After a few seconds, the girl closed the door and turned around, head down. Still no face. She was looking at something in her hand.

"It's a phone," Reni said.

"That little sneak," said Ava.

"Is that the guy from the dining hall?" Daniel asked.

The tech froze the image, enlarged it, zoomed in on the window in the door and the person outside.

Nobody could confirm.

"We don't know that he has anything to do with anything," Daniel cautioned.

"Can we at least ID the girl?" Reni asked. "By her clothing?"

"Those pajamas are given to all the girls. They're part of the experience package," Ava said.

Reni looked at Daniel and tried not to roll her eyes. "Of course they are," she muttered.

"We're going to need these files—all the footage you have from the time the girls were here. Send all of it to my email and I'll forward it to Digital Forensics. Maybe they can clean it up and get us a clearer image."

"Sure," the tech said. "I'll do it tomorrow."

125

"Do it now, while we're here." Daniel pulled out a business card with his email and placed it on the desk.

The tech wasn't happy, but he did it. Once he'd hit send, he said, "Let me know if you ever need another pair of eyes in your department." He glanced up at Ava. "Kinda doubt this job will be around much longer."

CHAPTER 19

Eliza was used to seeing hikers along Highway 2. It was California, after all, and living near the Pacific Crest Trail meant hitchhiking was common, the people with their thumbs out often seeking a ride into town.

She didn't consider herself a trail angel. Those were a special breed of givers who set up stations with food and water, clothing, medical supplies. Eliza was more of an accidental angel. She gave people rides when she spotted a thumb up and a backpack, sometimes driving them all the way into Phelan and the McDonald's they liked to stop at. She always helped if she saw someone in need.

When she spotted what looked like a small mound of clothing next to the road, she eased up on the gas pedal and leaned forward in the seat, eyes peeled. In the past, she'd helped a few hikers who'd passed out along the highway. They got dehydrated and disoriented and made it to the road before collapsing. Those were the luckier ones.

She stopped coasting and put her foot on the brake, pulling her Jeep to a stop behind pink fabric that snapped in the wind. She adjusted her glasses and peered through the dirty windshield.

There was a metal fence nearby, and even with her windows up she could hear it, the high wind causing the taut wires to vibrate. She called it singing. Some people hated the sound, said it creeped them out. She wasn't one of those people.

As she looked through the windshield, she thought she spotted what could be an arm. She blinked a few times to clear her vision. Maybe a leg. And then she remembered the missing girls. Her stomach dropped and her heart beat faster. The place the girls disappeared was about seven miles away. She turned off the engine, jumped out, ran to the pile on the ground.

Yes, it was a person. Lying still, although the fabric was going wild, and Eliza's gray hair was whipping around her face, disrupting her vision. She clutched her hair, securing it against her neck with the palm of her hand as she crouched near the body.

She touched an arm. "Hey," she said softly. Then louder. "Hey."

The pile moaned.

Eliza gasped and pulled out her phone to call for help, almost dropped it, caught it, only to find she had no bars. Not a surprise. A surprise was when she could actually make a call. She liked the remoteness of the town of Wrightwood, but when a person needed medical attention . . . well, most of the time you had to depend on yourself. She tucked her phone away and gently rolled the person over enough to see a face.

A teenage girl. Eyes closed. Barely conscious.

"Hey, honey. You okay?"

The girl moaned again, and Eliza tried to recall what the missing hikers looked like. She'd seen their faces on TV. This girl had brown hair. Had one or two had brown hair?

The girl tried to open her eyes. They just rolled back in her head.

Eliza scrambled to her Jeep, retrieved a bottle of water and a blanket—supplies she always carried in case she was either stranded or saw someone in need. She hurried back, opening the water as she ran.

It took a little time, but the girl came round enough to take several sips.

"We need to get you to a doctor," Eliza said. "Do you think you can stand up?"

The girl nodded.

At least she was semi-aware.

Eliza helped her up. She wasn't wearing shoes, and her feet were bruised and bloody. Her whole body was bruised and bloody, now that Eliza got a better look. It was hot out, but the girl's skin was like ice, so Eliza wrapped a blanket around her. She was tiny, less than a hundred pounds, but still certainly too much for Eliza to carry.

"What's your name?" Eliza asked.

The girl tried to form words, started over, swallowed, ran a tongue over her cracked lips, and whispered, "JoJo."

That sounded right. "You're going to be fine, JoJo. You're going to be just fine. My name's Eliza, and I've got you." She walked the girl to the Jeep, helped her in, and climbed behind the wheel.

With her head against the seatback, JoJo turned her face toward Eliza. Her eyes had dark circles under them and were sunken from dehydration. Her mouth hung open, and her hair was matted and tangled. She was probably pretty on a normal day. This was not a normal day. She wasn't pretty now, and Eliza felt bad for thinking that.

"She's dead," the girl said with no emotion.

Eliza knew one of the group had been murdered. She didn't like to think of something so horrible happening so close to her home. Or that whoever had done it was still out there somewhere.

CHAPTER 20

Reni held her phone in landscape mode while watching a livestream.

"Hello out there! Yes, I'm back, girlfriends, boyfriends, and bitches! I'm coming to you from beautiful San Bernardino Medical Center. You've probably already heard about how I was rescued by this awesome woman named Eliza. I swear I was almost dead when she found me along the highway!"

From the driver's seat of his SUV, Daniel glanced over Reni's shoulder. The live video was of JoJo McGrath, sitting up in bed, makeup perfect, twirling strands of dark hair. Her eyeliner precisely applied. Were those false lashes? It looked like it. The freckles were obviously fake, but Reni wasn't sure if they'd been applied by hand or if they were tattoos. The girl was wearing a hospital gown, and when she stroked her hair, Reni could see the oxygen monitor on her finger and the IV line attached to the back of her hand.

She'd cleaned up quickly. It had been only a short time since Daniel had been notified that she'd been found. She seemed uninjured except for dehydration and exposure, and had been taken to the same hospital as Portia.

Two girls alive.

"A million views already," Daniel said.

And the live comments were flying.

We're so glad you're okay!

I thought you were dead! I cried for hours!

I knew you weren't dead!

Prank!

Scam!

She almost died!

Stunt!

JoJo was reading comments aloud as they came in. "Some of you people are so mean!" she said. "I would never fake anything like this!" Pouty face.

Daniel pulled into the hospital parking lot and cut the engine. They got out of the vehicle and strode toward the building, Reni still watching her phone.

"I have another surprise!" JoJo said. "Look who's here with me!"

Someone leaned into the screen.

It was Portia, dressed in a hospital gown, and also tethered to an IV rack. She didn't look as if she should be out of bed. Pale, with circles under her eyes, but much better than when Reni had found her.

She waved and smiled.

Comments scrolled on the right of the screen too fast for Reni to read them all.

Tell us what happened!

Who did this to you?

Did you kill Janet Ravenscroft?

Who killed her?

Did you see it happen?

"We've got to put a stop to this," Daniel said. "Before she ends up sharing vital information that shouldn't be made public."

"And before she and Portia corroborate stories," Reni added.

It was never a good thing for people involved in a crime, victims or otherwise, to be interviewed together or talk to each other before getting their statements taken separately. Stories had a way of merging when they shouldn't. Ideas, details, had to be protected from cross-contamination, even when there was no intent to mislead anyone. The brain was a weird thing. They hadn't expected JoJo to be up and lucid so quickly, but teens could seem superhuman at times. And it was amazing what a little fluid and electrolytes could do.

At the hospital doors, Reni tucked her phone in a pocket. Inside, Daniel flashed his badge at the reception desk, and a woman there gave them the room number. It was on the third floor, just down the hallway from Portia's. That explained how Portia had so easily visited JoJo.

They took the stairs rather than wait for the elevator. The same sober-looking officer was still stationed in the hall, but now stood outside JoJo's room. From the open door of the room, Reni could see both girls, along with a hovering nurse, who seemed to be waiting to wheel Portia back to her room.

Daniel knocked.

Portia's face lit up when she saw Reni.

"Uh-oh," JoJo said to her live audience. She was talking to them with her smartphone. "There are a couple of people here who look like detectives. And one of them is a really cute guy in a suit!" She flashed Daniel a smile. "Gotta go, my lovelies, but I'll be back soon with makeup tutorials! Nobody's gonna keep me from the internet anymore!"

That comment alone made Reni wonder if the people who were screaming that it was a stunt might be right. Maybe not the murder itself. It was hard to think that JoJo or Portia would kill someone, or have someone else do it for them, just so they could get back online. But at the same time Reni wasn't going to discount that theory. Murderers all started somewhere.

Portia sank into her wheelchair, looking relieved that the live feed was over. She could go back to being a recovering patient.

"We'll be in to see you soon," Daniel said as a nurse wheeled her away.

He seemed to be doing a pretty good job of hiding any irritation he might be feeling at JoJo's behavior. And since the girl seemed to be responding to the male in the room, Reni took a seat in the corner, pulled out her sketch pad, and began drawing the scene while jotting down bits of information as it surfaced, much like a courtroom sketch artist. Her plan was to observe, since Daniel seemed to have more chance of being successful with the girl.

He produced a digital recorder and spoke into it with name, date, and location before laying the device on the bed table and wheeling it closer to the girl.

Reni often asked victims to write their answers down for her. Sometimes it was easier to write words than to speak them aloud. And sometimes thoughts could flow more clearly from the brain to pen or pencil. She wasn't sure why. With that in mind, she pulled out a lined steno tablet and pen from her bag and handed them to JoJo, who looked confused by the offering.

"In case you want to write down your answers too," Reni explained. "Or maybe draw something pertinent."

Reni returned to her seat, and Daniel began a routine set of questions meant to relax the girl. Things about how she'd felt on the day of the expedition. What the weather had been like. Had she enjoyed the day before everything took a turn, or had it been more like a punishment?

"I didn't expect to like it," JoJo admitted. "I was mad, but it ended up being okay. Of course I kept thinking about my channel and getting back to it. Wishing I had my phone so I could record it. Although I didn't look so great that day, so maybe not. It takes me two hours to prep for my videos. Sometimes a lot longer."

Daniel nodded seriously, as if he completely understood. And then they got to the night of the event. JoJo's story was similar to Portia's. As it should have been. They'd been sleeping in the same tent. JoJo confirmed that.

"What about Emerson Rose?" Reni asked.

"What about her?"

"Did you like her?"

"She seemed decent."

"Did you know her before you went to Kaleidoscope?"

"No. And I didn't know her very well until we went for the hike. We had a sharing campfire hour, and she told us she'd been in a school shooting."

"That's right," Daniel said, without adding that he'd been there. "I want you to think about anything else she or the other two might have shared that night."

"Well, you know, it was confidential. Like secret stuff, or at least Janet promised it wouldn't go anywhere else." She frowned. "But I guess she's dead."

Reni drew that frown. She drew the IV and the needle in the back of JoJo's hand. She drew the light coming in the window, falling on the floor in a triangular pattern. She drew Daniel, elbows on his knees, hands loosely clasped. It felt good to capture the moment. Not as good as drawing her father's burial sites, but satisfying.

JoJo started to say something, stopped.

Daniel leaned closer, and the girl said, "I keep wondering if it was somebody Emerson knew."

Reni controlled the urge to lift her head. Instead she gripped her pencil, kept her chin down, and stared at the paper, waiting.

With no change in his voice, Daniel said, "Why's that?"

"Well, earlier she was talking about how somebody was going to come and rescue her. And about how her dad was so mean, and he wasn't her real dad anyway. And he was going to be sorry. And somebody was going to save her."

"Somebody?" Daniel asked.

On the paper, Reni wrote: *Boyfriend? Friend?*

"Do you remember a name?"

"I don't think she ever said."

Then JoJo told them about hearing screams. She and Portia ran but got separated. "I looked for her, but I was so scared, and it was dark.

I kept hearing screams and I just ran." In her recounting, she seemed genuinely terrified, the happy YouTube-girl persona gone.

Reni shaded in JoJo's arms. She jotted in the light-blue design on the hospital gown. She could smell the gown. Hospital gowns all smelled the same.

"I hope you find her," JoJo said. "Emerson."

Daniel tried to coax a little more out of her with casually positioned questions.

"I might have heard her scream a name, but I don't know." She started crying.

Reni poured a glass of ice water for her from the beige plastic pitcher. So far, JoJo hadn't mentioned hearing Emerson speaking to someone.

JoJo took a few weak sips and put the glass down. "I think I'm done talking." She closed her eyes and leaned back against the pillow.

Daniel shut off his recorder and put his tablet away.

"I'm so sorry you had to go through this," Reni said softly.

If a genie gave her three wishes, she'd wish for predators to stop terrorizing young women, she'd wish no more children would ever go missing, and the last one? What would she do with it? Wish her father had never killed? Or would she wish to find Daniel's mother? Her first wish might possibly take care of the third, because even though Daniel's mother's name was not on her father's victim list, Reni would never believe that list was complete. Never. And that left a different use for her last wish. To find Emerson.

Reni gathered her things, along with the pen and paper she'd given JoJo. The girl had sketched something. A clumsy drawing of a person.

Reni held up the tablet. "Who's this?"

"A guy I saw Emerson talking to."

Daniel peered over her shoulder at the tablet.

JoJo gave them a description. "A little skinny, not very tall, brown hair, maybe some facial hair."

"Where?" Daniel asked.

"Kaleidoscope."

"How old was he?" Reni asked.

"I dunno. A little older than you guys."

"How old are we?" Daniel asked.

"Fifties?"

Daniel made a strangling sound. "Thirties."

"Oh, sorry."

JoJo's parents showed up. They had the air of people who were tired of waiting around the hospital and wanted nothing more than to take their daughter home. Belinda McGrath stayed in the room, comforting JoJo, while Reni and Daniel talked to the father.

"We gave up trying to keep her away from electronic devices," Jim McGrath said. He seemed sad and ashamed.

Reni wanted to reassure him that he'd done nothing wrong. "Comfort is comfort," she said. "I probably would have done the same thing in your situation." In the scheme of things, the device didn't rank up there very high.

"Has she mentioned anything of interest?" Daniel asked.

"She hasn't wanted to talk about it."

"I'm going to give her a little time, but then I have to take her formal statement," Daniel said.

They told Jim goodbye and walked down the hall to Portia's room, past the officer guarding both rooms.

They had no way of knowing if JoJo and Portia had already discussed the possibility of the killer being someone Emerson knew. Daniel asked Portia about it.

"Yeah, Emerson said she knew a guy who was going to rescue her," Portia said. "Well, I don't think she said *rescue*, but she said her dad would be sorry. I remember thinking it was a weird thing to say. And also thinking she could just leave."

Reni showed her JoJo's drawing.

Portia laughed, then got serious again. "There was some guy hanging around Kaleidoscope. I guess he *kind* of looked like that. I don't really remember."

They thanked her. Reni stepped close to the bed and gave Portia a smile. "I'm glad you're okay."

Portia smiled back.

"Did Emerson's mother mention a boyfriend?" Reni asked Daniel as the two of them left the hospital building.

"No, but you never know. It could be someone she was unaware of. Parents don't know half the stuff their kids do. Also, *was* it a stunt gone wrong?" Daniel asked, more to himself than Reni.

"I keep wondering the same thing," Reni said. "But I think it's dangerous to focus too much on that. We could miss some important information while we're looking in the wrong direction."

On the way to his SUV, Daniel made a face and said, "Fifties?"

He seemed to be aging well. Reni wasn't sure about herself. "We've got a lot of miles on us."

CHAPTER 21

That night, Reni returned home with a plan to spend several hours online investigating. Sometimes that could be just as or more effective than legwork. She took a shower, then got into bed with her laptop, Edward curled beside her. She logged in to the homicide department's database to see if anything new had been added to the files. There were a couple of interviews with employees of Kaleidoscope that she read and flagged so Daniel would know she'd seen them. Nothing that seemed of merit, at least not yet. Then she checked her email. Her heart sped up when she saw a message from her artist friend who did age progression. It included a JPEG.

Alice Vargas would have been about fifty-five now, and the attached drawing depicted her with shoulder-length hair, a touch of gray, a fatter face, smaller eyes, pinched mouth, slight jowls.

Age progression was a fairly broad supposition. A could be. A might be. Some drawings ended up being remarkably accurate; others were horribly off, bearing little similarity to the person today. Weight, stress, heredity, health—they all played a part. Of special note? This drawing was substantially different from the ones Reni had seen before.

She returned to the current case and visited Emerson Rose's Facebook page. Not a lot there, and it looked as if she hadn't been active on it for a few years. Same with Portia and JoJo. She visited the page of Deidra Lundy, the girl who'd posted the social media video of the murder scene. No recent activity there either. The page for the boyfriend, Jordan Rice, was private, so she couldn't see much. Reni had a bad feeling about them both.

From Facebook she went to Reddit and requested to join the Victims of School Shootings group Emerson belonged to. She'd have to wait for approval. She checked out Portia's and JoJo's YouTube pages, subscribed, and clicked the bell to be notified by phone of new content. Then, feeling as if she'd earned a little time away from the missing persons case, she logged into a fake Facebook profile she sometimes used. She could never have gotten away with the somewhat unscrupulous behavior when she was an FBI agent, but now she had more freedom.

She updated and tweaked her profile with interests and hobbies that suited the persona most likely to get her approved by the groups she wanted to access. Hobbies of sewing and crafts. Sewing was her only real lead. If Daniel's mother was still alive, and Reni leaned toward her being dead, she could be anywhere in or out of the country.

She searched seamstress groups and requested to join all she could find. Most of the Facebook sewing groups seemed a trusting bunch who didn't require approval from a real person. After replying to a few questions, she was accepted automatically.

Her plan was to go through member profile images and see if she could find a face that looked similar to the sketch her friend had come up with. A tedious process, but tedium was at the center of all private investigator work. Most endeavors were exercises in futility, but all were paths to follow until they ended. A lot of detective work felt futile until you hit a solid clue.

She spent the next two hours scrolling through hundreds of faces, noting several women who could be Alice. If any *were* Alice, it would have been smart to avoid listing interests that could be matched to her old, offline profile. But after thirty years, it would also be easy and even comforting to let down your guard and feel you could be yourself, at least a little.

Reni had spent a lot of time going over Alice Vargas's personal profile and had quizzed Daniel about his mother's likes and dislikes. That was before he'd decided he wanted to quit looking for her. Alice used to like crafts and had been an excellent seamstress. Unfortunately, many people listed those hobbies and skills, and the sewing-specific groups contained thousands of members. It would have been easier if Alice's hobby were digging up unmarked graves in the Scottish Highlands or creating jewelry from bugs. Or, like Reni, pottery with bird feathers. Or painting death scenes.

That's where tastes came into play. Books, movies, travel destinations, shopping, products. Of course, things like that could change after thirty years, but it was interesting to note the longevity of many favorites among the general population. Then you had preferred colors and flowers and trees and animals. Politics. Temperament in dealing with virtual strangers. Things like these tended not to change over time.

Using the gathered data, Reni narrowed her suspects down to a short list of ten people, at least for now. She had to begin somewhere. The ten were located all over the country, as well as out of the country. Sweden, the UK. But three were in California, and one in Las Vegas. These four moved to the top of Reni's list. As she had long noted, California people tended to stay in California or return there if they left. And Vegas? Coincidentally, Vegas was the city where Alice's now deceased old boyfriend, Kyle Kennedy, had eventually moved. He'd been interviewed after her disappearance, and again later by Daniel himself.

It would be easy to assume a person who wanted to vanish would travel far, and Alice probably had. But she might have come back once she felt it was safe.

In looking at the profiles, Reni noted most were married with kids and grandkids. But one of them, the one in Vegas, Penelope Ranier, had lost a child, a boy, when he was eight.

A chill went through her.

Reni felt bad for thinking the loss might not be real, but she was fully aware of how evil mothers could be, how someone might try to generate sympathy for something that had never really happened, maybe even absolving themselves of their sins by posting their loss on Facebook. Or it could be real. It could be the truth.

Reni reached out to the woman through Facebook Messenger, told her she was looking to hire someone to make matching dresses for a sorority reunion.

Do you have any openings? Could we possibly meet in person someday, in a public location, of course?

The reply was almost immediate. Reni hadn't expected such speed, especially in the middle of the night. The woman from Facebook, the woman who might or might not be Daniel's mother, said: *I'm available all this week.*

Now Reni had a dilemma. She couldn't leave in the middle of an investigation, one that was time sensitive. Yet she also didn't want to risk losing Penelope. She sent a vague reply, saying she'd have to check her schedule and get back to her. She didn't like keeping secrets, but for now she didn't plan to mention any of this to Daniel.

CHAPTER 22

He couldn't stop watching the news.

Every second he was home, the TV was on. Even when he wasn't home—in case she made too much noise. There were no nearby neighbors, and he hardly ever saw anybody around, but you never knew.

He loved watching reports about the missing hikers. He couldn't go for more than an hour or so without checking to see if there were any updates. Last night a channel out of San Bernardino had reported from a trailhead, the camera framing a woman with a mic in her hand. The live feed was broken up with drone shots of trails, that footage interspersed with a recorded interview of a detective working on the case. Detective Daniel Ellis, standing with a cop in a beige shirt. They both asked for help in finding the missing hikers.

Johnnie had immediately filled out something online and was told to show up to help search. He got excited thinking about it. And now he was driving through the early-morning darkness, heading to the mountain and the trailhead, where the search was supposed to start at first light.

First light. They really said that.

He was one of the first people there.

They checked him in with his ID. When he signed his name on the form, he was breathing hard and his heart was beating fast. But the woman at the table didn't seem to notice. She smiled and thanked him for coming.

He smiled back. "You're welcome."

He was given an orange vest, and a stick to poke with.

Good thing he'd come early, because too many people were just showing up, and they had to turn the extras away. When there were one hundred searchers, the cop in the beige shirt from the news report gave them instructions, told them to remain close together. They couldn't do a real grid search because of the terrain, but they'd have to do the best they could. Johnnie always did his best.

He hadn't come with a plan. He was just kind of winging it. And honestly, everything looked so much alike that he wasn't sure he could find anything even if he decided to. Pretty funny.

He was not an outdoors person. He hated it. The wind that never stopped, the sun that never stopped. He liked looking at pictures of pretty places, and he liked drone shots of anywhere because drones were cool, but he didn't like hiking or going for walks, and he especially hated bugs and he was afraid of snakes. There were rattlesnakes here. He knew somebody whose dog got bit in the face. That story didn't have a happy ending.

As he walked, he went over the mistakes people made after a bite. You weren't supposed to put a belt or anything tight on an arm or leg. You were supposed to loosen clothing. Didn't make sense, but that's what he'd read on Reddit. You were also supposed to keep the bite lower than your heart and try to remain calm. Funny about being calm. Like, who could possibly do that? He'd run screaming to his car and drive himself to the ER. That was his plan.

There wasn't much talking among the volunteers except for people who knew each other. And those conversations were annoying for the most part. Unless they were talking about the killer, trying to guess "who done it."

He done it.

"Old boyfriend," someone said.

"Just some random sicko," came a reply. "An opportunistic kill."

"They say they always return to the scene of the crime."

He almost laughed. But not at the sicko part. That made him mad.

Everybody moved forward slowly with their heads down, keeping their eyes on the ground for anything that might have been dropped by hikers. From watching the news, he knew nobody had found the person who'd posted the Instagram video of the dead woman in the tent, or her boyfriend. Using special software, he'd been able to download a copy of the video for himself before the cops made Instagram remove it.

"What if we find a body?"

The question came from a middle-aged woman who was poking at the ground several yards away, as if looking for someone right under her feet. He wanted to say a bunch of different smart-ass things, but he also didn't want to draw attention to himself.

"We report it to the people in charge." He pointed. "That guy." Pointed to another person. "Or her."

The search process was unsurprisingly annoying. He didn't like following orders, and this was all about that. Lining up a few feet apart. Moving forward at the same pace. Watching the ground, watching where you placed your feet. A row of orange vests moving through the forest, kind of near where the murdered girl had been found. Pretty funny because it was nowhere near where the other two hikers had been. They had names now. Deidra Lundy and Jordan Rice. It made him feel smug and superior, knowing he knew more than anybody else here.

Thirty minutes passed, but it seemed like hours. His hatred of nature increased. He was hot and tired. His boots were rubbing his heels, and he was sure he had blisters. They stopped for a break.

A search and rescue dog sat down near him, its front feet straight and close together, the eyes staring right at him. Someone said the dog's name was Betty. Dumb name for a dog.

Go away, he thought, staring back.

The dog didn't blink. *It didn't blink!* That kind of freaked him out because it seemed like the dog was reading his mind. And it continued to stare at him until one of the leaders asked for twenty people to come with him. They were getting into rougher terrain and wouldn't be able to maintain the row of searchers. They were going to disperse them. He and the middle-aged woman volunteered to join the pack.

As they walked, he came to a place that started looking familiar. A sharp turn in the trail, a point they had to get around. He'd turned the corner that day too. It had been windier, scarier, because of gusts that could almost knock you down. He took the corner now and recalled how he'd come upon the hikers. And so he'd done what had to be done. They'd left him no choice. They really shouldn't have been there at all.

Once the two hikers were no longer breathing or moving or screaming, he'd dragged the bodies to an overhang and rolled them off the side of the mountain. He wasn't used to physical activity, and it hadn't been easy.

Now he had to decide what to do. Somebody else was probably going to find them. Maybe that dog. Wouldn't it be better if that someone was him?

Yes.

He stepped off the trail and walked to the edge of a cliff and peeked over. He saw big rocks, and the tops of trees swaying in the wind. It made him dizzy.

Thinking about that day was like remembering a movie, or something he'd read about that had happened to somebody else. Not him. Because how could he have dragged the bodies and rolled them over the edge? But he'd done it. Pretty sure he'd done it. Adrenaline made a person crazy strong. He'd heard a story of a woman lifting a car. Snopes said it was true. People on Reddit talked about it. His memory of what had happened was real. Clouded by the emotions of the moment, the fog of panic.

He made up his mind and quickly descended the steep grade, boots sliding over rocks, using his poking stick for support. He grabbed a branch to slow his descent. The woman who'd asked about the body shouted at him from above, told him to watch out, told him he shouldn't be down there.

"Against the rules!" she yelled down at him.

"No rules!" he shouted up at her, not looking, keeping his eyes in the direction the bodies had gone.

Now he remembered laughing as they'd tumbled and rolled and bounced, looking like giant and goofy stuffed dolls. Had the girl laughed too? Had she helped him shove the bodies? Sometimes he thought of her as a partner, a friend. After all, he'd done this for her. Saved her. He was still saving her. He still had more saving to do.

"I'm going for help!" the woman screamed.

"I don't need help!" he shouted back once he finally quit sliding. He was fine, and for her to imply he needed help pissed him off. He especially didn't like women telling him what to do.

He scanned the area below. Maybe this wasn't the spot. Then he saw something. Hadn't the guy been wearing an orange-and-green shirt? Yes. Blood had blossomed, turning the green darker and the orange darker still. He hadn't laughed. Not then.

Without looking up, wondering if the woman was still around, his heart slamming, he shouted, "I found a person!" He swallowed, smiled, shouted again, louder, "I found a person!"

She shouted something back. After that came the sound of movement fading away, then returning. "Here! He's down there!"

He imagined the woman pointing in the direction he'd gone. Over the cliff like the dead bodies, except he'd been able to stop his descent. He wasn't comically dead. He put a fist to his mouth to stifle a giggle. Then, suddenly, he wasn't sure how it happened, he was kneeling next to the orange-and-green shirt, next to the guy who wasn't much more than a kid.

If you find a body, don't touch it. Call for assistance.

Shouldn't he be puffed up and stinky by now? This didn't seem right. Why, the guy didn't look bad. Not bad at all. Nothing like the dead person in his dreams, coming to sit on the end of his bed at night, all bloated, with flies swarming around his head. And then the body groaned.

It groaned!

Johnnie tumbled backward, nearly slipping farther down the slope, waited a second, the blue sky above him, then crawled back to the body. One eye was open and looking at him, the rest of the face slack, mouth hanging open. *This* was the creature from his dreams. He shook his head like somebody shaking off water. Looked at the guy again. No. Not a dream. Not a monster.

The guy was still alive.

Just when he thought things couldn't get more messed up and confusing, the guy in the green-and-orange shirt reached for him with clawed fingers encrusted with dried blood. His nails were broken. A couple of fingers bent oddly. Bet that hurt like hell. Johnnie realized the guy had been digging, trying to drag his body out of the ravine. Wow.

He got to his feet and looked farther down below. He couldn't see the other body. Had the guy managed to haul himself up the steep slope to this point? That was remarkable.

Kudos.

As he stood there trying to piece it all together, the guy's mouth opened and he let out a croak, speaking a single word that was hard to make out. Something like *Deidra?* Oh God, yeah. That was the girl. And he could talk. This was bad. Really bad. And people were coming.

Someone shouted commands.

He inched closer to the pathetic person in the bloody green-and-orange shirt. He looked into that one open eye and said, "Sorry, pal." He pressed a hand over the hiker's mouth and nose. The guy struggled and whimpered. "Really sorry, because you kinda deserve to live after all this."

A scattering of rocks hit him in the back. Searchers were already sliding down the cliff.

He pressed harder on the guy's face. That one eye was looking at him, bugged out now, but behind it there seemed to be a person. Like a thinking and aware person.

"Get back," someone told him from behind.

His body blocked what was happening. They couldn't see the full story. He had no choice but to remove his hand. The guy on the ground, the not-dead-guy with the green-and-orange shirt, inhaled a long and wheezing breath, then the eye closed and the body went limp.

"Is he alive?" one of the search team asked.

Johnnie looked over his shoulder. The question didn't come from the bossy woman. It was one of the official search and rescue guys. Johnnie briefly considered tripping him, then shoving him down the treacherous hill. But more people were on their way, seeming to grow out of the frame of trees and sky. There was the annoying woman, standing way up there, pointing, directing the rescuers down the steep incline. Some were carrying supplies. A metal litter for an injured person. And a medical kit to try to keep him from croaking.

Thinking fast, he shouted, "He's alive! Yes, he's alive! Hurry! Down here!" He made a motion like he was scooping water toward him.

"Good job," the first guy said.

They'd done this before. They were pros. Ropes were lowered. Before Johnnie was aware of what was going on, someone secured a thick braided rope around his waist and he was being pulled back up. He half climbed, lost his footing, slipped, was caught by the rope, and finally collapsed on his knees at the top. After he was on his feet and the rope was removed, the woman, the tattletale, handed him a bottle of water. She was smiling and looking at him like she was his proud mom. He wondered what his real mom would think. She'd be surprised but impressed. Maybe even proud too.

He smiled a little, drank some of the water, dumped the rest of it on his head like he'd seen sports bros do. From below came the sound of voices as they worked with the hiker.

"Another person!"

"One more!"

"Down here!"

"A girl!"

They'd found her.

A few minutes later an update was relayed.

Dead. She was dead.

Johnnie sent a silent thank-you to the universe.

Now that he thought about it, it seemed he'd maybe caught faint whiffs of something rotten. Yes. He'd been too distracted to give it the attention it deserved.

"At least one of them is alive," the woman told him. "You done good."

He *had* done good.

He conversed with her a little, then walked back up the trail in the direction they'd come, intent on getting back to his car and getting home. It took him a few moments to notice the clapping. And even longer to realize people were clapping *for him*. Smiles and cheers and even some slaps on the back. He was a hero.

"I'm sorry, but you're going to have to stick around awhile," the cop with the beige shirt said. The patch on his sleeve said San Bernardino County Sheriff's Department. "A detective will be coming to take your statement."

"I have to leave. I take care of my mother who has dementia. I told Search and Rescue everything already."

"I know." The cop almost rolled his eyes. They were on the same page. "But a detective wants to talk to you too."

The euphoria of being called a hero was fading, and he started thinking about the guy they were hauling up the mountainside. Had the hiker recognized him?

Johnnie needed to get home. Figure out his next step, if he had one. He wanted to reset the day. If he hadn't shouted, he could have killed the guy before anybody showed up. Not his fault. The lady's fault who'd been nagging him. And the guy in the green-and-orange shirt's fault, for still being alive.

"Okay. No problem," he told the cop. "I'll wait."

The cop gave him a nod and walked off to talk to someone else. And as soon as the man was out of sight, Johnnie left. He was surprised to see it was still morning as he hurried away to the trailhead and his car. Home, not to his mother, but the girl. What if the guy woke up and started talking? He didn't want to do it, but he might need to kill her too.

CHAPTER 23

The morning after getting the Facebook response from Penelope Ranier, Reni was heading to Joss's to drop off Edward when she got a call from Daniel.

"Jordan Rice has been found," he told her. "Alive, but unconscious."

She felt a jolt of cautious optimism. "That's promising news."

He shared a few more details about Rice's injuries, including two gunshot wounds, one leaving a bullet lodged in his brain that would require surgery. "The bad news is that Deidra Lundy was found dead, also a gunshot wound."

"What about Emerson?"

"Still missing."

"I'm sorry."

"We're keeping the news close until I can contact the Lundy family," he said. "They live in Enterprise, Nevada, and I'm heading there soon. Just wanted to give you a heads-up."

Enterprise, a suburb of Vegas. She pulled to the side of the road, dust flying. "I'll go," she said. "You have a lot on your plate, and your time would be better spent elsewhere. And there's a large span of desert between here and there with no cell service." He'd want to stay connected right now, and he was also going to have to deal with breaking the bad news to Rachel Rose. Reni knew how tough it was to tell someone their child was still missing when everybody else was accounted for. But at least it wasn't the news she'd be breaking to the Lundy family.

"You sure?" he asked.

"Yes. And I haven't left for San Bernardino yet, so I'm an hour closer than you."

"Sounds good. As soon as you've met with the family, I'll hold a press conference. I want to get accurate information released as quickly as possible." He gave her location details. She entered the Lundy address in her map app, told him goodbye, and contacted Joss to let him know Edward would be staying with her for the day. Then she reached out to the woman from Facebook.

Yes, she could meet today.

Reni turned the truck around and headed in the direction of Las Vegas. The drive was under three hours if she took a shortcut through the Mojave National Preserve, a vast wilderness of no cell service and a narrow road with no shoulders, a road that wound through mostly flat public land stretching as far as the eye could see. It was not a popular route, and the road was deserted. If you broke down anywhere, you were on your own and it could be hours before another soul happened along. But she didn't break down and she made good time and was soon crossing the California–Nevada line.

Following GPS directions, she took the Enterprise exit to eventually reach a development where all the houses looked new and identical, beige homes with red tile roofs laid out on curved streets. Front yards were raked sand and impressively large cacti, some saguaro. She felt a little guilt over using the trip to also meet with the woman from Facebook, but she took comfort in knowing this was one less awful thing Daniel would have to deal with today.

The temperature was close to one hundred, so she left her truck on with the AC running. She probably should have left Edward at home, but he loved road trips, and bringing him also gave her an excuse not to linger. Sometimes families of victims wanted the person breaking the news to stay, talk to them, keep going over the details because it was hard to process. Not that Reni needed an excuse, but it would be easier to say she couldn't stay if Edward was waiting outside.

In these situations, whenever she pressed the doorbell or knocked, there was a part of her that hoped they weren't home. Daniel was a firm believer in breaking this kind of tragic news face-to-face. Reni had mixed feelings about it because it felt invasive, but she might simply have been projecting. If it was her, she'd prefer a phone call.

The mother opened the door. As soon as Reni introduced herself, she saw fear fill the woman's eyes. Her husband appeared beside her, and now two faces were looking at her in terror, not wanting to hear that their daughter was dead.

Reni broke the news as gently as she could. She told them where the body had been taken. They would need to formally ID it even though there was no doubt. They asked her inside and they all sat down, but after five minutes that felt like two hours, Reni got to her feet and said she had to leave. "I'm sure you need to be alone." She handed them two business cards. "And I know you'll have questions. Feel free to call Detective Ellis or me at any time. And again, I'm so sorry for your loss."

Her departure was a blur. They always were.

She stepped outside into the heat. She heard the door close behind her. Maybe heard a loud sob and low murmur of conversation meant to comfort. She got in her truck. Gave Edward a pet and a hug. Sent Daniel a text to let him know he could proceed with the press conference, then replayed the last ten minutes in her head. Their immediate disbelief, then grief-stricken faces. Had she said the right things in the best way possible? Even though she knew there was no way to lessen the pain for them, she'd wanted to so badly.

She got back on I-15 and headed to an area northwest of the Strip. She and the Facebook woman were meeting at a safe location, an outdoor mall. She parked in a lot that looked new, but then most things in Vegas looked new. It was both wondrous and unsettling, a fake world with real people living real lives and feeling real pain.

Leather bag over one shoulder, large black sunglasses on—her attempt at a small disguise since she was sometimes recognized from the news—she snapped Edward's leash in place. After leaping from the truck, he lifted his leg on a signpost. There was no grass or dirt. It was hotter here than at her place, and she reminded herself to drink more water and give plenty to Edward.

She found a bench and sat in the shade of a cottonwood tree, watching people come and go from the coffee shop. When Reni saw Alice Vargas, a.k.a. Penelope Ranier, her stomach took a dive. When it came to detective work, Reni didn't always like being right. This could end up being one of those times.

The woman held herself like Daniel. She stood tall, shoulders back, moving with a lanky stride that was his. The age progression had been amazingly accurate, but this woman was much prettier. The real-life person had long brown hair, wavy, shiny, with a shade so solid and even it had to be dyed. It reminded Reni of her own mother's hair, but that was where any similarity ended. Alice was all about color. She looked like the desert in spring with her bright, flowing skirt, sleeveless pink top, bright scarf on her head. Bare legs and bare arms and feet in brown leather sandals, toes shiny with red polish.

Vibrant.

That's how many people, including Daniel, described her.

Reni adjusted her sunglasses, got to her feet, and spoke the woman's Facebook name. She was not a Penelope, and Reni couldn't think of her as such. In her head, she called her Alice.

Alice glanced around, spotted Reni, smiled.

Damn it. The smile was Daniel's too.

Alice approached, bent, and sweet-talked Edward, petting him.

Points for that.

Edward liked her. He wagged his tail and sat down quickly in antic-ipation of more admiration. Edward's response probably didn't mean anything. Despite Daniel's insistence that Edward would be lost with-out her, Reni hadn't had him long enough to know if he simply liked everybody. Watching Alice's interaction with the dog left Reni thinking that Alice appeared just as delightful as Daniel's shared memories of her suggested she was. She had a vitality, yes, but also a calm confidence—yet another thing that reminded Reni of Daniel. And along with confidence, a sweetness that seemed to emanate from her. Reni felt drawn to her. Everything about her felt perfect. And yet . . .

If this *was* Alice, and Reni was 99.9 percent sure it was, she'd abandoned her child. This person had left Daniel to spend the rest of his life searching, imagining the worst, wishing he'd been able to find her, save her, or bury her, whichever the case might be. Dealing with year after year of survivor's guilt.

Reni had been prepared to spend years searching for his mother, too. She'd been willing to do that for Daniel. And maybe for herself. To find her so quickly was a surprise. But it proved how important it was to interview witnesses, even witnesses who'd been interviewed a multitude of times, how one little thing could turn a case around.

Reni wasn't sure how she got through the next few minutes. Her brain was racing, her nerves humming, her emotions torn. They sat down at an outdoor bistro table. They ordered coffee. Reni filled a bowl for Edward and placed it beside him under the table in the shade. The coffee came in disposable cups.

Alice pulled out a heavy design book, opened it. It contained fabric swatches and drawings. Reni had almost forgotten the ploy and her fakery of needing a seamstress.

Alice passed the book to Reni. "See if anything here catches your eye." As she waited for Reni to look through the samples, she sipped her coffee.

Reni feigned interest in the swatches while her thoughts continued to race. How could Alice have done such a thing? And she had to know Daniel was still looking. It had been all over the news. So much that he'd been bombarded with women who wanted to be his mother, who wanted to feel that touch of fame, and maybe just wanted to feel they'd helped. It was hard to understand the reasons behind false claims, just like it was hard to understand people who claimed to have witnessed something they really hadn't. Maybe it was because people existed in a celebrity-worshipping culture, and they wanted to feel involved, whether through proximity or even, sometimes, murder. Like killers who murdered famous people. Maybe the women contacting Daniel wanted to be touched by a twisted version of celebrity.

They talked about fabric colors. Shoppers passed. Scents of perfume and leather wafted on the air, along with conversations.

"I was thinking red," Reni said, deliberately mentioning a fabric design that should have been very familiar to Alice Vargas, "with pink flowers." Alice had vanished wearing such a dress, a dress Daniel had helped her make, from fabric he'd picked out.

Alice stammered, composed herself. *Target hit.* "That's fine." She took a few more sips. Nervous ones now. Her hand shook. At least she felt something, some guilt over what she'd done.

The edge of the paper cup was red with lipstick. Without explanation, Reni grabbed it, dumped the remaining contents, then stuck the cup in a ziplock bag she'd brought just for that purpose. Confused, Alice looked from Reni to the dog to the fabric book, unable to process what was going on.

Reni could have ended it there. She wanted to. She wanted to get up and walk away from the woman who'd hurt her friend so deeply for so long. But she also wanted answers.

She settled her glasses on top of her head and spoke Alice's name. Not her Facebook name, not Penelope, but her real name. She waited for the jolt. It hit like an invisible wave, and Alice's face drained of color.

"You're Reni Fisher," she said. "I thought you looked familiar."

She probably *had* seen Reni on television, standing next to Daniel during a press conference. The recent deaths of both of her parents had put her back in the spotlight, and the old articles had resurfaced, and new articles had been written.

"That's correct."

"What's this about?"

"I think you already know. I find missing people, even missing people who don't want to be found."

Alice gathered her things, closing and shoving her design tablet into her bag. Getting to her feet. Looking down at Reni's dog. Wondering if Edward would chase her, perhaps. Ha. Ridiculous thought.

Reni waited a moment, hoping Alice would volunteer information. She didn't. "Sit down," Reni said. "Please. We need to talk."

Could be Alice had no choice. She was shaking. A lot. She dropped heavily into the seat.

CHAPTER 24

"It's not what it seems," Alice said.

Reni refused to cut her any slack. "I'm gonna bet it's exactly what it seems."

Alice shook her head. Cried a little. Searched for a tissue. Couldn't find one. Wiped her face with her arm. "My coffee cup. That's for a DNA test, right?"

"Yep, but you could save me some time by just sharing your story." Reni had to temporarily push aside the knowledge that this was about Daniel. Fixating on that was dangerous in such a fragile situation. Her emotions and anger at what Alice had done could blow this moment. She had to remind herself that every person had a perspective; every person had their own truth and reasons for their behavior. Reni didn't get the sense that Alice was a sociopath like Reni's parents. This woman seemed to feel pain and guilt and sorrow. She liked Edward. Edward liked her. Reni had to tamp down her urge to verbally wound her, she had to find some empathy, because Alice didn't have to talk to her. She could just get up and walk away. And maybe disappear again, though it was harder to disappear today than it had been thirty years ago.

Everybody thought their story was unique, but most were driven by many of the same things. In this case, Reni guessed Alice had been driven by poverty, fear, love, greed, loneliness. Loneliness was a bigger force than some people realized or wanted to admit, especially among single men and women. Reni knew Alice's story before she even began speaking. It was similar to that of Rosalind Fisher, Reni's mother. The difference was that Alice wasn't a killer, at least not that Reni knew.

"He didn't want kids," Alice said. "He said he would marry me if I didn't have a kid."

So common. "Kyle Kennedy?"

"Yes."

Alice was talking about the guy she had been dating shortly before she vanished. The guy who'd been her boyfriend for a while. Daniel spoke of him with respect, but he'd always viewed the situation with the eyes of a child. Kyle Kennedy had been the prime suspect, but he'd quickly been removed from the list since he hadn't been in town.

"He didn't even know I was coming," Alice said. "I wanted to surprise him. Don't look at me like that. With pity and disgust."

Reni hadn't realized she'd allowed her poker face to slip.

"Do you have kids?" Alice asked.

"No." But one thing she knew was that if she did, she would not abandon her child. She would not use her child as a pawn in murder schemes. She would not try to kill her child and leave her for dead.

"It's hard to be a single mom," Alice said. "And it was a lot harder back then. At least a lot harder for people to accept. Men don't want to date women with kids. Most of them don't, anyway. And I was in love. And stupid."

She would have been in her early twenties when she ran away. It was easy to forget how young she'd been at the time. Hardly more than a kid herself.

Alice didn't hold back. It seemed she'd been waiting decades to unload her guilt, and once she made the decision to let it out, it was like confession, an unburdening of sins, of secrets, dark and damaging secrets that had never been shared with anyone, not even spoken aloud in the privacy of a shower or screamed into her hand when she was alone in the car.

"He was a salesman," Alice said. "I know, I know. Who falls for a salesman? I decided to surprise him. I left home that night, left Daniel with a sitter, and I took a bus across the country, all the way to Florida. And I found out he was married! And he'd never had any plans to marry me, with a child or without."

"What about the red dress? I don't understand that."

"I made it for Kyle, but I couldn't stand to look at it, because it reminded me of Daniel. He helped pick out the fabric. He helped make it. So before leaving California, I changed clothes in a gas station and stuffed the dress in a Goodwill box."

What a strange journey that article of clothing had taken. It must have been purchased from Goodwill by Hanna Birch, one of Benjamin Fisher's victims, and it had ended up in a desert grave with her.

Reni hadn't painted that particular scene yet, even though the image of the mummified body would most likely never leave her. The red against a sea of beige. Daniel, certain the body in the grave was his mother, standing nearby, holding the long-buried dress in his hand, pieces of sand blowing away, the sun setting. But no. DNA had proven otherwise, and there he went again, to continue his quest while his real mother was alive and well and probably watching the news about his search.

At Reni's feet, Edward whimpered and shifted uncomfortably, looking up at her, wondering why she was upset, wondering when this fresh hell, to borrow the famous words of Dorothy Parker, would end. She reached down and petted him. "Good boy," she whispered. And he was. The best boy.

She straightened in her chair. Flexed her fingers under the table, then gave up and pulled out her sketch pad and paint pencils, flipped through the pages to a clean sheet of paper, grabbed a pencil, and began drawing. She had to draw. With the tablet resting against a crossed knee, she asked, "So why didn't you just come back? If the guy was married. And you must have seen the coverage about your disappearance."

"I saw a little, but there actually wasn't much coverage. Things were different then. No social media. Of course I was ashamed, but I was broke, and far away. And I *would* have returned right then if I'd had the money, but I had to take a job first, and then so much time passed . . ."

Self-justification, most likely. Reni saw that a lot in her work. It was the only way people could live with themselves.

"I got a job waiting tables at a marina in Pensacola. I started drinking and doing drugs, and just fell into oblivion. I was so ashamed. I couldn't go back. And I honestly thought Daniel would be better off without me. And he *was*."

Trying to reinforce her bad decision by lying to herself. "Your disappearance informed his entire life," Reni said. "It took away his choice to be anybody but the person who had to search for his mother."

It wasn't so much that she'd left. That might have been *somewhat* understandable, given the circumstances. The real sin was that she'd allowed Daniel to grieve and search for her his entire life. That, Reni could not forgive.

Alice cried. Most of the people passing by tried not to look. She wiped her nose with the back of her hand. Glanced at Reni.

"How did you end up in Vegas?" Reni asked.

"I wanted to move back to California, but I was afraid to. I met a guy. Yeah, another guy, and we moved here. I got some seamstress work and tried to get my act together. Got off drugs. He had a construction business. It was a good marriage while it lasted."

Reni kept wondering how she was going to break this to Daniel, while at the same time wanting to call him this second and say, *You won't believe this shit.* But maybe he would believe it.

"I used to drive to California to see the old house. It felt good to live close enough to do that. Something I could do in a day. I'd just drive past, sometimes even stop out front. And wish I could undo it all. But you can't take back a mistake like that. I don't even know if you can really live through it. I feel like something died in me back then, and never reawakened. I missed him. I miss him. The guy I followed was just some product of my longing for something better. He represented the world I no longer had. I thought I could start over. Do it right."

"By leaving your child."

"Yes. It's horrible, I know. But later, I found out Daniel had been adopted. I used to drive by that house too. I saw him more than once. One time he was riding a skateboard down the sidewalk and he looked right at me. I thought he recognized me."

Reni's true weakness was responding to people in pain, no matter what they'd done. She felt Alice's pain and wanted to take it away. Also, the idea of Daniel on a skateboard was compelling.

Alice kept talking. "I think, deep down, I wanted him to recognize me. But I was wearing big glasses and a wig. He glanced away and continued down the walk."

Poor Daniel.

"Are you going to tell him?" Alice asked. "I don't think I can stand it. Don't tell him. Let him think I'm dead. I want him to think I'm dead. Tell him I'm dead."

Would it be better if he never knew? Reni wondered. Maybe, but that wouldn't be fair to him. That wasn't Reni's way. And it would be no different from what Alice was doing. No matter how awful it was, he needed to hear the truth.

"How is he?" Alice asked, a pensive hand to her cheek.

She didn't deserve an answer. "All things considered, he's good."

"I did love him. I do love him. I guess I just loved myself more."

"Guess so."

Reni emptied what little water was left from Edward's water dish and collapsed it. Put her tablet away. While Alice just sat there, Reni got to her feet and noted the layer of smog and possibly smoke from a wildfire as she looked toward California. Then she and Edward walked away, in the direction of the parking lot and her truck.

After considering various locations where they could meet, she decided to break the news to Daniel at his house. There was no telling what his reaction might be. She didn't want to have to tell him about Alice in a public place, and she didn't want him to have to drive home after hearing the news. And she definitely did not want to break it to him over the phone. Daniel preferred sharing bad news in person. He would probably prefer getting it that way too.

CHAPTER 25

The wind never stopped blowing. How was that possible? Wind that didn't stop? And who'd have thought wind could be so horrible? It was *just wind*, and Emerson used to love the wind. Running and screaming through it while palm trees rustled overhead. The memory made her cry. But the sound of it, the wind, was one of the worst things about being in this place.

They'd hiked for miles, then he'd stuffed her in his trunk and they'd driven a long way over bumpy roads. Deeper into the mountains? She didn't know, because he'd blindfolded her and tied her hands before pulling her from the trunk. Then he'd grabbed her arm and led her to the bedroom and closet, where she'd been ever since, whatever amount of time that was, because the drugs and the dark had scrambled the clock in her head. Emerson thought about the photos of missing hikers they'd seen nailed to a mile marker on the trail. Would her mother nail a photo there? And what photo would she use? Hopefully not one Emerson hated.

Nobody prepared you for a kidnapping. They should teach kidnapping safety in school. Like what to do if someone tried to kidnap you. They had shooter drills, so why not kidnapping?

The wind was causing stuff to hit the building. Each crash made her jump and hug her knees tighter. The violence of the gusts made her think of her history teacher who'd died. They'd studied the Dust Bowl and learned about people who'd gone mad because of the wind. She'd always thought it was because the wind had kept them locked inside for weeks at a time. Now she wondered if the sound itself had driven them crazy.

Her mom said more crimes were committed when the Santa Ana winds blew. Emerson believed it. Day, night, howling, whistling, covering up more important sounds—like maybe someone coming to rescue her. But sometimes the wind stopped. Like now. The bottom dropped out and turned hollow and her ears tried to find another noise to latch on to.

She heard a door open and close, then footsteps. She heard the soles of his sneakers squeaking against the floor. Another door creaked open, then the familiar sound of him pulling heavy objects away and shoving the desk aside. He was strong, a lot stronger than Emerson. Stronger than he looked. She should be scared, but the drugs softened everything and made it more boring than scary.

Through the closet door, she heard his heavy breathing. And she could smell him. Some kind of body spray. But under that, she smelled fried food and heard the rustle of a paper bag. The fast food he always brought made her think they must not be too remote.

Another thought jumped into her brain. He'd killed Janet. Maybe the other girls too. And those people on the trail. Just random hikers. No reason to do that. No reason at all.

He opened the closet door, stood there. A big looming shadow. She blinked and waited for her eyes to adjust to the ceiling light that framed his head like a halo. He didn't look much different than he had the day she'd first seen him at Kaleidoscope. He didn't seem a lot different either. A little nervous. Shy around girls. Shy, period. He was older than she was. At first, she'd thought he was ugly with his thin hair and the bald spot on his head. His little eyes, straight mouth. But she was used to him now.

During the time she'd been here, she hadn't been able to figure out anything about him. She wasn't sure she wanted to. She guessed he was one of those guys who couldn't get a girlfriend and had maybe never had sex. What were they called? Social media had a name for them. So far, he hadn't tried anything with her. She wasn't sure how she'd handle that, because she didn't think he'd listen if she said no. It was like he owned her. She was his possession. A pet he didn't take very good care of.

He left every day, and she wondered if he still worked at Kaleidoscope. Maybe talking to other girls. Flirting with other girls. Following other girls. She wondered if he'd bring other girls here. She almost wished he would so she wouldn't be alone, but that wasn't fair. She shouldn't want another girl to have to go through what she was going through.

She accepted the bag of food and drink. Cola with a lid and straw. Took a long drink even though she knew he put drugs in it. She'd found it was easy to talk him into some things if they were harmless and simple. Like the other day she'd wanted a candy bar, and he actually left the house and came back maybe an hour later with a lot of different candy. That told her there was a place he went that was a half-hour drive away, probably less. A gas station, maybe, because the candy wrappers smelled like cigarette smoke and fabric softener.

Maybe her dad would come, her real dad. He rescued people. That's what he did. Maybe he'd figure out where she was and come for her. Break down the door and move the desk and weights aside. He'd pull her from the closet and ask if she was okay and when she said yes, he'd carry her away. Run through the house with her in his arms just like he'd done at school.

She opened the bag, pulled out a handful of fries, and stuffed them into her mouth.

"Hurry and eat. I have friends coming over."

He'd said that before, but she wondered if he really had any friends. Seemed like a lie. She'd never heard any other people. No conversation or footsteps. But then he turned up the TV full blast sometimes, so loud it almost hid the wind. She wondered if he had virtual friends he hung out with online. He seemed like that kind of guy.

"What would you do if cops showed up here?" he asked. "Would you scream?"

Of course I would. I'd scream and scream.

Had she said that out loud? Sometimes it was hard to know what was thought and what was spoken, because once the heaviness crept into her limbs and the numbness overtook her mind, she got confused about everything.

She stuck the straw in her mouth and sucked harder, visualizing the drugs hitting her system while he stood in the middle of the room, arms limp at his sides, head down. It seemed like he was thinking very hard.

"I want to show you something," he said abruptly, as if coming to a decision. He pulled out his phone, scrolled, and turned it around so she could see the screen.

She let out a surprised gasp. It was a photo of her sister, taken in front of their house.

He scrolled to the next one. Arial walking from her school building to their parents' waiting car. Arial was a brat and she was always lying and trying to get Emerson in trouble, but Emerson still loved her and didn't want to see her hurt.

"If you try to scream, if you try to get away," he said, shoving the phone in her face, "I'll kill your little sister. I know where she lives. I know where she goes to school. I'll kill your whole family. Just like I did that girl in the tent. Just like I did those people on the trail." Then his face changed quickly. He looked almost happy. "Oh, I almost forgot."

She got the idea he hadn't really forgotten anything.

He reached into his pocket and pulled out something small, hiding whatever it was in his hands. He held them out to her, fists down. "Choose one."

Under the odor of body spray, he smelled like sweat, nervous sweat. The kind of sweat that had its own special stink that almost burned your eyes. "I don't want to," she said.

"Do it." He raised one fist, touched her chin with it, pretending to hit her, pulled it back.

"I don't know." It didn't matter. She just wanted to sleep. She pointed. "That one."

He turned the fist over and opened his clenched hand. Lying in his palm was a button pin, the kind used for things like aspirational sayings and bands. He stuck the pin through the fabric of his shirt. The first pin was followed by two more. "I laminated them myself." Each one contained an image of a family member. Her mom, Arial, and her stepdad.

Emerson's heart beat faster and she started breathing hard through her mouth. She didn't know what it meant, why he had them, where he'd gotten them. "Did you make any for me?"

He snorted. "This is in case you try to leave here. Or if you shout for help." He formed a gun with his fingers and thumb, pointed at the pins, one at time, and made a firing motion. *"Pew, pew, pew."*

His meaning cut through the drugs that were making her arms and legs and eyelids heavy. She needed to behave, do what he said, not try to escape, or he'd kill her family. "I'm okay right here." She crossed her ankles and dropped to the floor, landing cross-legged, awkwardly slamming the drink down beside her. "I won't scream." She shook her head. "I'll never scream. Promise."

"I'd like to believe you."

He closed the door. He shoved the desk back. She heard him piling weights on it, hundreds of pounds. She'd tried to push her way out many times, but she wasn't strong enough. And now she had no reason to try to leave. This was her job. Stay hidden. Stay quiet. Keep her family safe.

CHAPTER 26

It was close to eight p.m. when Reni knocked on Daniel's door, Edward sitting patiently next to her. Daniel's SUV was in the carport, no sign of Bo's sedan. If she remembered correctly, it was his poker night.

Daniel's San Bernardino home was modest, with a curved sidewalk, white breezeway blocks that looked original, and a couple of huge palm trees out front, along with several varieties of cacti.

She'd had several hours to brace herself for this, but she still wasn't sure she could do it. Hopefully once Daniel knew the truth, he could move forward, even if the truth wasn't something he'd expected to hear. But when he answered the door, she felt a fresh pang of dismay. He looked as if he hadn't slept well in days, and now she was going to dump something else on him that would lead to more sleepless nights.

Edward and Daniel reunited, Daniel petting the dog, Edward's tail wagging furiously.

"I have some news." Reni closed the door behind her. She could see he already knew it had to be big for her to drive to his place late at night. But logically he would assume it was about the Pacific Crest Trail murders and the missing girl.

Rather than resort to "You'd better sit down," she silently suggested it by taking a seat on the couch, Edward settling at her feet. The living room was typical California modern. Big picture window, vintage-style drapes pulled shut, shapely green lamp in the corner, white shade. Low blue couch, a comfy chair, probably Bo's, facing the bookshelves and flat-screen TV. Eclectic, with a lot of teal and orange. There was a velvet painting of a yellow cat, and a framed gold-and-brown owl made from brads and colored string—a trendy craft from the sixties, popular at vintage stores in the area that often catered to tourists.

She knew the story of how the two men, adoptive father and son, had come to cohabitate. After Bo suffered a heart attack, Daniel packed him up and brought him to live with him. That was several years ago, and the arrangement seemed to be working out well for them both.

Daniel vanished, then returned with a bowl of water he placed near Edward before sitting down across from Reni in the big TV chair, swiveling to face her. From somewhere, a clock ticked as Edward lapped water from the bowl.

"There's no way to soften this," she said. Her heart was pounding, and she wished she could have just sent him a text or an email. She'd given bad news to the families of victims so many times before, so why was this so exceptionally hard for her? Because it was Daniel. And the story of his mother had been the driving force behind everything he'd done his entire life.

Light from the lamp fell across his face. His hair was rumpled, face needing a shave. He was working so hard. Was she doing the right thing? Should she hold the news about Alice close, at least for a while? She briefly considered making up some excuse for her visit, waiting until this case was either over or cold. But there would always be a case. There would always be nights of no sleep. And what if Alice contacted him before Reni broke the news?

He picked up on her anxiety. "What's going on?"

Her desire to run was cowardice. It wasn't about Daniel at all, and this should be completely about him. She pulled in a shallow breath and said what had to be said, no softening it. "Daniel, I found your mother."

He looked at her, struggling to understand, probably rerunning her words. "What?"

"I'm sorry. I know this is very unexpected. I found your mother."

Almost a mirror of the shock he must be feeling, she felt a fresh punch in her own stomach.

Not breaking eye contact, he asked, "Where's the body?" He jumped to his feet, looked around the room as if it could help him right here, right now, trying to figure out his next move. "I need to go there, be there."

He thought she was dead. "I have to tell you something else." And now she did give him the "sit down" suggestion. He ignored her.

Reni squared her shoulders. "She's alive."

"What did you say?" A fresh wave of confusion. He thought he'd misunderstood.

"She's alive. Alice is alive." She could see his mind racing, trying to put together what might have led to such an outcome.

"Is she safe?"

Oh, Daniel. His mind had moved from Alice being dead to her being kidnapped, abused, locked up.

Her heart was breaking for him. She wanted to rewind ten minutes, tell him she'd just dropped in to say hi. "She's okay." Reni got to her feet and faced him. "She's fine."

Reni wasn't a toucher, but she reached out, took his hand, held it in both of hers while she looked into his eyes. "Daniel," she said softly in an attempt to draw his focus, let him know she would be there for him. "The police were right." She spoke with a tug of apology and a crack in her voice. "Years ago. Alice left of her own free will. She ran away."

A face that was unreadable to many had become easy for her to decode. His subtle change of expression spoke more than words as he went from disbelief to rage, then back to disbelief.

"Are you sure?" he asked.

She'd come prepared for that question. He was a detective. "I met with her today after breaking the bad news to the Lundys. I collected her DNA in case you want to run it and see if you get a match. But I have no doubt it was her." She didn't mention all the things they had in common. The way they walked. Mannerisms. The smile.

He looked toward the door, in the direction of the street and Reni's truck. "Is she here?" He seemed near panic. Reni had never seen fear in him, but she saw it now. A child afraid of his mother.

"No, no." She put a hand to his chest. His heart was slamming. "I'm so sorry." He'd asked her to stop looking. And here he was, the one person she'd allowed into her life, and now she was hurting him. "She's well. She's living in Las Vegas. I met with her today. Let this sink in, and I'll give you more details later." She went to the kitchen and filled a glass from the faucet.

She returned to the living room, wished she could have stayed in the kitchen. His hand shook when she pressed the glass into it.

He swigged it down like it was booze. "No, I need to know it all."

She told him everything Alice had shared. As she watched, Daniel's face crumpled.

He turned his back to her, burying his face in his hands. He let out a shuddering gasp, and then his shoulders began to shake. A sound tore from him. It came from a place of deep, deep grief and almost real physical pain, something that ripped the bones from his body. She'd known this would be hard for him, but she'd had no idea how bad it would be. His reaction shook her.

Her own grief had always been silent and private, with very few tears. But that didn't mean she couldn't feel compassion. Maybe too much. Maybe this was allowing her to visit a place she couldn't visit for herself. His pain opened her own, and an avalanche of emotions hit her.

She put her hands on his shoulders, turned him around, wrapped her arms around him, and pulled him close, holding him while he cried it out and he clung to her. He would most likely regret this moment later. But maybe not.

After a time, they broke apart. He was no longer crying but was still stunned. His demeanor was similar to people who'd found out someone close had died. She'd seen the reaction many times when she'd had to give the news of a victim's death to a loved one. And yet Daniel had just found out someone was alive.

Reni had hoped to remove the pain from his eyes, but instead she'd caused more. Would it have been better for him to think Alice had died than to know she'd left of her own free will? And not only left, but never contacted him even though she'd known he was searching for her?

He was still shaking, though it wasn't cold in the house. She found an orange blanket on the end of the couch, something that appeared handmade. She wrapped it around him. He mumbled a thanks and clutched it. Nearby, Edward whimpered in distress. Daniel bent and tried to reassure him.

Would he try to see Alice? Either way, whatever happened, he had the truth. It would take time to get over the blow, and he'd never recover completely, but he could quit wondering.

He sat down in the chair and stared blankly in front of him. There was nothing she could say, so she just sat with him, Edward beside her, his chin on her knee, rarely blinking. She finally heard a car pull into the driveway. Seconds later, the kitchen door opened and Bo shouted a hello.

"In here!" Reni called back, relieved Bo was home, relieved that she could leave soon and fully face what she'd done.

After the sound of keys dropping on the table and shoes kicked off, Bo stepped into the living room and immediately knew something was wrong.

She stood up and snapped Edward's leash on his harness. "I found Alice," she told Bo in a soft voice, touching his arm lightly.

He pulled in a sharp breath. "Where's the body?"

"She's alive."

His eyes widened, then narrowed.

Was he thinking her visit and the revelation had been a bad idea too? Would he have protected Daniel if he'd known the truth?

"I'll let Daniel tell you about it," she said. She told Daniel goodbye and left. Now she had the double guilt of the shared secret and leaving Bo to deal with Daniel's trauma.

Outside, she and Edward got into her truck. She started the engine and drove down the dark street. She went several blocks before realizing she hadn't taken any turns on any streets that would carry her home. The truck rolled to a stop. She was the one shaking now. She pressed a hand to her mouth, holding in the noise and the pain. Then she rested her head against the steering wheel and cried.

She'd broken down in private like this when her father died, but she hadn't cried for their family friend Maurice when he died, and she hadn't cried when her mother had been shot by Daniel. By the time her mother's betrayal was exposed, Reni had gone numb and dead inside. But in her mind, it was all tangled now. Daniel's story, her own, the choices their parents had made. She leaned into the pain, using it to experience the grief she hadn't allowed herself to experience for so long. At the same time, she wondered if she'd used this moment to bring herself closure and hadn't considered Daniel in the way she should have.

She wasn't sure how long her truck sat idling in the middle of the street. Luckily there was no traffic. A whine and a paw on her arm pulled her back to the present, enough for her to tamp down her emotions, sternly stop the tears, put the truck in gear, and drive.

She found Highway 210, took it to Interstate 10, then 62 up the Morongo grade that led to Joshua Tree and the desert, until she was home, safe for now.

After a late dinner for Edward, she sat outside under the stars and remembered the comet that was supposed to be visible soon. She might not even go to bed, so there was a chance she'd see it. She hoped so, and hoped Daniel would be okay.

The desert healed, but it didn't feel healing tonight. After a couple of hours, as coyotes howled, no sign of the comet, she went back inside, the door slamming behind her. Unable to sleep, she pulled out her sketch pad, filled a tin with water, sat down at the kitchen table, and began painting.

Hours passed and she kept at it. Painting Daniel's agony when she'd told him the news. A painting of Emerson, created from newer photos she'd found online. But she also worked to enhance the drawings she already had. JoJo at the hospital, all the images she'd painted of the crime scene on the mountain. Daniel's mother.

Before dawn, her phone started vibrating on the kitchen table. She ignored it. It rang. She picked it up, saw it was Daniel. She stared at the screen as she tugged at her hair.

She couldn't talk to him right now. She didn't even know if she could continue working on the PCT case. She hadn't done anything that anybody else couldn't have done. Betty had found Portia. JoJo had saved herself. Jordan had been found by a rescue volunteer. They didn't need her. She turned off the phone and tossed it aside, then went back to painting.

CHAPTER 27

The morning after Reni stopped by with the news about Alice, Daniel decided to drop in on Johnnie May Moore, the guy who'd found Jordan Rice. The emergency tech at the scene where Jordan had been found had reported something interesting that Daniel wanted to follow up on. He could have sent someone else, but coincidentally, Moore lived in an area of the desert located not that far from Reni's house. Maybe ten miles. He'd tried to call her several times early that morning. No surprise that she hadn't answered, and then his calls began going straight to voicemail, indicating she'd turned off her phone.

The news she'd given him had been hard to hear, and it was going to take time to accept it, if he ever did. But through his distraught reaction, he'd seen the bleak look in *her* eyes. She'd regretted telling him. At the time, he'd wished she *hadn't* told him. Now . . . now he still wasn't sure how he felt about that decision. But he did know he needed to reach out to see if she was okay.

It was almost a hundred degrees when he stepped from his SUV, and he half expected to see a mirage shimmering in the distance. He checked his phone. Jumping between one and no bars. The desert was growing on him, but he still felt baffled by its popularity and by all the people who loved it. The sand, the heat, the weird creatures. Cut off from the rest of the world. But a person could see *so far*. So much sky. So many distant mountains. A place where the ground was close and hot, and the sky was big.

The wind was blowing hard right now, whipping Daniel's hair and tie, pulling his tucked shirt from the waistband of his pants, making the nearby wires on the fence sing. That same wind could sandblast the finish right off a car. Particulates made up of varying degrees of harm could settle in your lungs and eyes and teeth.

The GPS had brought him to a house that didn't look occupied, but a person could say that about a lot of desert places. Chain-link gate propped open with a big rock, several cars scattered around. None looked as if they would run, and they'd long ago been claimed by nature, their bodies turned a deep brown by the intense sun.

The desert had a history of attracting criminals or just people who wanted to be left alone. For some, like Reni, it was an escape, but others stockpiled guns and embraced conspiracy theories and congregated with like-minded people while working together trying to prove the earth was flat. One such man had recently died in a rocket that was supposed to take him high enough to finally see the flatness with his own eyes so he could report his findings. And yet, despite everything, even though Reni's father had killed and buried his dead in the desert, she still managed to love the place.

His phone dinged. Apparently he could still receive texts. It was an update from Davenport on Jordan Rice.

They removed the bullet lodged behind his eye and he's recovering from surgery.

Poor kid.

Daniel sent a reply; it didn't go through.

No bars now.

Turned out the house *was* occupied. Even with the noise of the wind, he could hear a TV blaring before he reached the door.

He knocked.

A guy with no shirt answered. Baggy camo pants, a silver bracelet on his wrist with an insignia he couldn't make out. The guy was pale for the desert, getting a little bald even though he was probably under thirty.

"You Johnnie May Moore?" Daniel asked.

"Yeah."

With the door open, the TV was even louder, with thundering bass. "I wanted to get your statement about the rescue yesterday," Daniel said. "And I wanted to thank you for your service."

"I heard they were asking for help in the search, and I just felt like I needed to do my part." He shrugged. "No big deal."

"You might have saved a life."

"So he's still alive?"

"Yes."

Moore let out a relieved breath. "That's good."

Daniel tried to see around him, but the interior of the house was dark. "Can I come in?"

"My mom's asleep."

"With the TV on?"

"She has dementia and screams at me if I turn it off."

Daniel looked around, searching for a spot of shade. One lone Joshua tree with a plastic table and broken chair under it. "Let's go over here." He walked to the table, and Moore followed.

Daniel placed his phone, voice recorder activated, on the table, then thumbed through a tablet to a blank page, clicked his pen, and silently cursed the desert as sweat rolled down his spine and soaked his armpits.

Aloud, he noted the time, location, and interviewee. Then he asked the most obvious question and the reason behind his visit in the first place.

"Why'd you leave the rescue scene?"

"My mom. I had to get back to check on her."

Things could be confusing in that situation. Everybody had most likely been focusing on Jordan Rice, and grabbing an interview with Moore wasn't high among their priorities.

"What made you look where you looked?" Daniel asked. "Did the victim cry out?"

Moore thought a moment. "I heard a sound. Maybe a moan. And I looked down the hill and saw something that didn't look like it belonged there. His shirt, I think."

"So was he conscious when you got there?"

Moore frowned, as if trying to remember. This was why it was best to get the details right away. "I don't think so."

"Did he say anything to you?"

"Maybe. Yeah, now that I think about it, he did. A girl's name. Darla, I think."

"Deidra?"

"Yeah, that was it. Does that mean anything?"

Daniel was asking the questions. "Did he say anything else?"

"No."

"Did you touch him? Because the SAR responder said you were leaning over him."

"I was just looking close, to see if he was breathing."

"And he was?"

"Yeah."

"So you didn't try CPR or anything?"

"No."

"And you didn't touch him?"

"No."

"Are you sure?"

"What is this all about? I found him and I called for help."

"We just have to have a detailed record of everything that transpired, to the best of your memory and everyone involved. I know it's harder when even a few hours have passed."

"I said I had to check on my mom."

"Could I talk to your mom?"

"Like I said, she's asleep. And like I said, she has dementia."

Daniel was beginning to think the mom wasn't real. "Okay, let's go back. We're almost done. The reason I keep asking about whether or not you touched him is because there was a handprint on his face." Faint, but noted by an EMT once Jordan had been carried up the mountain.

"Wow."

"That's why I asked about CPR. If you attempted CPR, that's okay."

"I didn't. I didn't touch him."

"Okay."

Moore looked over his shoulder in the direction of the house. "I've gotta get changed and get to work."

"Sorry to have kept you." Daniel shut off the phone's recorder. He really wanted inside Moore's house, but the guy had done nothing to justify going in without a search warrant. Daniel slipped his phone into his pocket. "I think I've got everything I need. Thanks for your time."

In his SUV, he texted Davenport and told him to run a background check on Moore.

Just like his last text, it was unable to be sent. He'd have to try later. Then he headed to Reni's place.

CHAPTER 28

As Daniel waited for Reni to ignore his knock, he re-sent his texts to Davenport. They went through, and Davenport replied with some positive news. Jordan Rice was coming in and out of consciousness. Which meant he might return to a somewhat normal life. And he might also be able to help with the case and fill in a lot of blanks—mainly ID the murderer who'd killed his girlfriend.

"I know you're in there," he said to the door.

A curtain shifted, and he spotted Edward peeking out. The dog barked politely.

He knocked again.

The dog vanished, barked, then reappeared.

The door finally opened, and Reni put a hand up to shield her eyes against the bright light.

She'd been painting. A lot. She had paint on her jeans, and it looked like she'd been using her shirttails to clean her brushes. Her hair was pulled back in an elastic band. She had circles under her eyes, and he wondered if she'd been up all night.

"I was in the area," he said.

"Really."

"Truth. I just came from Johnnie Moore's place. The guy who found Jordan Rice."

"Come on in." She backed up. "It's too hot to stand out there."

It reminded him of the first time he'd come to her home several months back, when he'd asked for help finding the bodies her father had buried in the desert.

He followed her inside, bent, and petted Edward. He was relieved to find Reni okay. Until that moment, he hadn't realized he'd been excessively worried about her mental state and well-being. He was glad she had Edward. Sometimes he wondered if she stayed alive for her dog, which was the reason behind his comment to her a couple of days ago about Edward being lost without her. He'd wanted to remind her that she'd be missed. And he'd wanted to hint at his own feelings for her.

After assuring himself of her semi-well-being, he looked around and gasped at the number of paintings in the small space. There were a hundred, maybe more. Some framed and hung, but she'd run out of space. There were piles of her work stacked on the kitchen table, the paper warped from the application of water. On the floor, leaning against walls, were more framed pieces.

At first, her painting had seemed a secret, something she didn't want anybody to know about. And the actual act appeared to be somewhat of an obsession, replacing the pottery. She always had her tablet and little paint tin with her, and it didn't seem she could sit long without digging it from her bag, pulling out a brush, opening a container of water. Sometimes just a drawing pencil or even colored pencils. When he thought about it, he realized she'd been doing it ever since her mother's death.

"I'm getting ready for a craft show," she said, as if to explain such a frenzy of activity.

"Is this her?" Feeling gutted all over again, he pointed to a painting that was obviously Alice. So bright, such a beautiful face.

"Oh God. I'm sorry. Yes."

He stared at it a minute and used the time to pull himself together. "Thank you for finding her."

She crossed the room and turned the painting around so it faced the wall. "The news could have been delivered in a better way."

"No, it was perfect. The only way, really."

"I think maybe I shouldn't have told you at all. I should have let you have the illusion. It was hurting no one."

"You did the right thing," he said. "It couldn't have been easy. It's good you forced me to see the truth. No more living in a state of limbo."

Rachel's reappearance in his life had reminded him of how much he'd given up in order to search for someone who wasn't even dead. "I think I might have even seen her once when I was a kid. I was riding my skateboard down the sidewalk, and this car drove past really slowly. The driver was a woman and she looked right at me. And I just looked away and kept skateboarding. What I mean is, I think I always knew."

"Oh, Daniel."

"It's okay."

"I should've known," she said. "You're too good to not have found her yourself. Of course it crossed my mind. I know all about denial."

"You did nothing wrong."

"I didn't listen to you, didn't abide by your wishes."

"You probably thought I was just trying to keep you from wasting years searching for a ghost."

"Kind of true. Maybe a lot true."

"We're okay, right?" he asked. "I want us to be okay."

"Yes. I'm glad you don't hate me."

"I know you've had very little stability in your life when it comes to people close to you, the people you should have been able to trust the most. But I want you to know I'll always be here. I'll never turn my back on you for telling me the truth. Or for any other reason. This probably just sounds like a bunch of words coming out of my mouth, but I mean them. I'm not your mother or your father. I'm not Ava Brown."

Her eyes glistened. "Thank you." Then, in an obvious need to escape the emotions of the moment, she ducked away. "I'll get you a glass of water." In the adjoining kitchen, she opened the refrigerator. A cupboard door slammed.

He took the opportunity to really look at the work surrounding him. And he suddenly understood the truly secretive nature of her work.

These were not creations, they were documentations.

He couldn't say for certain that they were all places where her father's victims had been found; he didn't have that kind of recall. But many contained recognizable landmarks and places where he himself had witnessed exhumations. One was a specific boulder with a bird carved on it, a location that had led to solving the Inland Empire case. Another was the Amboy Crater. Another, a park near Riverside, one of her father's favorite places to abduct women. What Daniel did know was at least *many* of the scenes were locations where bodies had been buried and found. This was how she coped. This was how she let the pain out.

She handed him the glass of water.

"You sure give me water a lot," he said with distraction.

"Would you like something else? I have soda."

"Water's fine. Just seems like you have a little obsession about it."

"I've run out a couple of times in the desert." She got an odd look on her face, and he remembered one of those times had been when her mother left her to die.

"It's not a bad obsession to have," he said.

His mind pivoted back to the paintings. It had always been obvious to him that Reni was an artist all the way to her soul. She'd worked hard with her pottery and had quickly built a name for herself, mainly due to her skill and the unique designs, most created by placing bird feathers against red-hot pottery fresh from the kiln. But she was always struggling between art and crime-solving. She would probably be better off mentally if she quit crime work altogether. He understood that, but selfishly he hoped she wouldn't. It would be a loss. Not just because he'd lose the one thing that connected them and always gave him a reason to see her, but because it would mean some cases might never be solved.

"I just got some good news. Rice is showing signs of consciousness," he told her.

"That *is* good news."

He took a long drink and eyed her work again.

"What do you think?" she asked in a casual voice. Much too casual.

"They're interesting," he said with care. "Very good. I don't know much about watercolor."

"My therapist approved."

"I don't know why she wouldn't. Are they all crime scenes?"

"I was hoping you wouldn't realize, recognize."

"Reni, I've been to some of them. Many of them."

"I know, but I thought maybe all desert looked the same to you."

Funny. His own words coming back at him. "It's a little bit . . . disconcerting, I'll have to admit."

It was hard to take them all in, but he tried. He focused special attention on a grouping of ten paintings in white frames, all five by seven in size, lined up on the mantel of the brick fireplace, all featuring beautiful skies and beautiful colors. All of the same murder scene. Each individual painting worked on its own and conveyed a simple camping trip. There was nothing in any that told the full story of death and murder. Just a person, a camper or hiker, sleeping in an orange tent surrounded by beautiful mountains.

He leaned closer. "I remember when you painted these." There was an uncanny, almost savant accuracy to the details in the scene. The clothing, complete with logos. The brand of tent, the colors mind-blowingly accurate. The individual frames, close-ups focusing on various objects, were like photos. More than photos.

"It's almost more accurate than a photo because you're highlighting and focusing on a single area at a time," he said.

"That's what I had in mind. Like when the whole thing is too terrible to handle, but each little piece can be beautiful and only tells a small story that evades the bigger story."

He finished the water and put his glass aside. Hands in his pockets, he leaned closer still, examining each work. Edward let out a heavy sigh and lay down nearby.

"I might have told you that when I was a kid, I used to love to draw birds," she confided. "Really colorful birds, with feathers that were unrealistic. I even gave some birds two heads. No idea why. I'm sure a therapist could explain it. Maybe the two sides to my father and even my mother."

He turned to face her.

"The birds were all bright, with the most amazing colors," she said. "My father didn't like that, and he chastised me for it. He worked and worked with me until I could create a bird that looked almost like a photo. In effect, he killed the joy I found in drawing and painting, but I learned to accurately reproduce what was in front of me."

Her father had touched every part of her life, even robbing her of this joy. "I'm so sorry."

He looked back at the paintings. Something was bugging him, but he couldn't put his finger on it. He went over the grouping again, pausing on the body lying on top of the sleeping bag, one hand curled, palm up, the body bloated and covered in flies.

"Obviously that won't be at the craft sale," she said.

"No." The wrist. "She has a tan line on her wrist," he pointed out. As if she'd been wearing a watch and someone had removed it. It was no secret that killers liked to take trophies from victims.

Reni nodded. "Yes."

"Are you sure these are accurate? To me, it seems the detail is excruciatingly precise."

"Fairly certain."

Daniel hadn't been involved in processing the scene. He'd been there, but he wasn't the one cataloging evidence and sealing and signing evidence bags. Maybe the watch had been in Janet's belongings. The video posted by Deidra Lundy had been pulled from Instagram shortly after the sheriff's department was made aware of its existence, but he had a copy on his phone. He scrolled through evidence photos, found the video, and played it. Not the best viewing situation, but he was able to pause and enlarge the frames enough to see, not a watch, but a wide silver band on the victim's wrist.

"She's wearing a bracelet in the video," Daniel said. "But it's not in your painting."

He lifted his phone and showed her the paused image that revealed something on Janet's wrist.

"We'll have to check the evidence," she said. "Also, Deidra or Jordan might have taken it after Deidra shot the video."

"Or maybe the killer returned and took it after he killed the hikers."

She nodded. "That's possible. Play it again."

He did.

"Stop it there," she said. "Enlarge that screen."

He did.

"That's not just a bracelet. It's a bracelet given to people who complete all three hiking trails. The Triple Crown. Janet was a Triple Crown hiker."

He looked closely, then said, "I think I've seen it. Recently—very recently. On Johnnie Moore."

"Wow." She looked appropriately stunned.

"Who, by the way, wouldn't let me inside his house, and was definitely lying to me."

"Looks like we might have found our killer. Hopefully Emerson is with him and still alive."

What an odd turn of events, all due to a random watercolor painting.

She grabbed a few things, filled Edward's water dish, and they both hurried out the door and ran for Daniel's SUV. While they moved and as Daniel slid behind the wheel, he called for backup.

Reni shot him a glance of apprehension. He nodded, reading her concern. They had to be careful. They couldn't have cops invading the area. No sirens, no helicopters, not even any squad cars. Sometimes such activity could open up a bargaining channel, but too often the kidnapper would panic and attempt to destroy the evidence. The evidence being Emerson, if she was still alive.

"Remain on standby," Daniel said into his phone. "We'll let you know if you need to stand down or deploy."

They took a series of dirt roads, some that split to circle around Joshua trees. Near the foot of a familiar landmark called Goat Mountain, Daniel pulled to the side of the road and parked a distance from Moore's house. He lifted a pair of binoculars to his face, then passed them to Reni.

"Homesteader cabin," she said.

The house had a chain-link fence with a bent and padlocked gate. Even from such a distance, he could hear the sound of a television. "The gate was open before," he said.

"What do you think?" Reni asked. "Stealth approach, or walk up to the front door and knock?"

"Both."

He'd heard the low rumble of an engine below what to him had become the white noise of the blaring TV. Now, holding binoculars to his face, Johnnie stood to the side and looked out the window at the white SUV parked on the dirt road, the same vehicle that had been there an hour ago. This time Ellis wasn't alone.

The passenger door opened and a woman got out. He watched her squeeze through the space in the gate and approach his cabin. With a soft curse, he locked the front door, strapped his holster around his waist, and ran through the house.

CHAPTER 29

Emerson had no idea how long she'd been in the closet. Sometimes it seemed she'd always lived there, spending most of her time sleeping. All she knew and all she hung on to was that she must keep her family safe. But her old life was fading. Maybe the drugs were making her forget, or maybe it was because she'd been alone in the dark for so long—sensory deprivation, it was called—but everything before her closet life had a dreamlike quality, a blurry life that had never really happened, not to her anyway. Somebody else's life. But this wasn't real life either. It couldn't be. This couldn't be the rest of her existence. The only thing she was certain of was the rhythm of her own breathing, and the wind.

Living in the dark with no visual clues, her ears had quickly learned to sort out sounds, almost feel them. Sometimes she even heard birds, and she could always hear his footsteps. She actually looked forward to them because there was nothing else, and he was the only break in the monotony. The steps she heard now were weird, different, not like his, and moving fast. Maybe somebody else. Maybe somebody to save her. But the steps were followed by a familiar jangle of keys and a scrape of the bedroom door against the floor. And then came the sound of weights being moved and the desk being dragged away from the closet. The door flew open. As her eyes struggled to adjust to the light, he jerked her out and shoved a pair of shoes into her hands. Big clunky things.

"Put these on. Hurry."

Standing made her dizzy. The brightness of the room hurt her eyes. Squinting, she dropped heavily on the twin bed where he usually slept. She tried to put on the shoes, but she was too weak and just didn't care. He made an annoyed sound, bent over, put the shoes on her feet like a prince putting on glass slippers. She looked down at the top of his head, at the spot with no hair at all. She ran her palm across it. He jerked away and gave her a weird look.

"It's smooth," she explained. Her tongue was thick and her words were slurred. It sounded more like she said *smoof*. She wondered who the shoes belonged to. Something an older person with bad feet might wear. Bubble shoes.

He pulled her off the bed, whispering harshly in her ear, "Don't make a sound." He tapped the buttons on his shirt. The pictures of her family.

They moved quickly through the house, Emerson stumbling after him, walls a blur, ending up in the kitchen, a room she'd never been in before. It was dark there too. Not as dark as the closet, but dark, and it smelled like rotten food. Dishes and carryout containers piled everywhere.

"We have to hurry," he whispered. "Bad people are coming for you."

Her heart fluttered, and confusion clouded her brain. He was the bad person, right?

He turned the knob slowly, then pulled the kitchen door open with more speed, like he didn't want it to squeak. They slipped out and he shut the door quietly behind them. He put a finger to his lips and pulled her along with him.

It was daytime. That was a surprise. She'd expected night, like maybe it was always night now. She'd forgotten the way the sun felt, and how it washed the color from everything. It was so bright it stung her eyes and made it hard to see. Everything was faded, but the big thing she noticed? *They weren't in the mountains.*

This place was like Mars. Like some alien landscape. Yet even though they were in the desert, she could see mountains. Hazy, far-away mountains that looked dreamy, like a Japanese watercolor. The mountains didn't seem real either. Maybe they weren't. Maybe they were a Hollywood backdrop and she was starring in a movie.

Her feet moved over dirt and sand and past prickly cacti. She was glad she was wearing shoes. In the brightness of outdoors, she saw how filthy her clothes were. But her immediate distraction was the heat. It radiated from everywhere. When she inhaled, the dry, hot air filled and burned her lungs, heating up her insides. Even her Kaleidoscope T-shirt and pink pajama shorts burned where they touched her skin. Like, just *touched* her skin.

Shade is a commodity, just as important as water.

Who'd said that? Somebody from that other life that probably wasn't real? Her stepfather.

"Come on," Johnnie whispered. He was getting mad because she couldn't keep up, but her legs were weak. She looked down and saw they were shaking. But somehow she managed to keep going, and they ran past broken and collapsed shacks and metal shipping containers, the kind you saw on trains when you were stuck at a railroad crossing.

They slipped under a broken fence and ran along a shed with a slanted roof propped up by wooden poles with almost no white paint left. No doors on the shed. The vehicles inside looked like they'd been parked there years ago. Most were rusty with flat tires.

He opened the passenger door of a gray car that didn't look as old as the others, and shoved her in. It was a relief to sit down, but it was just as hot in the car, maybe hotter.

After squeezing through the opening in the gate, Reni circled to the back of the house while Daniel approached the front. Summer brush

191

hadn't been cleared away. Now she could see the property was completely fenced. There was a pole shed in the distance, and another sagging gate with a chain holding it closed.

Bent at the knees, head down, she waded through a tangle of dead scrub, the kind that caught fire easily. Like many desert homes, the cabin had an outdoor laundry shed. At the kitchen door, she slowly turned the knob.

It was unlocked. That was unexpected.

She opened the door a crack and peered inside. From the direction of the front entry, she heard Daniel knocking. A television was blaring, the noise coming from the vicinity of the living room. A game show.

This was a case of exigent circumstance. No warrant was needed if a person's life might be in danger. She pushed the door open a little more and recoiled at the smell of rotten food. Sucked in a deep breath, looked back inside. The windows were covered in black trash bags, but some light managed to cut around them. Dishes were piled high in the sink.

Daniel knocked again. "Detective Ellis here!" he shouted.

She slipped inside and crept down a dark hall, moving slowly, her heart slamming as she strained to hear any possible noise over the blaring TV. She ducked around a blind corner to reach an open door, her mind documenting and banking several things at once. The sagging curtain hanging from a bent rod. A mattress on the floor. No sheets or blankets. Nobody there. Not the room with the TV.

Keep going.

Remaining close to the wall, her breathing fast and shallow, she moved to another door, this one slightly ajar. She paused, pushed the door open all the way.

No humans.

Trash bags here too. An unmade twin bed on a wooden frame. Various covers, most the kind that could be picked up at a discount store for a few bucks. Fuzzy blankets with deer and dogs. Halloween and Christmas designs. Giant black weights were scattered around, every single one more than she could possibly lift. A desk askew in the center of the room. She was familiar with cases in which weights had been used to contain victims.

She checked under the bed, then flung the closet door open—and recoiled again, this time at the smell of urine that burned her eyes. Nobody inside, but it was a place where a victim had been kept. Where was Emerson? Were they too late?

She heard footsteps. Through the crack next to the hinged side of the door, she saw Daniel. He came into the room on high alert, gun held in two hands, barrel pointed toward the ceiling. He lowered his weapon when he saw her. She motioned to the closet and he peered inside, swung back around with dismay on his face. The television in the living room let out a deep bass reverberation. A second later, Reni realized it wasn't the TV. She and Daniel looked at each other. From somewhere outside, an engine roared.

The car shot out of the shed, Emerson's head thrown back from the momentum. Johnnie made a quick turn and they bounced down a dirt road and headed straight for a chain-link gate.

He didn't slow down.

Emerson sank in the seat and put her hands to her face.

They hit the gate.

It clanged and the car shuddered. The hinged gates blew open, metal scraping and squealing down both sides of the car. Then it was dirt roads, dirt roads, dirt roads, the interior of the car filling with fine dust. It floated in from the vents and windows and every possible crack until they finally reached blacktop, tires burning as rubber grabbed hold of a highway that had a yellow line down the center.

CHAPTER 30

Reni and Daniel ran down the hall to the front door, arriving in time to see a car flying from one of the shacks that littered the property. Tires spun in the loose sand. Dust filled the air. The car blasted through the back gate.

They hadn't found anybody in the house. Did he have Emerson with him? If so, was she still alive? Without conversation, Reni and Daniel sprinted toward Daniel's vehicle, slipping under the chain and padlock, taking off again. As they ran, he tossed her the keys. "You drive. You know these roads better than I do."

In the car, behind the wheel, Reni made a quick three-point turn and they were off, after the little compact. One bad thing about the desert? Cars left a nasty dust trail that could linger for hours. One good thing about the desert? Cars left a nasty dust trail that could linger for hours.

She pressed the accelerator, turned on the wipers for a few seconds. Beside her, Daniel called for backup. "No service."

No surprise.

"What's he driving?" Daniel asked.

They needed a better visual to report, when and if he could get through. "Some little beater," Reni said. "Not sure of the make or model."

"A little beater is good," said Daniel. "We should be able to catch up."

Emerson squinted against the sun's brightness. Her eyes were still adjusting to being outdoors, but the colors weren't as faded now. And the air smelled so good after the closet. Like dirt and car exhaust. But the road. It was insane, and it made her wonder if this actually *was* a dream. She'd had so many in the closet. Maybe this was just another one. The road they were flying on was like a roller coaster, like something in a cartoon, like driving on the backbone of a dinosaur.

She clung to the seat and looked at the speed gauge on the dash. They were going eighty. The road climbed straight up until she could see nothing but blue sky. When it seemed they were going to launch into the air, they hit the peak, leveled out, and a vast valley opened below them. Now it was like being in a plane. Then they shot straight down, her stomach dropping. But she wasn't scared. Fear didn't seem to be a part of her anymore.

A stop sign.

Johnnie blasted through it, only slowing enough to make a right turn. Tires squealed. The car swiveled and fishtailed, tipped up on two wheels, dropped back down. He accelerated, engine roaring.

"Are they behind us?" he asked.

She turned and looked over her seat. "I see a white truck. No, maybe it's an SUV."

"That's them."

Their little car roared down the highway. The few vehicles they met pulled off the road, dust flying. Some threw them the finger. But no matter Johnnie's speed, they weren't going fast enough, and the white vehicle finally caught up.

Yes, an SUV. Two people in front, but she couldn't make out the faces. It dropped back, caught up, moved into the oncoming lane.

"They're going to try to pass," she said while at the same time marveling at how she'd gone from the sedentary existence of the closet to this. But dreams were like that. Soon she'd probably be flying like a bird.

Gripping the wheel with both hands, Johnnie wrenched the car to the left, straddling the yellow line, blocking the vehicle behind them. Seconds later he slammed on the brakes, tires squealing. The SUV lurched as it slowed, its tires squealing too, smoke billowing from the shredding of rubber against the surface of the hot road.

Johnnie stomped down on the gas and shot away.

The SUV didn't try to pass again. Lesson learned.

At one point in the chase, Johnnie slowed, gave the wheel another wrench, took a sharp left, and then they were blasting up a dirt road that looked like it would take them straight to a mountain peak.

The road was bad. Really bad. The worst yet. So bad that the car slammed the ground hard. They hit big rocks that rolled and tumbled under the floorboard as the car was tossed from side to side. Emerson bounced again. This time her body left the seat and she hit her head on the roof. She landed on the floorboard, then scrambled back into her seat.

"Who is it?" she asked. "Who's after us?"

"Cops."

Her heart leapt. Coming to rescue her.

The road got worse, bumpier and steeper and finally so narrow and rutted it didn't seem like a road at all, but more like a hiking trail.

She looked over her shoulder. "They're still behind us."

The fleeing car turned and went north on Old Woman Springs Road. Reni was trying to figure out how to stop the vehicle, possibly pass, when the driver took an unexpected turn onto a dirt lane heading west, barely slowing down, the car bouncing. Houses on the left. Church on the right. Some horses looking surprised before shrieking and bucking away, kicking up dust behind them. Then the road narrowed and climbed. Giant ruts that were hard for the high-clearance vehicle to manage, let alone a small car. And it got worse, continuing to narrow until it wasn't more than a trail, the car in front of them airborne at times, bottoming out with a loud crash at others as it climbed an off-road-vehicle path up Ruby Mountain, an area familiar to her, especially because of Willie Boy.

"He's leaking oil," she said.

Daniel lowered his window and braced his feet against the seat until he was sitting on the window frame, gun drawn. He fired. They hit a bump. He fired again.

Both back car tires blew.

As Emerson watched, Johnnie fumbled at his waist and pulled a gun from a holster. He lowered his window.

"Take the wheel!" he shouted.

She grabbed the wheel and kept an eye on the road in front of them. Every bump threw them left or right. Johnnie lowered his window and fired at the SUV behind them. The sound hurt her ears. She let go of the wheel, remembered she was supposed to be steering, and grabbed it again. Something was wrong. The car was slowing.

She looked down. Johnnie's foot was on the gas. Confused, unable to adequately sort out what was happening, she found herself moving her leg over, pressing her foot on top of his. The pedal was all the way to the floor, yet they were still losing speed. The tires were making a loud flopping sound.

Johnnie turned back around in his seat and focused his attention on the sick car. He pumped the gas pedal. Nothing changed. Just a steady drop in speed. He tapped a finger against the dashboard. "No oil pressure."

She didn't understand.

The car sputtered to a stop. Johnnie threw his door open. "Out. Get out!" When she didn't move, he grabbed her arm and pulled her across the seat after him. "Let's go let's go let's go!"

"Impressive," Reni shouted over the noise of the road as Daniel lowered himself back inside.

The car in front of them had stopped. Two people got out. The male was dragging the woman with him. Reni's heart beat faster. "Is that Emerson?"

"Think so," Daniel said, his voice full of hope. "And Moore."

They screeched to a halt behind the gray car. Even if not for the leaking oil and blown tires, it wouldn't have made it much farther, because the road would soon become a foot trail.

She and Daniel ducked out, both taking partial cover behind their doors.

"Police!" Daniel shouted, gun drawn, his arm resting on the open window. "Halt right there!"

Moore ran, leaping over boulders, pulling the girl along with him.

Daniel tried again. "Halt!"

Moore turned and fired.

The windshield shattered and safety glass rained around them. They both kept their faces down, then shook off the small cubes of glass.

The couple vanished behind a boulder.

Reni and Daniel ran after them, knees bent, heads low, stopping when they reached cover. The desert was often an open and vast expanse. Not so right here. Daniel pulled out his phone again. Instead of trying to make a call, he sent a text because they could sometimes magically go through.

"I dropped a pin so they can find us." He put his phone away.

"I don't think we should wait," Reni said. "He might kill the girl."

"Agree."

They ran. Emerson stumbled, caught herself, ran more. Johnnie turned and fired, swung back around, half the time hanging on to her, half the time letting her run on her own. They scrambled up large rocks, leapt over smaller rocks, ducked behind rocks as big as small buildings, the wind blowing hard.

A bird called from somewhere.

She remembered the wind on the mountain.

She remembered the bird.

Run, run, run!

Johnnie began shooting again.

She flinched and covered her ears.

He made a satisfied sound, stuck the gun in the holster, and took her hand again. They ran more, and rested, and ran, and finally came to a flat area of packed dirt and more boulders.

She dropped to the ground in the shade and rested her head against a rock. Johnnie was busy doing something. Fiddling around, his back to her. Unrolling a blanket, spreading it on the ground. Where had that come from? He must have hidden it nearby. Maybe he'd had this whole thing planned. The blanket had cartoon characters on it. That made her feel like crying; she didn't know why. But then she saw what was inside the blanket.

Guns. Big ugly guns. Not like the one he'd been using. She remembered something. AK-47. That's what they were called. They could shoot and shoot and shoot. They could cause a lot of damage. She heard a sob and realized it had come from her.

"Why do you have those?" she asked, her heart pounding.

"Because I don't want anybody to hurt you."

"I don't like that kind of gun. I don't like guns at all."

He slid in a curved magazine—the thing that held all the bullets. He had more than one. Handling the weapon looked like something he'd done a lot. "Thirty rounds in three seconds," he said smugly. "Six hundred per minute."

"I don't like it," she repeated.

"You don't have to like it."

He climbed to the top of the boulder she was resting behind, crouched and jammed the stock into his shoulder, rested his elbows on the rock, and looked through the sight.

Then he pulled the trigger.

The gun made him shake all over, the sound circling and so continuous it didn't seem like there was a pause between bullets. Above Emerson's head, birds scattered. She put her hands to her ears, closed her eyes, and screamed.

As Reni and Daniel remained covered by a boulder, a barrage of bullets chewed up the ground, the rapid onslaught laying down a pattern that moved in a straight line across the desert floor, shredding plants, blasting dirt twenty feet high, pinging off rocks, finally hitting Daniel's SUV, shattering what was left of the glass, blasting side windows, and blowing tires. The vehicle hissed and canted to one side, then dropped and leveled out as the remaining tires collapsed. Without letting up, the assault rifle continued to spit bullets, ripping through the hood and radiator. Sizzling water shot skyward like a geyser. Reni could smell the sweet, toxic scent of radiator coolant, and she could taste the dirt in the air.

Daniel pulled out a second gun and tried to give it to her. She shook her head.

The assault rifle didn't let up. Even in the vast openness, the sound was deafening. It echoed down canyons and seemed to bounce off the sky. Before the echo faded, more blasts joined; the sound, once set in motion, just kept going.

They heard a scream.

Using facial expressions and hand signals to communicate, Daniel pressed the gun into Reni's hand. Held it there with both of his, locking eyes, silently telling her she had to use it.

She shook her head again.

The rifle shots stopped. Dead silence followed. Not even a bird called. Not a breath of wind, as if it had been driven away by the noise. No more screaming.

"You don't have to fire it at anybody," Daniel said.

Either he was whispering, or her ears were messed up. She'd experienced temporary deafness in the past after gunshot fire.

"I want you to shoot . . . anywhere," he said. "Just draw his attention while I circle around back and come up behind him."

She thought about Daniel creeping around in the present terrain. She looked down at his dress shoes with their smooth leather soles.

"I'll do it," she told him. "You stay here." At his look of skepticism, she said, "I'm a better climber. And I know this area. I've hiked it many times."

She could see he understood there was no time to argue. Moore could be reloading, or he could be moving toward them or away. He could be getting ready to kill Emerson. He might have killed her already after she screamed. If he hadn't, Reni needed to do everything she could to keep the girl alive.

She wrapped her fingers around the gun.

Before Daniel could blink in acknowledgment, she took off, bent low, moving behind rocks, keeping herself hidden from the boulder from where the shots had been fired.

The mountainside was covered in low brush, California juniper, and boulders ranging from the size of a person to bigger than a house. Winding among them were a myriad of trails dipping in and out of ravines, circling steep inclines, all leading to the peak. So many places to hide.

Once Reni was a good distance away, she heard Daniel discharge three rounds. Those shots were immediately answered with rifle fire. Reni continued to move quickly, climbing, reaching an area where she wouldn't be visible from the boulder Moore was using as his watchtower. She focused on the trail, jumping from boulder to boulder, the weapon Daniel had given her tucked into the back of her jeans. Poor placement. Her old FBI instructors would be horrified. *She* was horrified.

The gunfire below was continuous now.

She was downwind and could smell hot metal and sulfur drifting in her direction. As she got higher, the wind kicked up, gradually increasing until she had to take care because it almost blew her over at times before dropping to nothing, the sound hollow, like the atmosphere had turned inside out.

As she moved, she kept her ears focused on the gunshots. Familiar with the Ruby Mountain location, she mentally visualized the spot where Emerson and Moore were hiding. A small level area surrounded by boulders. A little shade, sometimes water collected in rocks after a rain. A place hikers were known to camp.

The sound of the gunplay was good for covering her approach. Finally above the shooter, she scanned the terrain below, spotting them. Yes, they were in the camp location. The girl was crouched in the shade below the boulder where the shots were coming from, her hands to her ears.

Reni pulled out her phone. She was high enough to have two bars. She sent a text to Daniel, letting him know she had a visual and that Emerson was alive. She put the phone away and circled closer to the couple, crept around a rock, pulling the weapon from her waistband.

The weight was so familiar.

Muscle memory.

She'd spent so many hours at the gun range, practicing until the weapon became a part of her. This was the same make and model she'd used. Without even looking, she chambered the bullet. Then she took a deep breath, paused, and stepped into the campsite, low enough now to be visible to the girl but not the guy.

Emerson stared at her.

Reni put a finger to her lips.

The girl was filthy, wearing pajama shorts and a Kaleidoscope T-shirt. Strange-looking pink clogs. Her hair was stringy. None of that mattered, of course, because the most important thing was that she was not dead. But her eyes. The poor girl's eyes. Reni didn't like what she saw there. Or rather, didn't see.

She might have been drugged, but such a mental state could also be the result of kidnapping. Captivity and trauma could wipe out ego, a state of absence caused by whatever unthinkable things she'd been through. That blank stare, that intentional numbness. The way the mind built a cushion around a person, protected them. It also kept everything out. It was a reason people didn't run away or try to escape, and it didn't take long to succumb. For someone like Emerson, a person who'd been traumatized before in her young life, a second event could take her back and undo everything in a matter of days. Even hours.

Shut off. Shut down.

The only way to cope.

Above them, gunshots from the rifle continued. Both Daniel and Moore were firing.

Taking advantage of the continued distraction, Reni extended her hand to Emerson. The hand without the gun. She mouthed the words *Come with me.*

The girl stared.

Trust me.

More staring.

Reni motioned for her to come closer. They were maybe twenty feet apart.

The girl stood up. Hands loose at her sides, she didn't move forward. She finally shook her head. Reni thought of the photos she'd seen of Emerson and tried to see that person in front of her. The essence was gone. Moore was still firing from the boulder, but not as often now. And with fresh alarm, Reni realized there were no shots coming from Daniel.

Reni tucked her weapon in her waistband and took a couple of steps closer to Emerson.

The girl finally reacted with wide eyes and a shout just as the shooting from above them stopped. "Run!"

Reni heard movement on the boulder, rocks sliding.

"Let's go," Reni whispered. "Trust me."

The girl took a stumbling step, froze.

Moore jumped from the boulder to the ground to stand facing Reni, his weapon pointed at her chest.

The shooting had stopped. For now. And Daniel was out of bullets. Trying to push aside his deep concern and unhelpful speculation of what could be going on with Reni and Emerson, he focused on actions he could take to keep them safe as possible. Get to his trunk and his ammunition. He ran. Hunched over. Did a baseball slide behind the car, waiting to hear shots fired.

Silence.

Not good.

Crouching on the ground, he opened the trunk, grabbed his black weapon case, ducked back down behind the car, opened the case, and reloaded his handgun. Then he stuck several preloaded magazines in his pocket.

He didn't like the silence.

He didn't want to risk trying to call Reni and possibly alerting Moore, but he pulled out his phone to see if she'd sent another message letting him know she was okay.

Nothing new from her, but he had two messages with info on backup.

Squads on the way.

Helicopter on the way.

That was followed by an ETA of fifteen minutes.

He straightened quickly, fired off several shots to determine whether the shooter was still active and to distract Moore if Reni was in danger. Rounds fired, he ducked back down, waited, gun held in one hand, braced with the other.

No response from the mountain.

He bent-ran for the cluster of boulders he and Reni had hidden behind earlier, his heart pounding, not knowing when more shots would be fired, feeling exposed for an eternity. He dove for cover and felt a sting. Looked down. A snake was slithering away.

The girl jumped to her feet and screamed, "Don't hurt her!"

If she hadn't tucked her gun back into her pants, Reni might have attempted a shot, but Moore had the advantage. The man's rifle, a weapon that weighed over ten pounds fully loaded, wasn't even shaking.

Emerson suddenly lunged at him, grabbing at his shirt, appearing to rip something from it.

Moore faltered, and Reni took the only chance she might have. She drew her weapon.

Moore pulled the girl against him, using her for a human shield, controlling her by wrapping his arm around her throat. Her head was tilted back, her pupils near her lower lids as she tried to watch Reni. Yes, she'd definitely been drugged.

"I can help you both," Reni said, talking clearly but quickly. Where was Daniel? There were no more gunshots since the last few rounds, and the silence was telling. Dead, or at the very least injured.

"Don't hurt her," the girl pleaded again. "Please, please, please."

Surprisingly, Moore seemed to be listening to both of them. "We don't want your help," he said.

"You must need something. What do you need? I can get it for you."

"To be left alone."

"Emerson can come with me," she said. "And you can leave." She'd keep her word. She'd let him go. It was a good trade. The best trade. Bringing the girl home alive. Deal with Moore later.

He walked backward, keeping a grip on Emerson, glancing behind him to check his footing until he and the girl vanished behind an outcropping of rocks and shrubs. Reni heard scrambling feet and rocks skittering. They were heading for even higher ground.

Reni tucked her weapon back in her waistband and followed. She took long strides, the tread of her hiking boots gripping the smooth surface of rocks. She found handholds; she moved quickly over rough and difficult terrain. Maybe she could pass them, jump him, take him by surprise, avoiding gunplay entirely. She didn't want to risk Emerson getting shot.

The higher she went, the windier it got. Gusts moved through narrow channels of rocks and circled strange formations. It blasted through narrow valleys. Sometimes the sound of it was like a faraway jet, sometimes like someone blowing over the lip of a bottle, so loud that at first she didn't recognize the familiar whip-whip of a far-off helicopter. She hoped they hung back. Getting too close could cause Moore's behavior to escalate.

She'd managed to pass them, and now she spotted the two not far below her. They'd stopped in an open, level area with a drop on one side where the ground fell away and became blue sky. Moore still had a grip on the girl as he gestured toward the precipice.

Reni flashed on a memory of her father standing in his orange prison one-piece, a chain around his waist, his hands clasped together.

One second he was there in front of her, the next he was flying through the sky, orange against blue, the fabric of his prison clothing fluttering.

Was Moore going to jump, just like Reni's father? And was he taking Emerson with him? The girl was unlikely to resist, even if she could. Victims became reliant on their kidnappers. Emerson was his possession, and though she'd warned Reni to run, she probably was unable to fully think for herself, especially in her drugged state.

The helicopters were closer now. Two of them, their rotors beating the air, creating a dead and vacant sound in Reni's head.

The couple ran for the cliff. Hand in hand. As they ran, Moore dropped his weapon on the ground. He wouldn't need it where he was going, and it had to be hampering him. And he was taking Emerson with him if Reni didn't stop him.

She pulled her gun, steadied herself, aimed, hands clasped around the weapon, one arm straight, her supporting arm bent.

Moore was moving fast.

She blinked, inhaled, held her breath.

They were almost to the cliff.

She fired, felt the recoil. Moore staggered, screamed, regained his footing, began moving again, slowly now, dragging an injured leg behind him, still managing to keep a grip on Emerson.

Reni's hands were shaking violently. She'd never be able to hit a target now. The weapon useless, she dropped the gun and ran for them, pumping her arms, taking long strides, almost flying. Above them a helicopter with *San Bernardino County Sheriff* on the side hovered, creating a blinding tornado of dirt. She choked, kept going. Cut through an outer wall of swirling dust.

The pain must have been too much. Moore staggered and collapsed to the ground, rolled to his back, clutching his leg and screaming. Blood gushed from the gunshot wound.

And dear God. Emerson was still running.

"Go! Go!" Moore shrieked to the girl, waving his arm, directing her to the ledge.

Emerson ran.

Earlier, she'd briefly broken away from his control when she'd begged him not to hurt Reni, but Emerson was gone again, under his power, doing what her captor told her to do. But in her weakened condition, she couldn't run very fast.

Reni poured it on, her lungs burning. She caught up, charged, knocked the girl down, both of them landing mere feet from the precipice. And still Emerson clawed her way toward death, sobbing, dragging herself across the ground on her stomach, then crawling on her hands and knees.

This couldn't happen again. Reni couldn't lose another life this way. She swiped at Emerson's leg. Caught her. Until the girl's shoe came off and Reni lost her grip.

Emerson started to plunge over the edge. Reni grabbed the girl's ankle with both hands, felt her arms practically yanked from their sockets as Emerson slammed against the mountainside, dangling.

This time Reni held on. She braced one foot against a rock and dug her heel into the ground with the other as gravity and Emerson's weight worked against her, dragging her closer to the edge. At some point, she'd have no choice but to let go or fall with her.

The helicopter moved higher, the dirt no longer blinding. Two people were being lowered from the aircraft. Moore had stopped screaming. Wondering at his silence, Reni risked a quick glance over her shoulder. He was slithering across an expanse of ground, moving in a straight line toward the weapon he'd dropped. The officers in the air were halfway down. Moore would reach the rifle before they reached solid ground. There was nothing Reni could do about Moore.

She closed her eyes and gritted her teeth and hung on. Her fingers were cramping, her grip slipping. The girl was silent, no longer struggling, maybe unconscious. From behind her came the sound of a gruff exhale of air followed by scuffling. She opened her eyes, expected to see the rescue team. Instead she saw Daniel. Fighting with Moore.

Not dead. Not dead. Not dead.

In the struggle, Daniel managed to pick up the AK-47, leaving Moore weaponless as the harnessed officers touched down. Daniel ran for Reni, limping as he covered the ground between them. Just when Reni thought her arms would give out, he reached her side, grabbed Emerson's other leg. Gasping and straining, they pulled her back over the ledge, everyone collapsing.

Reni was spent, her legs and arms shaking. But no pain. Too much adrenaline for that. Pain would come later.

She rolled to her back, one hand to her stomach, gasping for air, and turned her head to see Daniel bent over the girl. In the distance, the officers from the helicopter were with Moore.

"Get his phone," Reni shouted. "Also look for a silver bracelet." Someone collected the gun Reni had fired. Per department protocol, it would be logged as evidence and a full investigation launched.

Emerson sat up, her legs cut and bleeding and straight out like a doll's. She had a knot on her head, but she managed to roll and push herself to her feet. Confused, she looked from Moore, on the ground, to the precipice behind her. Was Emerson still on Team Moore? She'd almost killed herself at his command. She might not be done obeying.

Reni whispered a warning, "Daniel."

Sweating and swaying and breathing hard, Daniel spread his arms, ready to block Emerson if she moved for the edge. "You're going to be fine," he told her in a low voice.

Emerson blinked.

"You're going to be fine," he repeated.

She let out a muffled sob. Then, appearing to recognize him, she started crying and threw herself into his arms. Daniel held her close while guiding her away from danger.

More officers arrived, appearing from around boulders. These must have driven in from the nearby town, probably parked below at the trailhead. They were followed by medics carrying body boards and medical supplies.

"Got his phone," an officer shouted, holding up the device in a gloved hand. "No bracelet."

Daniel grasped Emerson by both arms, trying to pass her to a medic.

She shook her head.

"They'll take care of you," he told her. "You'll be fine."

As Reni watched, Emerson finally allowed one of the female medics to coax her to an area of shade.

Daniel let out a sigh of relief, then looked at Reni. He had a strange and oddly unreadable expression on his face. "You know how I'm always saying I'm not crazy about the desert?" he asked.

Her reply came tinged with caution. "Yeah?"

He lifted his pant leg, then rolled his black sock down to reveal two red holes in a swollen ankle.

Her heart dropped.

She hadn't been *afraid* afraid all day, but she was now. For him. "Did you get a visual?"

"It had a rattle."

"How much time has passed?" she asked. A bite victim needed to remain calm and keep their heart rate low after a venomous strike. Daniel had climbed a mountain and joined her in dragging Emerson from death.

"Thirty minutes maybe?"

She signaled to the helicopter crew, shouting to be heard over a fresh wave of noise as the chopper above them shifted position. "Send Moore to Palm Springs in an ambulance." They needed to use the helicopter for Daniel. "We've got a rattlesnake bite, and that takes priority.

Detective Ellis needs to be airlifted." She looked back at Daniel, trying to keep the fear from showing on her face.

"Stay here," he told her. "Go back to Moore's house. Make sure they process it correctly. We don't want a compromised scene."

There was a good chance he'd be incoherent by the time he reached the hospital. Someone had to be there to make sure he was given immediate and rapid care. "I should come with you."

"We'll take care of him," the air medic said. That promise was followed by the name of the Palm Springs hospital where they'd take him. "It's too far to short-haul him all the way there," the EMT continued, referring to a method of leaving the body cage at the end of the tether without hoisting the victim into the chopper. "So we'll hoist him inside."

Reni recognized it as the best choice, but she was still torn.

"I'll be okay," Daniel said.

He couldn't know that. He'd need antivenom, which in itself was a huge risk. People often had reactions. Serious reactions, which was why it was never administered in the wild.

She realized she was holding his hand. She didn't recall grabbing it. Or had he grabbed hers? She wanted to give him some reassurance, and the most important thing was that they'd saved Emerson. And they'd saved her together.

"We got her," Reni said.

Daniel nodded. "We did."

It was a repeat of a scene Reni had been part of not all that long ago, although this time she remained on the ground. A member of the rescue team attached himself to the taut line connected to a winch inside the chopper. Another person covered Daniel's face with a clear shield to protect him from flying debris. A hand signal, and the chopper lifted the basket from the ground. Reni watched until Daniel was safely inside the aircraft and the door was closed. It turned slowly, then shot off in the direction of Palm Springs. He'd be there in less than thirty minutes.

Once the chopper was gone, she pulled out her phone and called Bo, telling him what had happened.

"I'll head there right now," he said.

He might even get there before the chopper.

Daniel would be fine, she tried to tell herself.

CHAPTER 31

A female officer had Emerson sit in the shade of a big boulder. Someone else, a guy who was part of the medical team, wrapped a navy-blue Velcro band around her upper arm, then clipped something to her finger to get her pulse. While the medic checked her vitals, Emerson thought about how her father had rescued her just like she'd known he would.

"Blood pressure and pulse low," the medic said. "Understandable," he added in a falsely cheerful voice.

"Why are they taking Detective Ellis away?" Emerson asked.

"Snakebite."

That didn't sound good. "Will he be okay?"

"I'm sure he'll be fine."

A litter was put on the ground beside her. It took her a minute to realize they wanted her to get in it.

"I can walk," she said.

"I'm sure you can," the medic said. "But think of this as a vacation. We'll carry you."

She got in, and they strapped her down. "So you won't fall out," he explained as he stuck a needle in her arm. "Just fluids." One of the other medics held an IV bag higher than her head.

The wind got louder and the sky above her swirled as she was lifted off the ground. She thought she heard a bird calling again, but when she looked, she saw it was the helicopter. Not far away, in another litter, was Johnnie Moore. People were working on him too. There was an IV and blood.

"Hey, Johnnie!" she called. Her mind actually felt a little clearer than it had in a long time. Maybe the adrenaline had blasted the drugs from her system.

Moore turned his head.

She raised her hand and threw him the finger.

CHAPTER 32

The siren yowled above his head as the ambulance raced down the grade toward Palm Springs. The noise wasn't as loud as it would have been from outside, but it was bad.

"You know who this is, don't you?" someone in the vehicle asked. "He's the guy who killed that hiker and kidnapped the girl they put in the other ambulance."

Johnnie's eyes were closed, and he'd ignored most of the conversation until now, just concentrating on shallow breathing and dreading each bump in the road. If he didn't move, didn't breathe deeply, the pain in his leg wasn't as intolerable. But now they were talking about him. Not discussing his blood pressure and heart rate, but *him*.

"And you know what's going to happen to him, right?" the same guy asked. "Our taxes are going to pay for his trial, and then we'll spend another several million on him while he lounges in prison and plays basketball and takes online classes to get a degree. I wanted to be a veterinarian but couldn't afford it. So here I am."

Another voice chimed in, a female. "This is nothing you should be talking about. We have a judicial system that will do what needs to be done. And yes, if found guilty, he'll probably get a life sentence, but California hasn't executed anybody in over a decade. I doubt they'll start again with him."

"Well, at least he's going to have to live with what he did."

That was a new voice. Also female. Closer. Maybe the person who'd put the IV in his arm.

"At least he's going to be one of the most loathed humans on the planet," said the first voice. "I guess that counts for something. What a loser."

"That's enough," said the second voice. "I don't want to have to report you, but I will if you keep this up. He's a patient in need of care. That's all he should be to you right now."

The guy mumbled something under his breath. It sounded like *bitch*, but Johnnie wasn't sure. Maybe *witch*. Nah, probably *bitch*.

"What did you say?" the woman asked.

"I said *bitch*."

Bingo.

Johnnie cracked his eyelids. Nobody was looking at him. All three of the people in the back of the ambulance were concentrating on one another and the drama the first speaker had stirred up. A female police officer, probably the one who'd yelled at the guy, was sitting nearby. But the guy was one hundred percent right. There would be no life outside prison for Johnnie after this. And he would never see Emerson again, or at least not until she was eighteen. And what about the look of hatred she'd had on her face when she threw him the finger? He sure hadn't been expecting that from his girlfriend. Would she ever *want* to see him again?

Once they got to the hospital, any chance of escape would be gone. With very little movement, he pulled out the cable from the heart monitor on his finger.

"No pulse! He's coding!"

People scrambled.

He almost laughed.

He snatched the IV from his arm, blood spurting. He grabbed the gun from the officer's holster and jumped to one side, keeping his weight off his injured leg, waving the weapon at them. Everybody yelled and ducked.

They'd managed to stop the bleeding, but now that he was upright, the bandage around his upper thigh began to turn bright red. He could feel the wet heat spreading and running down his leg like hot piss.

The ambulance lurched, throwing everyone to one side. He caught himself, pleased to find he still had the gun in his hand and that they all looked scared. Panting, in pain from the exertion, he unlatched the back double doors, threw them open, and jumped out.

He hit the pavement at sixty miles an hour, rolling and bouncing—kind of like the bodies had bounced when he'd tossed them off the mountain. His bones snapped and cracked. Coming up on him was a semi. It laid on its horn. Brakes shrieked. The last thing Johnnie saw was a front grille that seemed to be grinning at him.

CHAPTER 33

Still feeling uneasy about leaving Daniel to fly to the hospital by himself, Reni caught a ride to Moore's house with a police officer. They arrived just before the San Bernardino County crime-scene van, which came bouncing up the road behind them to stop in the front yard. More police cars followed, and a staging area was set up in the shade of a Joshua tree. From that location, Reni could still hear the blaring television. She and several of the crime-scene team put on shoe covers and black vinyl gloves and went inside. The plan was to do a quick overview inspection before the in-depth one.

The sun wasn't quite down, but the rooms were especially dark now. They turned on ceiling lights with gloved hands. Reni had already done a brief stint inside the house, so she wasn't shocked by the smell. Not so with the others, who made choking noises while struggling to hide their disgust. Judging from the piles of trash, it looked like Emerson had been living on fast food, although there was some evidence of cereal—bowls piled up in the sink along with an odor of sour milk. Reni shut off the TV. The silence was a relief.

They found a stash of weapons in a closet, mostly handguns. One was the model and caliber Reni had suspected to be the murder weapon during the Ravenscroft autopsy. The last room of the initial sweep was the bedroom where Emerson had been held captive. Someone would bag and log the laptop found in the desk. Digital Forensics would carefully go over it back at Headquarters. Reni was still looking for more evidence to tie Moore to the murder of Janet Ravenscroft.

She got a text message from an unknown number. Anxious for an update on Daniel, she opened it and found it was from Davenport.

Weird development. Moore is dead.

Her knees threatened to buckle, and a wave of heat washed over her. Moore's injuries hadn't seemed life-threatening. "I have to take a call," she said. But what she really needed was air. Outside, as people came and went, some carrying processing kits, she pulled off her gloves and replied to the text.

Need more details.

Things are sketchy, but it sounds like he fell from the ambulance and was hit by a semi!

What the absolute hell? While she was trying to figure out how something like that could possibly happen, she released a tight breath. Her shot hadn't killed him. She knew she'd done what was necessary, and later she could even let herself bathe a little in the fact that she'd fired the weapon in the most professional manner possible. But taking a life, any life, was something she never wanted to do ever again—*again* meaning being part of her father's kills, however tenuously.

Her own reaction aside, they now would not have Moore's confession and story.

She sent a reply: *Let me know as soon as you have more information.* Then she added: *Any news about Daniel?*

Haven't heard anything. Sorry.

Despite Daniel's orders, she couldn't stay at the cabin any longer, not when he might be in crisis. She needed to get to Palm Springs.

She found an officer to drive her home to her vehicle. On the way, she tried to call Bo. No answer. Her anxiety increased. She knew she might be in for a bedside vigil at the hospital, so once she got to her cabin, she packed up Edward and dropped him at Joss's house. Then she headed to Palm Springs and the hospital.

CHAPTER 34

There was a common misconception that a person with a snakebite could be given antivenom and sent home to live happily ever after. Not true. Reni had never experienced a bite herself, but she'd known people who had. Not all bite victims survived. Even when they did, they might lose a leg to an emergency amputation done to save their life. And many had reactions to the antivenom itself. Best-case scenario—no severe reaction, or a reaction that could be controlled in a medical setting— still usually meant a gradual recovery that could take weeks.

All these thoughts were in Reni's head as she sped toward Palm Springs and the hospital where Daniel had been taken. The fact that Bo hadn't picked up when she called was alarming, but she told herself there could be many reasons behind that. Maybe his phone had died. Maybe he'd forgotten it. Maybe he was in a restricted area of the hospital that didn't allow cell phones.

Maybe Daniel was in crisis.

As her headlights cut through the darkness, illuminating the yellow lines on the highway, she spotted her customary gas station and pulled over to fill her near-empty tank. She tried Bo again. Straight to voicemail.

She hadn't eaten in hours and didn't know if the shakiness she felt was due to that or worry over Daniel. Even though the last thing she wanted was food, she went inside to grab water and something she could eat while driving. That ended up being a comically large peanut-butter cookie.

In the station, people were standing around, their attention glued to the TV mounted high on the wall among the cigarettes. A YouTube feed was following the recent events, moving between live footage being recorded at the Moore cabin, Ruby Mountain, and the site where Moore had died. Citizens were often the ones getting the news out there before local stations arrived. Social media wasn't all bad, and it had proven itself again and again during catastrophic events, keeping the world updated.

Reni paid for her food and left, hitting the road again, getting back on Twentynine Palms Highway. Not long into her renewed journey, she saw a string of red taillights. Cars were creeping as officers directed traffic around a semi. It wasn't until she neared that she realized she was looking at the remnants of the ambulance scene Davenport had texted about. She pulled over and parked at the side of the road, got out, and found an officer who recognized her.

"Word is, he opened the back doors and jumped out," the officer said.

"Suicide."

"Looks that way."

The scene was under control and there was nothing she could do. Someone asked if she wanted confirmation of the victim. She did. They stepped closer, and the bloody sheet was pulled back.

She'd seen some mangled bodies in her life, but she wasn't sure she would have been able to ID Moore. There wasn't much left of his face. She spotted something on his shirt and remembered how Emerson had attacked him on the mountain.

She held out her hand. "Can I borrow that flashlight?"

The beam of light exposed two photo pins attached to his shirt near a ripped hole. She was able to make out an image of Rachel Rose and a young girl, probably Emerson's younger sister.

They needed to question Emerson about the pins.

She left the scene and continued to the hospital, where visiting hours were over. The man behind the check-in desk at the ground-level entrance surprised her by saying she was expected on the second floor. He gave her the room number.

"Details?" she asked, heart pounding.

He leaned closer to his monitor, then shook his head. "Doesn't say." She thanked him and took the stairs. She wasn't one to have irrational thoughts, but what she was thinking now was that Daniel was in bad shape and maybe wasn't expected to make it.

She located the room. His last name was on the patient ID slot on the wall. The door was propped open, a faint light flickering from within. She stepped inside, quietly in case he was asleep, but seconds later she found herself standing at the foot of an empty bed. The room was clean, as if it hadn't been occupied.

Or had been cleaned after moving a dead patient.

She stood there breathing hard. Beyond the roaring in her ears, she heard someone outside the door. A nurse was removing Daniel's name from the slot she'd spotted earlier. Reni forced herself to remain calm. She clung to logic rather than emotions. That didn't last long.

"I'm looking for the patient who was in this room," she said.

"The snakebite?" the nurse asked.

The woman's nonchalance collided with Reni's panic. She tried to read the nurse's face. Couldn't. "Yes," she croaked.

The nurse turned and walked down the hall, slipping the name into another slot by another door. "In here. We had to move him due to an issue with the plumbing. Gotta get maintenance up here."

Reni wanted to melt to the floor. Instead, she walked to the room and looked inside, her heart slamming. The space was dark, but light fell from the hallway, enough for her to see that Daniel was asleep, an IV rack beside him, a monitor and digital display tracking his vitals. She slipped into the room and eased herself into a chair and waited for her panic to recede.

Words came out of the darkness. "The doctors thought it was most likely a baby rattlesnake since I didn't have an extremely lethal toxin load." No movement from the bed, just Daniel's voice, his wonderful voice. "I'd always heard the baby ones were bad."

She got to her feet. In the dim light, she could see the paleness of his face. "Babies are good," she said. "Babies are *really* good." She was talking fast, euphoric to find him alive. "And cute. Really cute."

"That's what they told me. Not about being cute, but better than being bitten by an adult. That the baby rattlesnake thing about having more venom than an adult is a myth."

"Total myth."

"So I didn't get much venom in me."

"Good. That's good."

"They watched me in the ER, I didn't react to the antivenom, so they just want to keep me overnight for observation."

He probably didn't realize it could still take a couple of weeks to fully recover. She wouldn't mention that now. The important thing was that he'd experienced the best possible outcome. "I couldn't get in touch with Bo," she said. "I thought things were bad."

"I would have called, but they took all my belongings. I think they're around here somewhere. Bo's battery died. I told him to go home for the night. No need for him to sleep in a chair."

She found Daniel's phone in the patient closet. She dug a charging cable from her bag, plugged in his phone, and handed it to him.

She filled him in on Moore. He filled her in on Emerson.

"She's one floor above me," he said. "Tox report showed drugs in her system. No surprise. They ran a rape kit. No results yet, of course, but the initial report says no obvious physical signs of it."

"Sometimes incels, and Moore seems to fall into that category, are actually fearful of sexual encounters," Reni said. "A lot of bravado goes along with their behavior and mistreatment of women."

"I was hoping you could interrogate him, but now, with him dead, we'll never know the full details," Daniel said. "But I'm planning to interview Emerson first thing in the morning. I'd like you to be there."

"I don't think you should."

"It was a little snake."

"You still have venom in your system."

"I'll be fine. By the way, excellent job out there today. You saved Emerson's life."

"I should have ridden in the ambulance."

"That was my call. You can't be everywhere."

Now that the rush of adrenaline had faded, Reni felt drained, weak. Even in his condition, Daniel noticed. "Been a long, weird day."

"I'm glad you aren't dead."

"Me too."

"Get some sleep," she said. "I'll check in tomorrow morning."

The long walk down the hallway and out of the building would have been so much different if he'd died. In the parking lot, Reni got in her truck and dug a protein bar and drink from her backpack. She lay down across the seat, tucking a jacket under her head, and covered up with Edward's blanket. As she ate, she opened the browser on her phone and began searching for information about Johnnie May Moore.

CHAPTER 35

Early the next morning, Reni got a text from Daniel.

They found the bracelet and a self-defense ring at Moore's house.

That was followed by more information that didn't come as a surprise—the hospital was keeping Daniel another day. And he was waiting for Reni before visiting Emerson. Reni had to wonder if he wanted to avoid seeing the girl by himself, given how awkward it might be.

Reni met him in his room. Bo must have brought him a change of clothes. He was dressed in slacks and an untucked white shirt, sleeves rolled up. He had dark circles under his eyes, but all things considered, he looked good.

"You should take some time off once we wrap this up," Reni said.

"I will."

"Good."

"You're wearing the same clothes."

"I didn't go home. I slept in my truck."

He looked concerned about that. Like he wished he'd considered the possibility. She was glad he hadn't.

"You could have slept here. Or at my house."

She didn't tell him she'd needed time alone. "I'm used to sleeping in my truck. It's not a big deal. And I wanted to do some research on Moore because we really haven't had a chance to do a deep dive into him."

"What did you find?"

"He fits the incel profile. I found his Facebook page, and someone on Reddit who sounded like him." Much of it was private, and they'd need a court order to thoroughly examine Moore's profile in both places, but she'd seen enough to get a solid idea of who he was. "He followed school shooters and also people who kidnap. One thing of particular note was that he was a fan of the killer from Barron, Wisconsin, who kept his victim secured with the use of weights."

"That was a random kidnapping, which made it so hard to solve."

"More than eighty days, and she got out herself. Not to disparage their police department, but we got this guy in five, so I feel good about that," she said.

He nodded. "It's interesting that these people who consider themselves such outliers use the blueprints of other criminals."

"It's disturbing that we're seeing an uptick in young men who feel society and women in general have nothing to offer them. And they have nothing to offer in return but rage. Moore definitely fit that profile. He seemed to hate women, but for some reason he was drawn to Emerson."

"I feel bad for her," Daniel said. "Victimized twice."

"She seems pretty tough. I think she'll get through it as much as anybody can." She pointed toward the hallway. "Someone left a wheelchair out there. I'll bet it's for you."

"I'll walk. They want me to walk."

"I think *walk* might mean a few steps down the hall. I'll bring the chair along."

They took the elevator to the third floor, Daniel moving slowly, Reni following with the wheelchair, which she parked outside Emerson's room. Conversation and laughter could be heard coming from inside.

They found Emerson sitting up in bed, blanket over her legs, freshly showered, her hair clean, skin shining. She had a bruised area on her forehead, where she'd slammed against the rock face, but her eyes were brighter. Standing beside her were Portia and JoJo, both looking camera-ready in stylish clothing and perfect makeup. JoJo had some new freckles. Upon spotting the adults, the girls stopped laughing and tried to pull serious faces. But then Portia let out a little squeal and took short tiptoe steps toward Reni, arms raised high in an invitation to hug.

Reni started to dodge the arms, caught herself, and let the girl hug her. Daniel shot her a wink.

"I'm so glad he's dead," Portia said, obviously meaning Moore. "Like my dad said, none of us have to live in fear now."

Before leaving, Portia and JoJo both leaned over and gave Emerson a kiss on the cheek. Portia whispered something to her, and Emerson, with an odd look on her face, smiled and nodded.

"We'll have a pool party when you feel better!" Portia said as she and JoJo breezed out the door.

Despite being alert now, Emerson's recall of events was patchy. Understandable due to the drugs. She did remember gunshots and screams and running. Being told to get in Johnnie's trunk. A long ride to the desert.

"After we got there, even though it was scary, it was also super boring," she said. "Not a lot happened. I mainly just remember the closet, and the wind, and the dark. And how bright the sun was yesterday when we ran."

"You were drugged," Reni said. "Combine that with light and sensory deprivation, and I'd say you've done remarkably well."

"He really is dead, right?" Emerson asked. "Like Portia and JoJo said?"

Daniel answered a little more bluntly than Reni would have. "Yes."

Emerson's eyes filled with tears. She wiped them away with the back of her hand. "I know he was bad. I'm not crying about him. Well, maybe I am."

"It's a confusing time," Reni said softly. "Don't push yourself or overanalyze right now." Then she asked, "What can you tell us about the photo pins on Moore's shirt?"

"He wore them to remind me that I needed to behave or he'd kill my family."

That's what Reni figured.

"I was afraid he'd kill me, but I was more afraid for them and that he'd maybe even kidnap my little sister." She fell silent, then added, "I was nice to him at the retreat center. I talked and smiled at him. I don't think I'll ever be nice to someone again."

What a shame. Hopefully this hadn't hardened her against all men.

Emerson's parents appeared at the door. Her mother was carrying two shopping bags. She put them on a vacant chair, kissed her daughter, turned to Daniel with tears in her eyes while Emerson's stepfather hovered uncomfortably in the background.

"I should leave," Reni said. This was personal, private, between Daniel and Emerson and her family.

"Stay," Daniel said.

"Yes, stay," Emerson echoed. "I didn't thank you for saving my life." She glanced shyly at Daniel. "Both of you."

The parents chimed in. "Yes, we can never thank you enough."

Daniel had a look of panic on his face. Was this why he'd wanted Reni to be there? To help deflect a possible awkward situation? A teen who thought he was her father.

Stanley glanced at Reni. She could see he was recalling the conversation they'd had outside his house. He had to be relieved that Emerson had been rescued and was alive, but he was clearly still in pain. Daniel had become every bit the hero Stanley could never be, and Reni hoped the girl's stepfather would one day realize it wasn't a competition.

"I'm going to get a cup of coffee," he said, leaving the room. It was obvious to Reni that he simply couldn't be there right now. Once he was gone, Reni redirected her concern to Daniel. He looked ready to drop. She scooted a visitor chair close to him, pointed to the seat. He didn't argue and eased himself down. He was sweating. He should still be in bed.

"Can we hang out sometime?" Emerson asked him, not seeming to notice his physical distress.

Daniel glanced at Rachel, then back at Emerson. He shouldn't have to be the one to clarify Emerson's misconception, but then again maybe she'd believe him, since she'd obviously never believed her mother.

"I'm not your father," he said softly, a level of kindness in his voice that made Reni want to cry.

Emerson pressed her lips together and hung her head as she looked down at the white-knuckled grip she had on the hospital blanket. "I know," she whispered in a heartbreaking voice of final acceptance. "I know."

Rachel stepped closer and squeezed Emerson's arm in an attempt to comfort her. Emerson's reaction shifted from sorrow to anger. Reni could understand the anger to some extent. Rachel had to realize that keeping Emerson's birth father's identity from her daughter had backfired in a big way.

"Then who is?" Emerson asked. "Tell me. I just want you to tell me."

Reni wanted to say that blood wasn't everything, and love and caring could come from many different places. But it wasn't her place to speak platitudes to this child. Any words from her would be an intrusion.

Rachel shot Daniel and Reni an uncomfortable glance. "We'll talk about that soon. I promise."

CHAPTER 36

Daniel spent the days following his hospital release working from home. The news was filled with Emerson's story, and it was hard to go very long without someone knocking on the door hoping for an interview. He'd managed to attend a couple of press conferences, but he was still feeling the effects of the snakebite, or more likely the antivenom. Reni said it could take weeks to feel his normal self. He just had to take it easy and let his body heal.

Sitting in his office, logged into the department database, he heard the doorbell ring. Doubtful it would be press this time of the evening. He heard Bo's footsteps, then low conversation. It became clear from the sound of the closed door and continued low voices that someone was inside. Reni? She'd been checking in frequently, either by text or actual visits.

A moment later, Bo poked his head into the office, a strange expression on his face. "She's here."

Bo's face said it all. Daniel had no doubt who "she" was. Definitely not Reni. His heart started to slam. His breath quickened and his face flushed.

"I can tell her to get the hell out of here and stay away." Steady, calm Bo was shaking. "I'd like to say a lot more to her, I'd like to give her a piece of my mind, and I will with your okay."

From the time an eleven-year-old Daniel had taken the bus to Bo's office, slapped a newspaper about the Inland Empire Killer on his desk, and demanded Bo help find his mother, Bo had been his champion.

He was softer now, older. Daniel stood and put his hand on Bo's shoulder. "*You're* my parent, not the woman out there." He took Bo's hand, squeezed it, feeling the need to reassure him. "I'll talk to her. It'll be okay."

"You sure? Because I can toss her out."

Of course he'd never do that; he'd never manhandle a woman, even Alice, but Daniel appreciated that Bo was still defending and looking out for him. "I'll pass on that offer."

"Do you want me in the room with you?"

Daniel didn't want Bo to become more upset. Not that he was in poor health any longer, but he'd had one heart attack. "I'll talk to her by myself. It'll be fine."

They split up in the hallway, Bo heading toward his bedroom and Daniel for the living room. He felt an odd sense of calm, a blanket of self-preservation.

She was sitting on the couch not far from where Reni had sat when she'd broken the news to him. Wearing a bright dress in shades of turquoise and red. She'd always liked bright colors, especially red. Her hair was the same shade of rich mahogany he remembered. Some feathered lines around her eyes, but she was still beautiful. Seeing her spurred a surge of resentment that lifted some of his protective haze.

He did not sit down. "Black might have been a little more appropriate." His voice was steady. He'd learned how to control it in his job as a detective. Cover up the quake.

"I haven't been able to sleep since I talked to Reni Fisher," she said. "And then I heard the news about you, about how you saved that girl."

Her voice was his undoing. He so easily recognized it, and it made him feel as if he were falling through a tunnel. He'd replayed it in his head a million times over the years as he'd relived his early childhood. Finding comfort in it. Not now. Why was she here? To be forgiven? To step into the spotlight that was now shining on him? He hoped she wasn't that shallow, but who could say?

Her eyes teared up. "I'm sorry, Danny. I'm sorry I left."

Anger flared, along with a fresh feeling of foolishness for the waste of his life and the years of searching for her. The saintly pedestal he'd had her on for so long. She'd been his quest. Her disappearance had shaped him and directed his life from that morning he'd gotten up and found she was gone. Every breath, every decision, had been because of her absence.

"Why?" was the only word he managed. He wanted to hear it from his mother himself.

Agony in her face, she said, "I needed out. I couldn't be a mother."

He'd dealt with people like her in his years as a detective. Mothers who couldn't handle the responsibility. Mothers who wanted a different life, a do-over, without the baggage. *Baggage.*

He was tired. He couldn't deal with this right now. Maybe there would never be a time he could deal with it. "What are you doing here? Do you need a kidney?"

She flinched, then said, "I guess I wanted to explain myself. I wanted to tell you I didn't know you were looking for me. I wanted to make sure you were okay."

"Are you kidding me? Most people can't just turn off the people closest to them and forget they exist."

"I thought about you all the time. Every day. And I thought about coming back, but I'd changed my name. I was a different person by then." She gripped her skirt with both hands, her knuckles white. "And I was ashamed, unworthy of you. I told myself you'd be better off with someone else."

Now he wished he'd told Bo to send her packing. He'd expected to be able to handle this better. Instead, he felt the strong need to get away from her.

He left the room, confused, heading where? He didn't know. The house was small. Definitely too small for the two of them right now. His bedroom? Like some little kid? He wanted to drive away, but he was shaking inside and knew he shouldn't get behind the wheel. He thought about calling Reni, not surprised to find he wanted to reach out to her. He made it to the kitchen and out the side door, where he stood on the step in the dark.

He hadn't thought about having to see Alice again so soon, but moments after standing across from her inside, the front door slammed and she walked across the lawn to a parked car on the curved street. "Nice that I get to actually see you leave this time," he said softly, but loud enough for her to hear.

Without looking at him, she paused, then ran for her car, struggled to open the door, got in, and drove off. But she didn't go far. The sedan came to a stop a few houses down, brake lights on, middle of the street.

He waited. He'd have to crack open a bottle of hard liquor once he was back inside, no glass. Just drink it straight from the bottle. He watched the silver car. Nothing changed. Red brake lights. Palm trees silhouetted, and a moon that was near full hanging in a blue velvet sky. Same everything that had been there days ago, but it was a different world now. His mother was not dead. His mother had not been killed. She'd run away. From him. His biggest resentment might have been how her leaving had stunted him emotionally. Even though he'd become a detective, he was also still the bewildered boy he'd been that morning she'd vanished from his life.

He came to a decision. With purposeful strides, he walked to her car and opened the passenger door, dome light illuminating. Her arms, arms that were no longer youthful and toned, were wrapped around the steering wheel. Her face, a face with creases at the corners of the eyes and mouth, was partially hidden. Her sobs were dangerous and cut deep into his bones. The pain of another living thing, no matter what or who, would always break his heart.

Reckless and ill planned of him to become a detective.

If not for his mother, he probably would have gone into something that didn't involve dead people and having to tell relatives that a loved one was gone. He almost laughed at that thought. How her "death" had made him more compassionate. How he'd relived her disappearance with every homicide.

His hands no longer shook.

He knew how to deal with someone in pain. It was the thing he unwillingly excelled at, thanks to her. With a sigh, he slipped into the car, reached across the seat, and turned off the ignition. For the moment, he would not tell her she'd stunted his child heart and mind and that she deserved every ounce of pain she was feeling. For the moment, he would not talk or tell her he forgave her. For the moment, he would just sit with her.

CHAPTER 37

Emerson got a text from Portia begging her to come to her house in Palm Springs for a sleepover. She didn't know if she was ready for something like that, and she really didn't know if she wanted to hang out with Portia and JoJo. She just wanted to move on, and she was afraid they might want to talk about what happened. She didn't. But she felt like she had to go.

"I think it's a good idea," her mother said from the bedroom doorway. "You can just call me if you want to come home."

Emerson looked up from her phone. Yeah, she had her phone back. Kinda funny when she thought about it. "Maybe it'll be okay. It's not like I'll be hanging out with people who don't understand."

"That's what I'm thinking. It could be good for all of you to talk about it."

Her mom might be right. A classmate had come over yesterday, probably forced by her parents. They'd sat on Emerson's bed, and the girl had wanted to talk about her new boyfriend. Emerson hadn't cared. All she could think about was what had happened out there on the mountain, and later in the desert. None of it seemed real, and she wondered if it ever would. And yet she kept replaying things in her head, especially how it had ended. How Detective Ellis had saved her. Dragged her from the edge of a cliff. It was like a movie, but better. And yeah, they'd told her he wasn't her father. Not the first time she'd heard that, but she wasn't ready to let go of the idea. It had driven her, given her hope.

When the classmate finally left, Emerson had been glad. But it might be nice to be around people who'd been through what she'd been through. Who understood.

"What about my real dad? You said we could talk about it."

"We will. I promise. Stanley and I have discussed it, and it's time you knew everything. But not right now."

"My bio dad isn't like a serial killer or something, is he?" Because why else would it be such a secret?

"No." Her mom smiled. "Absolutely not. But go have fun with your friends tonight, and we'll have a long talk when you get back."

She packed a few things. Cute pajamas her mother had gotten for her. They had bunnies on them. She'd almost cried at the innocence of that image, and how her mom had wrapped them in pretty paper, along with the phone.

Emerson stuffed the pajamas, toothpaste, and toothbrush into her backpack. She also included a swimsuit because Portia said they'd go swimming. She'd actually said *skinny-dip*, but Emerson was bringing a suit anyway. The last item to go in her bag was a black metal ring with sharp cat ears.

Reni's microwave dinged. She opened the door and pulled out a bowl of nachos. The cheese had melted evenly. Always a challenge. The kidnapping case was almost wrapped up, and she was celebrating with her own version of cooking. One positive regarding her mental health—she wasn't itching to paint death scenes quite as often, and she and Edward were going to start search and rescue classes with Nadine once the weather cooled down.

Right now, she had an evening looming before her, but she'd recently purchased not only a TV, but a *smart* TV, which meant she could stream anything she wanted from the middle of the desert. She could even watch things like YouTube. So much to choose from, and now she was into the second season of a show she was really enjoying.

She got a beer from the fridge. With the drink that had been brewed right in Joshua Tree and a bowl of chips, the bowl one of her designs, she sat down on the couch in front of the new TV, one foot tucked under her.

It was still hot out. Almost ninety degrees, not all that unusual for a desert night in early summer. Her swamp cooler was blasting away, too noisy, blowing dirt, stirring her hair. She wondered what Daniel was doing, and thought about giving him a call but didn't want to risk waking him in case he'd gone to bed early. He was still feeling the effects of the snakebite and antivenom. It would take time.

Edward jumped up beside her on the couch, curling against her thigh. She petted him, sweet-talked him a few minutes, then picked up the remote. She'd just aimed it at the TV when she got an alert on her phone letting her know that Portia Devine was live on her YouTube channel. Instead of watching the show she'd planned, Reni navigated through apps to YouTube and Portia's feed.

It looked like the girl was streaming from her bedroom. Makeup like a mask, hair perfect, long purple nails. The kind of fake beauty that was so popular right now. Portia was staring at her screen, watching and reading comments as they came in.

So glad you're okay!
So glad you are alive!
Beautiful as ever.
OMG, I was so worried about you.
Love you!

Portia smoothed her hair and responded to some of the remarks and observations rolling up the screen. She thanked people for donating to her channel, revealing some of the figures in amounts that were astounding, especially considering her viewers must be mainly teens.

"Hi, Jen from Illinois!" Portia said. "I missed you too! And Toby from Santa Barbara! Peace, brother! I want to thank each and every one of you for believing in me and never giving up hope. I want to thank my parents for being cool and never giving up. I want to thank my friends, especially my girl pals who were on the trip with me."

Two faces appeared behind her, JoJo and Emerson. They waved and smiled and group-hugged.

Emerson looked out of place. She wasn't wearing makeup or fancy clothes, and she didn't seem enthused about being filmed. It made Reni wonder if they'd ambushed her into a public show of solidarity for views.

"We've had so many questions, and we're going to try to answer some of them tonight," Portia said. "The big one is, *Were you scared?*"

All three looked at one another, laughed, and turned to the screen, all answering in the affirmative: "Oh my God, yes!"

JoJo: "But it also seemed like a movie. It didn't seem real. I kept thinking it couldn't really be happening."

Portia: "Or that it was a sick joke somebody was playing."

Emerson: "I knew it was real when I heard the gunshots."

"Oh, I'm so sorry." Portia hugged her and looked into the camera. "Emerson is a school shooting survivor."

Hearts and hugs filled the chat window on the side of Reni's screen as viewers reached out with sympathy. The girls talked more, answered questions, more sympathy donations came in. Then Portia began to wrap up. "We're going to go for a swim." She aimed the camera so the viewers could see out the patio doors that led from the bedroom to the pool. Then she turned it back around, the camera panning the room. Emerson had moved and was sitting on the bed brushing her hair, an odd expression on her face. The hand that held the brush kept giving Reni tantalizing glimpses of a ring. Black, with what looked like two points . . .

If Reni were to paint Emerson, she'd note a blankness in the eyes that only appeared on occasion, and only fleetingly, and could very well be a simple trick of the light. But like a photo, a painting stopped the inhale and exhale, stopped the blink, stopped the quick smile, the nervous gesture that could often divert attention from the eyes. Unlike a photo, a painting allowed for an expansion and an artist interpretation that didn't always exist in a photo. Like most art, the artist brought herself to the journey. All good art came from that place. The blankness could be Reni herself. But she hoped not. She'd also paint the shine of Emerson's hair, her golden skin, the top lip that curved and was probably thinner than Emerson would have liked, but beautiful nonetheless. The thick black eyebrows. But most of all Reni would try to capture that hint of something wrong, something off, something hidden, something secret, something she might not want anybody else to see. And in this acknowledgment, Reni saw what she should have seen much earlier.

Reni had been a profiler. She'd taught the skills it took to recognize evil. But deep down, she wanted people to be good, to be more than they were. And she could admit that even though she'd been a decent instructor, she'd had bad radar when it came to people she liked. And people she loved. It wasn't until she looked in the rearview mirror and spotted their faces behind her seat that the ugliness became apparent.

She was a decent detective. And she was good at finding missing people. Very good. There was at least that. No reason to despair and mentally wring her hands. Daniel hadn't seen it either. The mother hadn't seen it.

Just a sweet girl.

Lost girl.

Good girl, with a big secret.

Reni called the digital forensics tech at the sheriff's office who was working on the security footage from Kaleidoscope.

"How's that going?" she asked.

"Case is closed, right? I put it aside."

239

"The case *is* closed, but I'm trying to tie up a few loose ends. Especially the footage at the security door. I'd like to have a firm ID of that person."

"No problem. I was actually working on it when I got notice that the case was closed. Then I was sent a new project that's the most boring time-suck I've ever seen. Give me a sec, and I'll log into the database."

She heard the clatter of keyboard keys.

"I was able to clean up the image and remove the window glare. I'm sending it right now. Check your computer, and let me know if you don't get it."

She thanked him and hung up. Then she opened her laptop and clicked on the email.

Two JPEGs. And now she had another surprise.

He'd done a good job. So good that nobody would dispute the faces on the screen. Both the person standing outside the emergency exit, Johnnie May Moore, and the reflection of the person inside. The girl who'd been handed a phone.

She tried to call Daniel. He didn't answer. She sent him a text. Then she called Emerson's mom and told her to meet her at the Devine residence.

"Why?"

"Just meet me there."

CHAPTER 38

Thirty minutes after he'd joined his mother in her car, Daniel checked a text from Reni.

I'm heading to Portia Devine's house. Meet me there if you can. Something isn't right.

"I'm going to have to go," he told Alice.

"Do you want me to contact you again? Ever? I wouldn't blame you if you didn't, but I'd like to see you again."

"Give me your phone."

She did.

He entered his cell number and passed the phone back. "Call or text me anytime." He opened the door slightly and the dome light illuminated. His heart crashed. She was still his mother. He still loved her. He almost wished he didn't. He wished he could hate her, but that wasn't who he was. He forgave. Even with criminals, he tried not to think of them as bad, but as humans who'd made horrible choices.

"Goodbye," he said, getting out, closing the door.

She started the car and pulled from the curb. He watched until the taillights disappeared, then he returned to the house, tried to call Reni, got her voicemail. In his office, he grabbed his badge, poked his head in Bo's room. He was in bed watching television.

"I've got to head out."

Bo muted the show. "Homicide?"

It made sense he'd think so. Daniel never did anything at night other than his job. "Just something that maybe shouldn't wait until morning."

"I'm really sorry about your mother, kid."

"She's not dead." He shrugged. "That's good."

"I guess. You're more generous than I am. Be careful. Don't let her visit distract you."

"I won't." He left by the kitchen door, locking it behind him. Then he headed for Palm Springs and the Devine house.

CHAPTER 39

"Come on!" Portia was in the pool treading water. "Take off your dress and jump in! Nobody will see you."

Emerson had already told them she wasn't going to swim naked, but Portia didn't believe her and kept pushing for clothes off. "What about your parents?" Emerson asked.

"My dad is driving back from Hollywood, and my mom is watching television in her bedroom. And look." Portia waved a hand at the solid wooden fence surrounding a backyard that looked like a movie set. Everything perfect, with more than one pool, each with a different water temperature, fountains that gurgled gently, palm trees silhouetted against blue-black sky. "Nobody can see you." She'd already turned off the outdoor and underwater lights. The only illumination came from the house, and it wasn't much.

JoJo removed her bra and panties, screamed, and jumped in, water splashing.

Without comment, Emerson turned and walked back to Portia's bedroom. She thought about calling her mom and asking her to pick her up like they'd talked about. But it was a long drive, and she'd probably just gotten back home.

In the bathroom, Emerson put on her swimsuit. It was black, one-piece, gathered a little in front, and it had a skirt. It looked like something from the fifties, which was why she loved it. Most people didn't know about her scar and didn't know she'd been shot during the school shooting. She didn't want people to make a big deal out of it. But that wasn't why she didn't want to skinny-dip. Being naked around people she didn't know very well would make her feel too vulnerable. What if she needed to run? Or fight for her life? A person had to be prepared. Always.

From her makeup bag on the counter, she pulled out a stretch band and tied up her hair. She checked her face, dug into her bag, found her red Hollywood glam lipstick, and applied it.

She pulled off the cat ring. The girls had made fun of her earlier for wearing it.

Why do you need a defense ring here?

She paused and put it back on.

She grabbed a fluffy towel, tossed it over her shoulder, and walked barefoot back through the open patio doors to the pool area, where the girls were splashing and laughing.

"Not fair," Portia said when she saw Emerson. "Can't get in unless you take off your clothes." And true to her style-conscious mind, added, "Awesome suit, though. Not anything I'd wear, not sexy enough, but cute."

Again with no response, Emerson waded into the shallow end of the pool. Even the steps were elegant, four in all. When she reached the bottom, water hit waist-high. The night was pretty, and with the lights off, she could see a lot of stars. Maybe even Venus. And a little of the Milky Way. There was enough of a moon to reflect off the water and make the girls' faces recognizable.

"I'm not a great swimmer," she said.

"I've got something for that." Portia swam to the side. With a gush of water, she got out, padded away, and returned from a cabana with three small rafts she tossed in the water, jumping in after them. Portia and JoJo launched themselves onto their rafts with the ease of people who'd grown up swimming almost daily. Emerson hadn't been a part of any pool scene. She knew how to swim, but even when her family was enjoying their pool, she preferred to stay inside and read.

It took some awkward tries, but she finally got onto her raft. The girls were on their backs, but Emerson chose to lie facedown, using her hands to paddle like someone on a surfboard.

"So your dad's a cop," Portia said.

On the mountain around the campfire, she'd told them about Detective Ellis being her father. So far, she hadn't told them he wasn't. Maybe she never would. This didn't look like a lasting friendship. These were not her people. "He's my biological father, but I don't really know him," she said. She decided to continue to pretend with them. What did it matter? "We might start hanging out a little."

"He's working on the kidnapping case, right?"

"He said he has to tie up some loose ends, but I think he's almost done."

"What about us?"

"What do you mean?"

"Like, are you going to say anything?"

"There's nothing to say. Johnnie killed Janet and kidnapped me."

"Have you ever heard of being an accessory to a crime?"

"Yeah, but—"

"That's what we are. I looked it up, and we can go to prison for a long time."

"I won't say anything. There's no need to. It's over. Johnnie's dead."

"Your dad is a cop. He knows how to get information from people," Portia said.

JoJo joined in. Sometimes they almost seemed like one person, but Portia was definitely the leader.

"He'll do it and you won't even know," JoJo said. "Like, you'll just be talking and he'll ask you questions. And before you know it, he'll be knocking on our door to arrest us."

"Maybe I should tell him the truth," Emerson said. "We didn't mean for it to happen the way it happened."

"That's the worst idea ever," JoJo said.

245

"And it's what we were afraid you might do," Portia said.

An invisible bird called from a palm tree. *What kind of bird is awake at night?* Emerson wondered. But she'd heard that city birds got confused and didn't have normal sleep cycles.

Portia rolled off her raft, grabbed Emerson's, and tugged one side, flipping Emerson with so much force that she shot deep into the water.

It was dark and black and hard to tell up from down. She flailed, finally surfaced, gulped for air, swallowed water, choked, started to dog-paddle toward the edge of the pool. She felt a hand on her arm. She grabbed at it. Instead of helping, the hand pulled her deeper, toward the bottom of the pool.

CHAPTER 40

Two weeks earlier, Pacific Crest Trail

So. Much. Blood.

The smell of it filled the tent. A camp lamp glowed, almost too bright for the space, washing out the dark corners and illuminating the tent walls. The guy from Kaleidoscope, Johnnie Moore, stood over the body, a gun in his hand. Panting, eyes glowing, mouth grinning as he turned to look at Emerson. Behind her were the two other girls.

What have we done? Emerson asked herself.

Yes, she was guilty. She'd flirted with him even though he'd put off a bad vibe. Used him as Portia and JoJo had suggested. All of them had been furious about having their phones taken and about being locked up at the center—for doing nothing. Portia and JoJo had wanted to be kidnapped, fake kidnapped, for more likes on their YouTube channels. It would be recorded, and they'd put it up on the internet.

Nobody was supposed to die. Nobody was supposed to be killed.

Emerson had wanted her dad, her biological dad, to see she was in danger and come rescue her, like before. The school shooting rescue had been unsatisfying because he hadn't hung around. He'd passed her to the people in the ambulance and vanished. But that's what superheroes did until you needed them again. Flew away, then came back.

Everything got blurry and crazy. They scrambled away from the tent. All of them ran through the darkness and the trees, feet pounding, lungs burning, branches crashing, Emerson's brain screaming, her mind trying to grapple with what she'd seen when she'd looked inside Janet's tent.

And the killer ran with them.

Finally, after what seemed like a long time, they had to stop. Bent over, panting. Portia started laughing, but it wasn't real laughter. More like hysteria. In a movie, somebody would slap her, and she'd shut up.

"I'm going back," Emerson said.

All three shouted, "No!"

"I have to see if she's okay."

"She's not okay," Moore said.

"We have to go back. This is not what we talked about."

She'd known he might bring a gun, but it was only supposed to be used to scare Janet. Just *scare* her.

"Did you get a video?" Portia asked.

"I sure as hell did not," Moore said.

"Oh my God!" Emerson said to Portia. "Is that all you care about?" She was evil. "We have to go back. I'm going back." Emerson started walking.

Moore followed, grabbed her arm. "I did this for you. I killed her for you."

"And we're all complicit," Portia said.

Emerson was surprised Portia even knew what *complicit* meant.

"*All* of us," Portia said. "If we don't go through with this, make it look like a real kidnapping, we'll go to a real prison."

Emerson wasn't sure about that.

"I don't care about you two bitches," Moore said. "I don't care if you get caught. If anybody arrests me, I'll tell them it was all your idea. I'll tell them you bought the burner phone and you hired me to kill that woman in the tent. Because you did."

"Is that true?" Emerson asked. Had Portia and JoJo planned to kill Janet all along?

"I said I didn't care, and the more dangerous the better," Portia said in a flippant voice.

"You told me to kill her," he said.

Somebody was lying, and Emerson was afraid it wasn't Moore. That's how screwed up social media was. Likes were more important than a life.

"She's right," Portia said. "We have to go back. We need to make sure she's dead, and we need to make sure there's nothing left behind. We need to stage the scene. That's what it's called." She glanced at Moore. "So nobody will suspect us."

"I'm not going."

That was from JoJo. Then she did something very risky. She ran.

Moore pulled his gun from a holster he wore like a gunslinger and fired after her. Emerson and Portia screamed. Emerson dropped to the ground, covering her head, her heart pounding. *This isn't real. This isn't happening.*

No sound from JoJo.

"Dumb bitch," Johnnie said.

Nearby, Portia was sobbing. The kind of sobbing that Emerson remembered hearing years ago during the school shooting.

"Shut up! You want to run too?" he shouted. "You want to go after your friend?"

Emerson peeked from under her arm. He was waving the gun wildly at Portia. "Run, bitch! Run!"

"Don't shoot her!" Emerson cried.

Her plea worked as a distraction. He turned.

Portia ran.

He shot into the dark again.

Emerson flinched and screamed, covering her head for a second time. She could hear Portia moving through the trees, screaming the whole way, the sound eventually fading. Moore fired again, and Portia stopped screaming.

Then it was just Emerson, alone with him.

"She was right about the campsite," Moore said. "I forgot to pick up my casings." He grabbed her arm and pushed her in front of him.

They walked, the gun sometimes pressed to the back of her head. She kept stumbling. That made him mad. She was so cold, shivering. Walking, walking, walking. "Are we l-l-lost?" she finally asked through chattering teeth.

"I hate nature," he muttered without answering her question.

She didn't mention that he should have brought a compass and more light.

"We're going to have to wait till morning," he finally admitted.

So they did. They sat on the ground and waited.

At one point, Emerson pulled her knees to her chest and hugged herself. She kept thinking about Portia and JoJo and how they seemed to have had a plan of their own that she hadn't even known about. And she'd helped them. And now Janet was probably dead. And maybe Portia and JoJo were dead too.

"What do you want?" she asked. "Why are you doing this?"

"I'm doing it for you."

"I don't understand."

"I rescued you. You asked for help and I rescued you."

"I don't know what you're talking about. We wanted you to pretend. This was supposed to be fake."

"I'm not talking about that. I'm talking about in the dining room, when I got you water. You asked for my help."

"I didn't."

"You did. Not with words, but I could tell that's what you were thinking, asking."

He was delusional, crazy. Would he kill her too? Would she never see her family again? "Have you ever done this before?"

"You're my first and only."

"Why me?"

"Girls usually hate me. You didn't. You were nice to me. And then you started talking about your stepfather, and I could see he was a bad man."

"He's not." Stanley had always been good to her, even when she screamed at him, saying he wasn't her real father.

"I could see you needed me," Moore said. "Here. Listen to this."

He pulled out his phone and played an audio clip. It was of a man answering the phone. The voice was one she recognized, the sound of it making her want to cry.

"That's my stepfather."

"Indeed it is. I pretended to be doing a county survey, and we had a nice chat about some current environmental issues in California."

She started crying for real, talking while she sobbed. But eventually she came to a decision and jumped to her feet. "I'm leaving."

"If you leave, I'll kill him. I'll kill your whole family. And you know I won't have any problem doing that."

He wouldn't. She could even imagine him parking outside her house and knocking them off one at a time like he'd just done to Portia and JoJo.

She sat back down and managed to stay awake the rest of the night, waiting for him to fall asleep. When he finally did, she adjusted her ring and charged him, aiming at his neck, hoping to hit his jugular vein. But he hadn't really been asleep. He kicked her and kept kicking her. When he finally stopped, he grabbed her hand and twisted it so he could see the ring.

"What's this?" He pulled it from her finger and put it on his.

"It's what I use to kill assholes."

"I guess we'll have to find some assholes."

She didn't want to display weakness, but she hurt all over from his kicks, and she'd used her only plan.

He didn't tie her up. He didn't have to. He would just pull out his gun and shoot her if she tried to get away.

251

At dawn, they were able to find the trail and head back in the direction of the campsite. She hoped to find Janet gone. Like maybe she hadn't been that hurt, and she'd gotten up and run for help.

Now that it was light, birds were singing and singing and singing. So happy. Was it the same bird? Laughing at her now? Was it the same wind, almost knocking her down? Her teacher, the one who'd been killed in the school shooting, had once told the class about a kind of bird that never touched land. Was that right? Could that be right? That they were born in a high nest and flew away, into the sky, and they slept up there on the wind and ate up there and dreamed up there. Was that true? Could it be true? She liked to think of it whenever she was scared. Birds sleeping in the sky.

They turned a corner. Moore stopped and she almost ran into him. Two hikers were coming their way, heading straight for them. The hiker in front stopped and clung to the shoulder straps of his pack. He was wearing an orange-and-green flannel shirt and had dark-blond hair pulled back in a ponytail.

"Whatever you do, don't go that direction." The hiker jerked his thumb the way he'd come. "We found a dead body."

Moore stiffened. "Thanks for the tip."

A dead person. Janet didn't get away. What if they'd been able to call 911 immediately? Would she still be alive?

Moore pulled the handgun from his waistband.

Emerson screamed. "Run!" She felt the blood rush into her face, felt the veins pop out on her neck, saw the guy's startled face. "Run!"

Moore fired.

Now that it was light, unlike last night, she could see he'd hit his target. The guy dropped, then fell forward on his face. Moore proceeded to do the same to the other hiker, a woman. And Emerson just turned her back to it all and thought about her family and the birds that slept on the wind.

The gunshots finally stopped. "Get over here."

She turned. Moore pointed. "Help me push these over the cliff."

Like a robot, she did what she was told. She helped, because what other choice did she have? As they worked, she tried not to look at the faces. They got rid of the girl first, then came the guy in the orange-and-green shirt. Moore tugged at his ankles, and she grabbed the arms. She didn't mean to, she tried not to, but she glanced down at the face.

He blinked.

Her eyes widened. She spotted his broken sunglasses on the ground. She grabbed them and stuck them on his face, hiding his eyes. Then she and Moore pushed him over the side.

"We must be going the right way," Moore said cheerfully as he wiped his bloody hands on his sweatshirt.

At the camp, Emerson looked in Janet's tent, hoping to see some sign of movement like she'd seen on the hiker. But flies were already crawling around Janet's eyes and up her nose. She was dead. Very dead.

Moore searched, finding the two gun casings left on the ground where he'd fired his weapon. Then he took Janet's bracelet and put it on. After that, he pierced her with Emerson's self-defense ring. "To make people think it's vampires." He laughed at that. "People love vampires."

CHAPTER 41

On her way to Palm Springs, Reni's phone rang. It was Daniel, calling to tell her he'd gotten her message and was heading to the Devine house. He gave her his ETA, which was close to hers.

"You gonna tell me what's going on?" he asked.

"I'm afraid this case might not be over." Before she could expand on that comment, she hit an area of the Morongo grade where there was no cell service. Conversation over.

Fifteen minutes later, she arrived at the guard booth perched on the edge of the Devine property, where she supplied her driver's license. The guy at the window made a call, then told her to have a good night, and activated the lift gate.

When Reni reached the house, Gwen Devine, dressed in pink sweats, hair wet, was already waiting at the door. Her face was clean and shiny, free of makeup, and she was still beautiful. Maybe more beautiful without.

"Where are the girls?" Reni asked as Daniel's SUV pulled in behind her truck. He jumped out and quickly joined her at the door.

"In the pool," Gwen said, confused, looking from one person to the other. "What's going on?"

Reni didn't have an answer to that question, because she wasn't sure herself. "I just need to talk to them. It could be urgent."

They followed Gwen through the house. Past a shelf of Oscar trophies and a wall of photos of Phillip Devine posing with other famous actors. Also photos of him with presidents and dignitaries. A wall of glass off the kitchen. Beyond that, darkness.

"The lights are off," Gwen said. "They're probably skinny-dipping."

"Turn them on," Reni said.

"I don't feel comfortable doing that."

"Well, then . . ." Reni looked around, spotted a set of controls near the french doors. Using her palm, she flipped all of the switches at once. Outdoor lights flooded the patio area.

Gwen let out a little cry and put a hand to her mouth.

The water in the pool was churning. It looked like a shark feeding-frenzy.

Without pause, Reni opened a door and ran outside, Daniel behind her. A boy of about twelve stood next to the pool watching the struggling girls. They all seemed to be fighting to stay alive. Hands appeared above the water. Mouths gasped for air. Faces vanished and reappeared.

The kid began babbling. "I heard a scream, and I came out to see what was going on. I know I'm not supposed to be out here when they're swimming naked." He put one hand behind his back like he was hiding something.

"Turn on the pool lights," Daniel shouted.

In unison, Reni and Daniel pulled and kicked off boots and shoes, both running for the water. Reni dove in while Daniel jumped feet first. The lights came on, banishing some of the darkness from the water. Reni swam toward the mass of bodies in the deep end, striking out with long strokes, scissor-kicking for an extra boost. Daniel was nearby, not moving as fast.

Both of them were vulnerable. Every water-safety class highlighted the importance of remaining out of the water for a rescue if at all possible. Getting in was a last resort—a flailing person could take you down, climb on your head, drown you in order to save themselves.

Reni executed a surface dive, going deep. She managed to grab someone, anyone, in the churn. She tugged at an arm, then tugged again, freeing one of the girls from the underwater fight and swimming away with her. Upon breaking the surface, she glimpsed blond hair. Portia.

Daniel had another girl, his arm cupping her chin to keep her face out of the water as he sidestroked for the edge of the pool. Gwen tossed him a life preserver. He grabbed it. With Gwen's help, he got JoJo out of the water.

"Emerson is still in there!" Gwen pointed to a dark, motionless shape at the bottom of the deep end.

CHAPTER 42

Reni dove again, using rapid strokes to reach Emerson. She grabbed the back of the girl's suit, bent her knees and planted her feet against the bottom of the pool, and shoved hard, propelling herself upward. They shot through the water and surfaced.

Daniel tossed the preserver. Reni caught it. He pulled her to the shallow end, then jumped in to help. Together they dragged and lifted Emerson's limp body from the water and laid her out on the concrete. Reni leaned over her, braced to begin CPR, when Emerson coughed. Daniel rolled the girl to her side, and water poured from her mouth. Portia and JoJo stood nearby, swathed in large white towels. JoJo was crying. Emerson sat up, still coughing as Gwen draped a towel around her shoulders.

Daniel looked at the two girls standing there. "Who wants to tell us what's going on?"

"Everything was Emerson's idea," Portia said. Her makeup wasn't perfect now. Thick trails of mascara and eyeliner were running down her cheeks, dripping onto her shoulders and the giant towel.

"Really?" Emerson was still trying to catch her breath. "They just tried to kill me."

"Oh my God!" Portia said. "You're such a liar! She knocked us off our rafts and tried to drown us. She's a total psycho!"

"Don't say anything else," Gwen warned them. Then, to Reni and Daniel: "I don't know what's happening, but you need to leave. We're getting a lawyer." She pulled out her phone, looked at the screen, then announced, "Phillip is here."

Reni grabbed a couple of towels and handed one to Daniel.

"I'll tell you what happened," Emerson said, still trying to catch her breath but defiant at the same time. "I'll tell you everything. We planned a kidnapping. All three of us." She inhaled, coughed, continued. "It was our idea, and Johnnie helped us. I didn't think anybody was going to be killed, but Portia didn't care if Janet died. I think it was part of her plan."

"She's lying!" Portia screamed.

"Quiet!" her mother warned again, prepared to defend her child no matter what.

But Reni knew the truth, at least part of it. The cleaned-up security footage had shown Portia standing at that fire door.

She thought about how many parents never really saw their own children. And you could say that went both ways. Reni had never seen her parents as evil. But this might be a situation of parental denial. The psychology of it was interesting. It might not have been that they couldn't handle the truth as much as they couldn't handle the fear of acknowledging the truth. But you couldn't make something go away by denying its existence.

"She tried to stab me with her stupid ring!" Portia lifted her arm to reveal two puncture wounds.

"Janet had puncture wounds just like that," Reni noted.

"Johnnie used my ring to stab Janet," Emerson told her. "He said it would look like vampire bites. He kept the ring, but Stanley got me a new one."

"She lies about everything," Portia said. "She lies all the time. She keeps telling us you're her dad. Who lies about something like that? Only somebody who lies about everything. I had nothing to do with any of this."

"Stop it! All of you!"

Everybody turned to see Rachel and Stanley Rose standing near the open patio doors, Phillip Devine behind them. The shout had come from Rachel.

"Emerson is telling the truth," she said. "About everything." With anguish in her face, she looked at her daughter. "I'm so sorry. I didn't want you to find out like this. I was going to tell you when you got home."

"Everything?" Emerson glanced at Daniel, then back at her mother.

"Yes." Rachel's admission was stated quietly, with the kind of flat tone that went with revealing something painfully unbearable. It didn't seem she could bring herself to say the actual words, but they all understood the unspoken. And now that Rachel had revealed the secret she'd been carrying for all of Emerson's life, she continued to unload. "I'm the liar," she said. "I lied about your date of birth." She looked at Daniel. Her face changed, softened, became pleading. "I didn't think you deserved to know. Because, well, I won't go into that here."

Not the place to bare everything, but it was easy to guess. Daniel hadn't been into the idea of kids, and Rachel had been pregnant.

"But I wanted to tell you the other day when you came to the house," Rachel continued. "And when Emerson got older, I wanted to tell her." She looked at her daughter again. "Tell you, but so much time had passed. It had gone on so long it seemed easier to not say anything. To continue the lie that didn't seem like a lie anymore."

Stanley buried his face in his hands, his shoulders shaking, a sob escaping him.

Emerson got to her feet and walked over to her stepfather and put her arms around him. "You're my dad," she said. "You'll always be my dad. I just wanted to know. I just wanted the truth. That's all."

Maybe Rachel hadn't kept everybody in the dark. Had Stanley always known? He was the only one who didn't seem surprised, just heartbroken. And it explained why he'd been so threatened by Daniel, who looked stunned, but was remaining wisely quiet. This was not his time to intrude. Despite what they'd all just learned, he was not part of their family. This strange and unexpected turn of events would undoubtedly take him time to process.

"I'm no hero," Stanley said.

"That's not true," Emerson said. "You've always been there for me." She was crying a little, but exhibiting self-control. "You taught me to ride a bike. You taught me how to drive. You helped me with my science projects. You took me to the doctor when I was sick, and you didn't get mad that time in grade school when I vomited on you."

Heroes took many forms. A quiet hero who was kind and always there could never be discounted.

The silence was abruptly broken.

"What are you *doing*?" Portia shrieked.

All eyes shifted from Portia to the direction she was looking— which happened to be at the smartphone in her brother's hand.

"You better not be recording this!" she screamed.

The boy smiled smugly. "I am. I'm gonna have more views than you! And I hope you go to jail and I get your room."

Portia shrieked again.

CHAPTER 43

Reni gently rolled the plump brush across the porous paper, watching the dark-blue shade bloom and spread, the edge of the color bleeding from dark to light as the pulp reacted and partook in the application. Paper was every bit as important as paint. And the correct amount of water almost as important as the paper.

The eight-by-ten piece had been removed from her tablet and taped to the wooden painting board braced against her knees. She taped when she was really serious about what she was doing.

Two weeks had passed since the revelation at the Devine house. The girls were all being held in juvenile jail in San Bernardino, where they awaited trial. Portia seemed to be the guiltiest, but people loved their celebrities, so she might end up with the shortest sentence. JoJo seemed like a follower who'd gotten in too deep. Emerson . . . It was hard to say. The hiker, Jordan Rice, had backed up her story once he was able to share what had happened. Emerson might have saved his life. Yes, she'd helped push him over the cliff, but she'd seen that he was alive and had hidden it from Moore. Stanley had confirmed that he had indeed supplied Emerson with a new self-defense ring.

And Reni was back to painting desert landscapes, not burial scenes, Edward lying at her feet in the shade of the white umbrella she'd brought for him. He was awake, watchful, but relaxed. Just chilling. She hoped Edward did well enough in his search and rescue classes for them both to join Nadine Clark's team, and Reni was planning for him to hike the PCT with her. Right now, he seemed to be enjoying the sound of birds coming from the nearby cholla cactus featured in her painting. The birdsong was so blissfully happy that it almost seemed part of an old-timey cartoon. Most likely wrens with a nest of hungry babies.

Chollas made excellent places for birds to hide because most logical creatures preferred to avoid the needles—nasty things that resulted in the chollas' nickname of "jumping cholla." They didn't really jump to attach themselves to people, but they were so good at grabbing hold at the slightest disturbance by the casual passerby that it seemed that way. They had a plan, and that plan was to attach, dig in, stay there. They were only upstaged by the occasional wait-a-minute bush, also known for grabbing someone and not letting go. Such a great nickname, because that's exactly what it did. Pulled a person right back until they could untangle themselves.

Not long ago, after coming across the napkin drawing she'd stuffed into the back pocket of a pair of jeans, Reni had followed up on the breakfast date that had been interrupted by Daniel's text and call. Greil had wanted to pick up where they'd left off, but she told him she didn't think she was ready to see anyone. He was disappointed, but he understood. She hoped he found somebody, because he seemed like a nice guy.

She dipped her brush in the tin can, tapped off the water, wiped a firm edge, and was ready to choose a shade for an agave plant when she got a text.

It was from Daniel.

Not again, she thought.

I'm going to need your help.

Was she ready to deal with this?

She looked up from her phone.

Daniel waved.

He was about twenty feet away, sitting on a blanket he'd spread on an elevated piece of ground. Painting. He was dressed in jeans and a light-gray T-shirt, leather hiking boots. As always, he looked a little out of his element not wearing a suit. But maybe that was just because he'd been wearing one the first time they met, when he'd shown up at her cabin uninvited and unannounced.

He seemed to be doing okay, all things considered. He'd spoken to his mother on the phone and had visited Emerson in jail. He didn't seem to hold Rachel's lie against her. In fact, now that Reni knew the full story, she kind of understood why a young mother would have done such a thing. At the time, she'd been looking out for her child and herself. But good lies had a way of turning into bad lies as time passed. And yet Reni wouldn't have been so forgiving as Daniel, especially concerning his mother.

Both Alice and Emerson seemed repentant, but one never knew if their behavior had been an anomaly, driven by fear and despair, or something embedded in their DNA to be repeated. It would take care, caution, and time to figure out all the players and decide if they deserved to be a part of his life. Reni didn't want to see him hurt again.

Daniel studied his work. "I don't think this is how this should be going."

She walked over and stood behind him. Hands on her hips, she surveyed his first attempt at painting.

It wasn't bad for something abstract, but maybe he wasn't going for that. Bright colors, very little bleed. "It's the wind," she told him. "It's drying the paper too quickly, which is why a lot of people don't like to use watercolors out here."

He squinted up at her. "But you enjoy the challenge, is that it?"

"And I like how it can't be fixed. It is what it is."

"I like to fix things I screw up."

She sat down beside him on the blanket. Edward seemed to realize she wasn't returning soon. He got up and moseyed over.

They weren't painting a murder scene. She was done with those. Hopefully. This was a view she'd always loved, looking west from Joshua Tree National Park in a section called Indian Cove. The monsoon season had brought an unusual amount of rain, awakening plants until so many were in bloom it almost seemed like spring again.

When you lived in the desert, it was often easy to forget the good months. The months of magical and riotous flowers. Reni always had to remind herself that the barrenness was temporary. But when you were in the middle of it, it could feel permanent and endless and inescapable. Now she marveled at how the terrain appeared to have been perfectly landscaped by a human hand. The different blooming plants seemed to have been arranged by size and shape, flowers clustered together in mounds of color, the desert senna almost orange, crowded next to larger shrubs of deep-purple Mojave indigo. Sun going down, a pastel blush to the sky. And something that smelled amazing. Woody and sweet, maybe coming from blooms so small a person needed a magnifying glass to see them. The rock under her was still warm from the sun, the air a cool breeze. All senses stirred, all senses soothed.

She felt something here. In this particular spot. Felt it from the top of her head to her toes. Almost like having finally eaten an edible from Edward's pet sitter, but she hadn't. This was just right. In the moment, inexplicable inner peace came over her and let her know that everything might not be perfect, but it might be okay. And there would still be these moments when the world embraced and sheltered her.

Daniel put his painting aside and leaned back on his elbows, ankles crossed. "It's really peaceful out here."

They enjoyed it in silence for a few minutes. Then she asked, "Ocean or desert?" He was an ocean guy, but she was always trying to convert him.

He smiled at her, then turned back to the pink sky. "Still ocean," he said with wry conviction. "You? Although I know what you're going to say."

"Desert. Of course. But I'd like to see more of the California you love."

"Let's make that happen."

"Soon."

"And bring Edward."

"Of course."

He rolled closer, took her hand, looked up at her as if he wanted to say something but wasn't sure if she'd want to hear it. She wasn't sure either. She hadn't forgotten what he'd said about being lost without her.

A burst of wind came out of nowhere, almost gale force. It attacked the pages of her watercolor tablet, ruffling them like a deck of cards. A gust tipped over water containers and ripped the hat from her head. It grabbed Edward's white umbrella and carried it high to toss it into a swirling mini tornado that grew bigger as they watched. The circling, funneling wind picked up debris, ripped up cacti, and lifted sand and small pebbles.

They jumped to their feet and staggered from the force, braced themselves. Reni grabbed Edward and held him against her chest, her hair and clothes whipping and stinging. At one point, it felt like the air was being sucked from her lungs. She closed her eyes and waited for it to pass.

It finally did, to leave them standing side by side on the rock, watching the tornado move across the valley floor, continuing to rip up plants and lift dirt. And then it just collapsed. The dirt dissipated as if it had never happened, leaving a faint cloud.

"Edward's umbrella." Daniel pointed. It lay mangled in the distance.

"A small casualty," she said.

"What the hell *was* that?"

"Dirt devil."

"I guess I'm honored." Then he repeated her earlier question with a smile in his voice. "Ocean or desert?"

"Still desert."

He took her hand again, gave it a squeeze. Then, with the sun reflected in his eyes, he brought her fingers to his lips while watching her mischievously.

So strange how a person's mind could hide the truth. Her mind should have known what she truly wanted, what she truly thought. It seemed like seeing the truth should be one of the mind's easier jobs. Apparently not. It hadn't been the case for Daniel and his quest for his mother. Not for Reni and how blind she'd been to the people closest to her. And mothers who didn't realize their daughters were capable of plotting murder. Maybe the mind protected a person from everything that might hurt. Even love.

"It's a perfect evening," she said. He was still holding her hand. "Even with the wind."

He smiled. "Especially with the wind."

AUTHOR'S NOTE

What a year. *Tell Me* was a very strange book to write. I'd just arrived in California for location research when the pandemic hit. The governor's safe-at-home order put an end to my research plans. When it became apparent the pandemic wasn't going anywhere, I revised the book's plot and changed the setting from an area I'd never been to my safe-at-home location, the Mojave Desert, more specifically a little unincorporated town near Joshua Tree. Not a terrible place to be stuck, but odd how, out of necessity, my real-life location became the location of the book.

The desert is a magical and wonderful place, but it's also a place in peril. With that in mind, I'd like to direct your attention to the work being done by two wonderful organizations: Mojave Desert Land Trust and the Center for Biological Diversity. Please do check them out and consider supporting their conservation efforts. I'll also include some other deserving organizations of note: Theodore Payne Foundation, California Native Plant Society, Joshua Tree National Park, Joshua Tree National Park Association, Leave No Trace Center for Outdoor Ethics, Joshua Tree National Park Search & Rescue (JOSAR), San Bernardino County Sheriff's Search and Rescue, Search and Rescue Dogs of the United States. Check out their websites and consider supporting one or more of them! And, as always, thank you for reading!

~Anne

ACKNOWLEDGMENTS

I'd like to thank the state of California for legalizing recreational marijuana. Edibles helped get me through the lockdown, but alas, they weren't much help when it came to writing this book. I'd especially like to thank my daughter, Martha, for all of her assistance, going above and beyond in an abnormal situation, hauling supplies to my remote writing location, a place where there was no mail, no UPS, and no Amazon. Did my year of simple living result in deep reflection and personal growth? Nope. It was just about getting through each day, and I applaud everyone for doing the same. I wish you peace, love, and healing.

ABOUT THE AUTHOR

Photo © 2018 Martha Weir

Anne Frasier is the *New York Times*, #1 Amazon Charts, and *USA Today* bestselling author of the Detective Jude Fontaine Mysteries, the Elise Sandburg Series, and the Inland Empire Thrillers. With more than a million copies sold, her award-winning books span the genres of suspense, mystery, thriller, romantic suspense, paranormal, and memoir. *The Body Reader* received the 2017 Thriller Award for Best Paperback Original from International Thriller Writers. Other honors include a RITA for romantic suspense and a Daphne du Maurier Award for paranormal romance. Her thrillers have hit the *USA Today* bestseller list and have been featured in the Mystery Guild, Literary Guild, and Book of the Month Club. Her memoir *The Orchard*, which earned a B+ review in *Entertainment Weekly*, was an *O, The Oprah Magazine* Fall Pick; a One Book, One Community read; and one of the Librarians' Best Books of 2011. Visit her website at www.annefrasier.com.